—————————— PRAISE FOR

THREE MARYS

"Robin Somers makes the Sierra foothills as compelling and full of oh-so-human nature as CJ Box's Wyoming, Tana French's western Ireland, or Attica Locke's East Texas. It's that good. I felt like I'd moved fully into reporter-heroine Eleanor's existence, took up her traumas, swung into her horse's saddle, adopted her firmness under pressure; she's a thoroughly real person caught up in a world of wildfires, violent men, sheer canyons, subdivisions, ancient Native secrets ... what a nuanced way to execute a thriller."

—Bruce Kelley, editor-in-chief,
San Francisco Magazine* & *Reader's Digest

"In this second of Robin Somers's *Wild Horses Mysteries,* journalist Eleanor Wooley rides again into danger and High Sierra beauty as she covers the story of a woman found murdered at the edge of an unseasonable forest fire. As with *Eleven Stolen Horses* - the first in the series - *Three Marys* weaves together the romance between two damaged people, the commitment women have to one another, and a love of horses into a landscape so masterfully evoked that the smell of sage and the sound of snowmelt tumbling over rocks remain in the senses long after the story is done. If you crave a mystery with a strong female lead, a can't-put-it-down plot, and an important message for today's world, *Three Marys* is for you."

—Kate Woodworth, author of
***Little Great Island* and *Racing Into the Dark*.**

"A fire breaks out in the Sierra Nevada high country, a dead woman is pulled from the river, and Eleanor Wooley, a reporter for the *Gold Strike Tribune*, is on the scene. Report, don't investigate, her boss reminds her. But Eleanor cannot separate the two. Something smells dreadfully wrong. Danger lurks in the Sierra Nevada mountains. Robin Somers has written a riveting novel full of mystery and intrigue. Through compelling storytelling, surprising plot twists, and rich detail, Somers weaves together the many threads of the Gold Strike community and Eleanor Wooley's life. She writes *Three Marys* with pitch-perfect passion and timing. It is a novel with a big heart and a strong pull for justice. I loved this book. It kept me up into the wee hours of the morning."

—Milana Marsenich, author of *Copper Sky* and *The Swan Keeper*

"In Eleanor Wooley, we find a protagonist as strong and resourceful as the wild horses she fights to protect. When a wildfire ravages the High Sierra, Eleanor discovers she must trust her instincts to catch a serial killer in a wilderness just as dangerous as the people in it. Set against a scorching Gold Country landscape that is burning and choked with smoke, Robin Somers masterfully weaves an atmospheric, high-stakes mystery that explores the rugged edges of Western culture and the resilience of the human spirit."

—Karen Nelson, author of *Last Summer at Feather River* and *The Sunken Town*

"I would love to see the murder board that Robin Somers used to create this intricate, thrilling tale. *Three Marys* is a mystery with a social conscience. Bad guys unleash environmental mayhem, and religious psychosis drives their scheming. Feminist pathos and journalistic chops reveal the wisdom of an author who has lived many lives and has sharpened her craft to its fullest. Robin Somers is a brilliant raconteuse. I can't wait to read more."

—Elizabeth Kadetsky, author of *On the Island at the Center of the Center of the World*

THREE MARYS

A WILD HORSES MYSTERY

ROBIN SOMERS

Sibylline Press

Sibylline Press

Copyright © 2026 by Robin Somers
All Rights Reserved.

Published in the United States by Sibylline Press,
an imprint of All Things Book LLC, California.

Sibylline Press is dedicated to publishing the
brilliant work of women authors ages 50 and older.
www.sibyllinepress.com

ISBN Trade: 9798897400102
eBook ISBN: 9798897400119
Library of Congress Control Number: 2025940869

Cover Design and Layout: Alicia Feltman
Book Production: Aaron Laughlin

Sibylline
Press

For Dennis, Jennifer, Joe,
and Buster

THREE MARYS

A WILD HORSES MYSTERY

ROBIN SOMERS

1

MCKENZIE WILSON TORE OUT OF the arena gate on her buckskin horse Scotch and thundered down the inside rail of the fairgrounds at a full gallop, the American flag aloft. McKenzie was this year's Gold Strike County Rodeo Queen, and her run launched the official opening of the town's annual Mother's Day rodeo.

As she rode, the Master of Ceremonies on a tall black and white paint faced the bleachers and introduced another young woman, who began to sing "The Star-Spangled Banner." The spectators rose. Eleanor Wooley, who stood at the rail covering the event for the *Gold Strike Tribune*, steeled herself, anticipating the off-key notes to come. But the soprano hit the high note *free* at perfect pitch, and the even higher bonus note floated above the fairgrounds at the exact moment McKenzie and Scotch streaked by on their final pass. The crowd went wild. Eleanor held up her camera. She took the shot and, despite her disdain for rodeos, wept from the thrill of the moment.

Behind the grandstand roof, the hum of a spotter plane grew louder. The red and white aircraft passed overhead, flying east toward the Sierra Nevada high country. Eleanor checked her phone for Cal Fire notifications. There were none, which meant the fire, if there were a fire, was under ten acres. She watched the plane disappear into the blue horizon, headed toward the mountains.

Over the loudspeaker came the booming voice of the MC announcing the Wild Horse event. More than a dozen horses poured out of the livestock gates. They ran kicking and bucking into the arena, their coats gleaming, muscles rippling. Each two-man team, consisting of a rider and a shanker, tried to catch a horse and control it long enough for the rider to throw on a saddle and mount. The first to ride across the finish line won. The horses' anguish, mixed with the cowboys' testosterone, created a stew of entertainment for the attentive crowd.

Eleanor watched a bay gelding drag a hopeful rider across the dirt clods. The rider held tight to his rope and managed to get his feet under him and dig in his heels. He pulled the horse to the ground, where it lay on its side, huffing. The panicked whites of the gelding's eyes shone like two small ghosts.

"This can't be legal," Eleanor said.

The shanker ran to assist his partner, adding his strength to the rope and forcing the horse to his feet. The horse kicked out, bucked, and broke free of the men. In a panic, he charged toward the metal fence where Eleanor stood, hit the rails hard, and crumpled to the ground.

Rodeo hands ran toward the horse, who struggled to lift his neck and issued a painful cry, dropping his head back onto the dirt. The rodeo veterinarian walked briskly into the arena with his medical kit. He bent a knee and ran his hand over the horse's jaw and poll, along the slight curve of his crest and down to the withers, over his chest, and up the neck, pausing at each vertebra. An official in a black Western shirt with Bull Livestock Co. stitched in red above the pocket stood beside the vet. Eleanor heard the vet say to the official, "Broken neck."

She'd snapped photos of the horse, knowing these weren't shots her editor would print. *For Christ's sake, Eleanor,* he'd say, *this is a community paper.* He'd choose the roping team or the bronc rider. Maybe the one of McKenzie on her buckskin, leaning over her saddle horn, everything flying.

Just then, a Cal Fire helicopter whumped along the same flight path the spotter plane had flown minutes before. The chopper confirmed wildfire, and although it was early in the season, every resident in this mountain town knew fire had become a year-round scourge.

But it was the horse who broke Eleanor's heart. His breathing was labored, and he remained on the ground. The equine ambulance drove into the arena while the vet conferred with the livestock official. She heard the word *euthanize*. A freeze brand of white symbols resembling hieroglyphics had been stamped on his neck just beneath the mane, identifying the horse as a BLM mustang. Apparently, he'd been sold at auction to this livestock outfit. The vet pulled a syringe from his bag and injected the poor four-legged.

A wave of nausea came over Eleanor and she fought to keep down the spit flooding her mouth as the livestock official glared at her like she was the one who'd done something wrong.

Her cell phone pinged. She glanced at the screen. The Forest Service reported fire in the river canyon off Brown's Ferry Road, not far from where she lived.

* * *

Firefighters created a fire break and cleared brush around the perimeter of the blaze. When flames hit bare dirt with nothing to consume, the wildfire stopped advancing. By evening the fire was controlled. A crew would remain overnight to extinguish flare-ups.

The expectation of another catastrophic fire season was now imprinted in Gold Strike's collective consciousness. The county was still reeling from the devastating Rim Fire in 2013 that devoured roughly two hundred and fifty thousand acres of Sierra because a bow hunter was unable to control his illegal campfire. The more recent Caldor Fire was nearly as huge, started by a single hot bullet. Last summer, the smoke from Caldor's pyrocumulus clouds had hounded Eleanor when she crossed the Sierra pass to scour Nevada in search of her missing best friend, Rette. Both fires had started in August during bone-dry drought weather. It took months and thousands of firefighters to put them out.

Eleanor reminded herself this was only May. Fire danger was low. The high country was still too wet to bring in cattle, and the rivers raged from a long winter of severe storms. This Brown's Ferry fire was a freak, possibly a prescribed burn that got out of hand.

2

AT DAWN THE NEXT MORNING the Sheriff's Office reported a body. They had discovered the victim in the river's fast-moving water a short distance down mountain from the wildfire's charred perimeter.

The smoke chafed Eleanor's throat as she descended the potholed gravel road. The chaparral was reduced to a blanket of ash. Conifers were blackened spears. She hoped her 1972 red and white Chevy Blazer would make it to the bottom without burning out its brakes.

When she reached the bottom of the gorge, a thin layer of smoke hovered over the reservoir. Every Gold Strike resident who didn't drink from a well drank from this lake. Its minerals and life-giving force coursed through communal blood and bones. This was the Little Bear River, the lower fork of the Bear River Watershed. The river's three branches were born of one oceanic plate squeezing under another until the ground leaned west and the glaciers moved with it, carving the river canyons through which ice melt flowed from the snow-capped Sierra Nevada crest.

The water before her was pure. It spread a mile on either side, beginning at the river inlet and moving across the reservoir toward a small, curved spillway. From the spillway, the river continued down the mountain through the gold-veined foothills to the plains and the Great Central Valley. Anglers and hikers could usually cross to the reservoir's opposite shore via a walkway on top of the spillway. But not this spring. The winter snowpack had created record high-water flows in all Sierra

Nevada rivers. Eleanor had already reported on four drownings, despite daily warnings to stay away from all bodies of water. The danger was far from over. As the high country snow continued to melt, the speed of the rivers would accelerate and the water continue to rise.

She was driving up the fire road between the reservoir on her left and the charred forest on her right when she spotted the first responders. They were dressed in heavy yellow jackets and stood in clusters, some leaning on trucks, others sitting on fenders. She noted the emergency vehicles. Two black and white California Highway Patrol cars, two dark green Sheriff's squad cars, one light green Forest Service rig, a red Cal Fire engine, and a gleaming new water tender.

Eleanor shut off her car and turned around to her Aussie, who sat in the back seat, wagging his tail, expecting to go wherever she was going.

"Granite," she said. "Stay." He twitched his ears and tilted his head, let out a small bark.

"No barking." She exited her car, and Granite's barking was quickly muffled by the roar of whitewater moving at five thousand cubic feet per second.

Deputy Perelli of the Gold Strike Sheriff's Office glanced at her, then her Blazer, and looked away. She walked up to him, and the first thing he said was, "Hope you can hike out of here. That pile of junk isn't going to make it back up."

Perelli was a dick. Eleanor had learned the hard way any attempts to be friendly only made him more of a dick.

She asked him if he'd identified the body, and he responded with a stare. She repeated the question, shouting above the roar of water. "Have you ID'd the body?"

"The victim's a woman," he said. "That's all we know."

"Her approximate age?"

"Can't tell," he shouted. "Not a gray hair."

"Who found the body?"

Inmate, she thought she heard him say, but she didn't see the prison's fire crew van among the emergency vehicles.

"The Con Crew mopped up and they're back in the slammer," Perelli shouted.

"You said an inmate spotted the woman?"

"Had to take a piss."

"Where'd he find the body?"

Perelli tilted his head, and she turned her gaze to a pair of first responders, who knelt on the ground a safe distance from the river, hovering over gear. The diver was storing his rope and carabiners in his wet bag. His fingers shook with cold. His skin was pale, lips blue. The other, a female, helped the diver roll down his wet bag and clip the sides. Her uniform and badge identified her as Fire Technician for the United States Forest Service.

Eleanor introduced herself. "Reporter from the *Gold Strike Tribune.*"

"Nice to meet you." The firefighter's face was covered with soot.

"Anything you can tell me about what happened here?"

The woman gestured with her chin to the river where mats of debris and beards of grass hung from branches that stretched over the river.

"That's where I pulled out the body," said the diver.

"She was in an eddy, caught up in strainers," the woman said.

"I heard an inmate from the fire crew spotted the body," Eleanor said.

"That's true. The victim was wearing a red jacket. The jacket caught an air bubble that floated above the surface, or he might not have seen her."

"Have you ID'd her?" Eleanor asked.

"No ID, but," his words slurred from the cold, "the river above the reservoir is designated wilderness. A person is supposed to take out a permit. Check the Forest Service to see if they have a name."

Eleanor thanked him and asked if there was anything else notable about the rescue.

The woman and diver glanced at each other as if they shared a secret and quickly looked down at the gear.

"Nope," said the firefighter. "But between you and me, there's a sicko out there planning more of the same."

"I won't quote you on that."

"Please don't." The firefighter inhaled and looked at the diver as Eleanor made a mental note to ask them another time what was so significant they couldn't speak it.

"Here's the thing, from my experience," said the firefighter. "A dead body raises suspicions. A dead body plus fire? Even more suspicious."

Eleanor asked for their names and contact.

"Adelia Shepherd, U.S. Forest Service." She thrust her hand forward and Eleanor registered the strength of her grip and the rough texture of her palm.

"Josh Richards." The diver gave her a quick nod while he gathered his gear. "Gold Strike County Search and Rescue."

Eleanor thanked them and walked to the river until its mist wet her face. The roar of whitewater walled out the world behind her as she photographed the spot on the river where the body was retrieved and the place where the inmate might have stood when he spotted her jacket.

The smell of granite and oxygen anointed the air as the raging water swept everything in its path down mountain.

She spotted Perelli in his patrol car. She walked up to the car and saw he was writing notes on an iPad. She stood there until he rolled down his window.

"What is it?"

"Two questions."

He tapped his pen twice and looked up at her. "Yeah?"

"Have you found her vehicle?"

"Next question."

"Are there any signs of foul play?"

He looked straight out his windshield and scowled. "C'mon, Wooley. A body, presumably drowned, next to a forest fire in early May."

"Are you saying you haven't ruled out foul play?" she asked.

"I'm not saying anything." He rolled up the window.

3

ELEANOR WROTE UP THE STORY from home, gazing now and then out her living room window:

> AN UNIDENTIFIED WOMAN WAS FOUND *dead in the lower fork of the Little Bear River, hung up on submerged branches in treacherously high, fast-moving water. Her body was discovered mere yards from the Brown's Ferry wildfire that broke out yesterday afternoon. An inmate from the Sierra Conservation Center firefighting crew spotted the victim early this morning, according to Gold Strike County Sheriff's Deputy Perelli, who did not rule out foul play. The woman's body was pulled from the river by a Search and Rescue diver. She was pronounced dead at the scene. The Gold Strike County Sheriff's Office has not confirmed the cause of her death.*

She called Adelia Shepherd. The call went to voicemail. Her next call was to the prison public information officer to request an interview with the fire crew member who'd discovered the body.

"I'll relay the message to our inmate," said the PIO. "He's allowed to call you. If he does, you'll receive a pre-recorded message from the prison identifying the inmate and you can choose to accept or deny the call."

She thanked him as she studied her photos of foaming whitewater scoring the riverbank at the site of the recovery, raising the obvious question, *Why would anyone get close enough to this river to fall in unless they were an idiot or wanted to die?*

Adelia Shepherd was returning her call. They exchanged pleasantries and Eleanor asked if there were any updates on the fire.

"Not much," Adelia said.

"Do you think it was a prescribed burn that got loose?"

"That it was not. We're not burning in there."

"Lightning strike?"

"No lightning. High humidity, no wind, mild temperatures. None of the factors that create red flag conditions."

"A bullet?"

"Like the Caldor? Unlikely."

"What about a spark from a car on the scenic highway?"

"Probably not. The fire started too far below the highway for a vehicular spark or cigarette butt."

Adelia's voice was calm and forthcoming. Eleanor searched for the right questions.

"Could the victim's campfire have gotten out of control and forced her to the river as an escape route?"

"We don't know that yet," Adelia said. "Off the record, possible. A lot of crazy hillbillies hiding out in the forest cooking meth, growing weed without permits, getting loaded, if you know what I mean."

"Not sure I do."

"Let me put it this way, Eleanor. Anytime you don't have a natural event igniting the fire, it's human-caused."

"May I quote you?"

"It's common knowledge."

"Is your official title 'firefighter for the US Forest Service'?"

"Fire technician," she said. "If we were called firefighters, they'd have to pay us more."

"Do you have any leads on possible arson?"

"Our investigators are considering everything."

"It's early in the season for fire."

"These days wildfire's an all-season hazard."

Eleanor finished her interview, hung up, and stared out her living room window, processing the conversation. Two crows swooped from the lowest limb of a cedar, glided across the ground, and rose to the ponderosa, cawing. Next, a bluejay soared from a higher branch, followed by a woodpecker. Finally, a family of quail emerged from the brush, parents in the lead, chicks following, topknots bobbing behind as they skittered across the open space to the nearest patch of brush. They did this every day—ordinary birds with a communal ritual of succession.

Across the small patch of crabgrass, Dolores, Eleanor's landlady, was opening the screen door to her double wide. She emerged rear end first, holding a Dixie Cup in one hand and securing a lid in the other. She limped to the corner of her short, white picket fence as if her hip were bothering her before tossing the cup and whatever was inside over the fence. Probably another wolf spider. Dolores had a thing about rescuing wolf spiders, who seemed to gravitate toward civilized amenities, especially sinks and shower curtains. Wolf spiders never failed to shock Eleanor. She'd be bending over her bathroom sink to brush her teeth and there it'd be, this meaty beast that always elicited a shriek. Because Eleanor hated killing anything, she'd begun following Dolores's example and kept an empty jam jar on the counter to capture and toss the arachnid into the forest, where it belonged.

Dolores examined the purple and amber bearded irises she'd planted in her flower bed last fall. The flowering bulbs had survived because of her watchful eye and various putrid concoctions she used to repel deer, gophers, and squirrels. When she looked up, Eleanor waved through the glass in silent greeting. Dolores returned the wave and remained in her small front yard, weeding her irises.

Dolores lived alone, like Eleanor, and living alone seemed to suit both women. Eleanor's boyfriend Easton Jode had asked her more than once to move in with him, and she was tempted. But it had taken her four years to become a woman who was able to live alone contentedly, and she didn't want to risk losing herself by moving in with her lover. Worse, she feared living together would damage their relationship because she didn't trust a man to stick around once those salsa hooks began to slow dance, although theirs were far from settling. They spent every night they could together, yearning for each other when apart. Tonight, she'd yearn for him while she ate dinner standing up, in the company of her own thoughts.

Eleanor went over her workday, the people she'd dealt with. How she could have handled situations better, like restraining herself from flipping off Perelli when he rudely rolled up his window. And the diver, his hands shaking so badly he could barely unfasten the carabiner and was so thick-tongued from cold his words were slurred. She wished she'd offered him a blanket. And what about that knowing look between him and Adelia when she'd asked if there was anything notable about the recovery? She should've pressed them.

She spread a whole wheat pita with hummus, sliced a perfect avocado, and laid it on top. She ate voraciously and afterward texted herself a note: *wilderness camping permits @ forest service.*

Granite twitched in his sleep. He'd spent yesterday hanging out by himself and a good part of today remaining in the car, which he preferred to staying home. He probably needed a walk. And soon, she'd have to pay a groomer to shave him down in a summer cut.

"Walk?" is all she had to say.

He lifted his head and stepped out of his dog bed, wagging his tail. She clipped on his leash and headed out through the screen porch door, down the duff-covered path, and toward the fire trail.

The native dogwoods behind her cottage had bloomed like fairy lanterns in a dark green forest. At the first tree, she paused beneath its canopy of perfect white blossoms and visually traced the adjacent dogwood's spindly limbs vining upward, through a slim fir, seeking light. The bloom was fleeting. Too soon the petals would brown at their delicate edges and drop to the ground. By autumn, the leaves would have fallen, leaving barebone, pencil-thin branches, their life cycle a testimony to beauty's fragility.

She thought of her friend Rette Kenny, who'd vanished this time last year. Rette remained officially listed as missing and endangered. Eleanor pined for her friend, but the pain had shifted from a physical sharpness to a tolerable mental ache.

She was staring at the dogwoods when her phone rang. Her screen said Easton. They talked while she walked down to the fire trail that ran horizontal to the mountainside. She unclipped Granite's leash and the dog romped ahead.

"Sounds like you're doing sit-ups," he said. "The service is great."

"Sounds like you're walking right beside me." She passed a stand of cedar saplings, their sweet scent lacing the air, and headed toward the cutoff to the abandoned Boy Scout camp.

"You okay?" he asked.

"About the dead woman? I'm okay. We don't know who she is or what she was doing so close to the river or the cause of the wildfire. Have you heard anything?"

Easton had been born and raised in Gold Strike County. He ran a working horse and cattle ranch and paid the ranch bills with the profits from his grading business. He was also an equestrian Search and Rescue volunteer. He knew a lot of people in just about every corner of the county.

"No," he said, "but I'll keep my ear to the ground."

"Thanks. How's the day going for you?"

"Compared to yours, uneventful. One of my mares could foal anytime. I have to write up a bid for a grading job outside Merced, and I gotta get the cows and calves vaccinated and ready to haul up mountain. What's the rest of your day look like?"

"Mac expects an action shot of the bull riders. I have to go back to the fairgrounds."

"You know what they say about bull riders."

"Don't tell me."

He laughed. "It's a saying is all. 'Rodeo's not over 'til the bull riders ride.'"

"Not what I expected. I'm stealing it."

She came to the abandoned Boy Scout road and turned around, keeping her pace brisk as they talked. She loved their conversations, so different from talking to her ex, who invariably manipulated the conversation to himself.

The ordeal of living with that lying, cheating man had taken four years to process, and he still lived in Eleanor's psyche, which hardened her resolve to stay single and live alone.

"Lee." Which was what Easton called her for short. "Once you're done with work come on out and we—"

His voice cut out and she lost the call. Her phone said no service, so they'd have to wait to try again, and knowing him like she did, he'd worry until he heard from her. Also, the opposite of her ex, who had never cared about her well-being.

Granite sniffed coyote scat—fresh, judging from the moist gray fur. A sugar pinecone lay on the side of the path. Its light brown thorns and drops of amber sap made the cone at once beautiful and dangerous. She hadn't noticed the cone on her way in. As she perused the surrounding brush and trees, nothing looked familiar. The section of mountainside on her left was too steep, the slope different, the path newly cut. She checked her phone. Still no service.

"Granite."

The dog sat at attention, ears perked, head tilted. She must've taken the wrong path and dropped down mountain at the fork. All she had to do now was bushwhack straight up the mountainside and she'd run into the main fire trail. She wasn't lost, but an edge of anxiety skated in nonetheless.

She pointed up mountain. "Go."

Granite bounded up mountain, over thistles and grasses and sticks as Eleanor trudged, carefully avoiding jagged branches that jutted out of the dirt, slash from winter storms. She lifted her feet to avoid snagging her laces. Tripping could cause serious damage if she fell on any one of the thousands of splintered spears of wood. Her breathing was rapid, and she felt dizzy.

4

WHEN ELEANOR OPENED HER EYES, Granite lay on the ground pressed to her side. Her head ached. She covered her face with her hands and swore softly.

Granite growled, baring his teeth and staring at a gap in the chaparral where Eleanor discerned a dun face, small ears, large snout, and eyes that stared straight at her. The dog charged, ignoring her commands. The creature turned tail, and as it humped down mountain she saw it was a bear cub. The mother bear had to be close by.

She followed the animals' faint trail until the ground leveled, where she noted an empty fifth of cheap vodka and an aluminum beer can, but no sign of the cub or Granite. Beyond a marsh of reeds and wildflowers sat a small wooden shack, most likely a remnant from the old Boy Scout camp. Smoke billowed from the chimney. A mound that was actually a dog rose from the ground. He was on a leash attached to a cable strung between the trunks of two trees. A man emerged from the shack. He was tall and burly, dressed in striped engineer overalls and a long-sleeved shirt. His hair was cut close, his beard long and pointed. Eleanor ducked, her face pressed to the ground, inhaling dirt. When she looked up, the man and dog were gone.

She abandoned Granite to his chase and hustled up mountain until she arrived at the spot where they'd encountered the cub. An animal roar pierced the air—mama bear. Seconds later Granite appeared, running scared between the trees toward Eleanor.

She and the dog pushed through the cedar saplings and hit the main trail. Once the cottage was in sight, she ran until her side ached and burst through the screen porch, pulling Granite inside. She latched the door, threw the deadbolt, slid the brass chain, and was about to slam the front windows shut when she spotted Dolores, who stood inside her own front window and waved for Eleanor to come over. She had to call Easton, but if she told him what had happened since their call ended, he'd worry even more. She filled Granite's water bowl at the sink and set it on the floor. As she crossed the lawn toward Dolores's mobile, the treetops above swayed in a high breeze, as if the conifers spoke among themselves. She bent to unlatch the short, white gate. Dolores opened her screen.

"We had a bear encounter," Eleanor said. "And I saw a man who lives in a shack down the mountain." A chill ran up her arms, and she entered the mobile's interior.

Overstuffed couch. Recliner, antique dining room set. A print of *The Crucifixion* hung over the fireplace. The brilliant gold leaf colored the top half of the painting above Jesus being tortured on the cross and women grieving at his feet.

"I'll make tea," Dolores said, and proceeded into the kitchen.

Eleanor took a seat at the breakfast nook with the view of the forest as Dolores whisked from one end of the kitchen counter to the other, filling her electric kettle, reaching into her cupboard for a yellow Lipton's tea box and a pink and white box of C&H sugar cubes. Dolores set two matching teacups decorated with yellow and pink peonies and periwinkle daisies on the table in front of Eleanor.

Dolores grabbed a small carton of hazelnut creamer from the refrigerator and placed it on the table. "Are you sure it was a bear? A family of Sasquatch live down there way on the other side of the river."

"You mean Bigfoot?"

"I hear them knocking some nights."

"It was a cub," Eleanor said. "But this very big man and his pit bull freaked me out a lot more than the bear."

Dolores poured boiling water from the kettle into the teapot. "How many years have you lived here, Eleanor?"

"Four."

"Four years and I've never once had you in my house," she said. "We don't know the first thing about each other."

"I'm sorry."

"I wasn't guilt tripping you."

"Even so. I work. When I'm home, I'm working. And when I'm not working, it's my horse or Easton. I don't mean to be unfriendly."

"You're a private person, and I was just making a point."

Eleanor waited for Dolores to finish making her point.

"We should reach out to each other a little more. The highlight of my day is reading my Tarot cards. I could use some company every now and then."

Tarot?

"I've been using the cards for decades. If I count the years, I'll be forced to admit I'm an old lady."

From Eleanor's perspective, time had been relatively gentle on Dolores. Her skin possessed a rubbery porcelain quality from staying indoors except when she threw out spiders and tended her small garden. If she were to guess, Dolores was a Baby Boomer without the cultural tags of the Bay Area, including the age-defying availability of Dysport, Juvéderm, and face lifts. She wore her sable hair in something between a bun and a messy French twist, bouffant on top. She liked big earrings, necklaces, bracelets, and rings. Though widowed, she still wore her diamond engagement and wedding rings.

"I think of you as ageless," Eleanor said.

Dolores liked that and poured tea. "Yes, well, women of all ages go missing around here all the time. What they find are our abandoned cars, our purses with wallet and ID, but no trace of the woman. *Poof.* Gone."

Eleanor hadn't thought about the dead woman for the last few hours. She wondered if Dolores had heard.

"Yes, I read the paper online," Dolores said. "The world is a dangerous place, especially around here. Be cautious when you're out there. Be aware of your surroundings." She dropped three cubes of sugar into her teacup—plop, plop, and plop—and poured creamer to the rim.

"To live in fear isn't living," Eleanor said.

"Unless you want to keep living. You can't go outside willy-nilly and think you're safe. Men are like mountain lions stalking their prey. And there are more of them than you think."

"Granite was with me."

"That's a good dog but no match for a predator. I wouldn't go on those walks, even with the dog."

The dog, as Dolores called him, was probably on her bed right now, scared after their incident and feeling very alone. Eleanor finished her tea and stood to leave. Dolores ushered her to the door.

"Be careful," Dolores said. "We never know if the beast is friendly or wants to eat us."

* * *

That afternoon, Eleanor made it to the rodeo as the bull riding event was about to start. She positioned herself on the side of the arena near the chutes where the riders prepped and the bulls gathered steam.

The final contestant in the bull riding event dropped from the top rail of the fence into the chute and sat the bull. He tied down his hand and gave a nod. The gate opened. The bull charged out of the chute in a mean twist of muscle. He spun, and Eleanor snapped a succession of shots, catching him at the apex of a buck, rider's arm extended. The whistle blew. The bull rider slammed to the ground and the rodeo clown leapt over him, prancing wildly to distract the bull until the rider escaped to the rail.

Eleanor found the bull rider sitting on the fence with his cowboy buddies. She asked his name and the proper spelling.

"Robbie Cartright from Bakersfield." He was twenty-two and liked the photos she'd taken.

"How'd you feel about your ride?" she asked.

"I made the whistle, and the judges scored me pretty high and my bull did good, too."

"What's your secret, Robbie?"

"I felt good, and when a bull rider is mentally strong going in, the moves follow."

"That looked like a perfect ride to me."

He looked at his friends bashfully and laughed.

"The only perfect ride was Wade Leslie on Wolfman. Google it."

"I'll be sure to do that."

"Thank you, ma'am." He tipped his hat.

He was a nice young man who would've changed her opinion of bull riders if she'd had one.

* * *

Easton was in the barn checking on the mare who was near foaling. He asked if Eleanor would bring in her paint mare Jessie to keep the mare company. She gathered Jessie from the outside paddock the mare shared with her buddy Fred, who whinnied as Jessie was led into the barn to the empty stall between the mare and Easton's horse Chester. The two mares sniffed each other's muzzles and that was the extent of their exchange.

"The mare knows she's here and that's enough," Easton said.

Eleanor slipped her arm around his waist, feeling his slim, muscled flesh through his T-shirt.

"Let's go inside," he said. "I'll throw dinner together and we can talk about stuff."

* * *

Easton had a whole chicken and russet potatoes roasting in the oven. He'd set the table with knives, forks, and spoons on top of two worn placemats. He set out sour cream, bacon bits, and chopped green onion tops. His salad was iceberg with avocado and tomato, tossed with Girard's dressing.

She smiled at his efforts to please her, and while they sat and ate, she told him about the bear cub and the hermit.

"All that after our call went dead?" He leaned on an elbow and pushed zucchini around his plate.

"I couldn't call you back, figuring you might worry about me."

He glanced up. "Can't imagine why."

She stifled a laugh. "He was creepy. One minute he was there and the next he and his dog"—Snap—"vanished." Think he could've started the fire?"

Easton shook his head. "Probably not. It doesn't stand to reason a man would set fire to his own backyard."

He stretched an arm across the table, and she laid hers gently over, touching the inside crook of his elbow with her fingertips.

"I'm sorry I wasn't there for you," he said.

Her eyes stung as tears welled up. "I'm sorry I didn't tell you sooner."

"Chalk it up to a good suppertime story." He cupped her hand in his. "You're something. You face trouble like a buffalo. You're the most beautiful, courageous person I've ever known."

She blinked and wet splotches stained her placemat like blessings.

5

THE USFS GOLD STRIKE DISTRICT opened at eight in the morning. Eleanor pushed the front door of the rustic ranger station. A woman rose from her desk and stepped up to the front counter. *Kate Barton, volunteer* was engraved on the pin over the breast pocket of her uniform. Her shoulder-length wavy hair was brown with strands of silver. She had an honest, intelligent face and wore no makeup.

"How can I help you?" she asked.

"I'm Eleanor Wooley from the *Gold Strike Tribune* reporting on the female body recovered yesterday from Brown's Ferry."

"A tragedy," said Barton.

"Have you identified the victim?" Eleanor asked.

"I'm sorry, I don't have any information, but if you call our Forest Service public relations officer, he might have more to say."

"One of the first responders at the scene," Eleanor said, "suggested we ask because the woman's body was found in designated wilderness, so she may have taken out a wilderness permit. I'd be so grateful if you could pull up the permits from this past week to find out if anyone took one out in the Brown's Ferry area?"

Barton typed something into the computer and pulled a lined yellow notepad toward her. She jotted some notes with a pencil. "We issued one permit but not in that area." She finished writing down names and contact numbers, tore off the yellow note, and passed it to Eleanor.

Eleanor read the names, both male.

"That doesn't mean she wasn't there," Barton said. "People often go out for a day trip or an overnight and they don't think of permits, or their hike is a spur-of-the-moment decision, and they've traveled too far from the ranger station to get one."

"It sounds like you heard about finding the woman," Eleanor said. "Could you tell me what you heard? Anything at all will help."

Barton looked a bit taken aback, as if Eleanor had crossed a professional boundary.

"I'm sorry if I'm being aggressive. It's just that the Sheriff's Office isn't forthcoming."

She tapped her pencil on the counter. "One of the rangers—" she started to say, but a man entered the room from the inner office. He offered a robust, "Hello, ladies."

"Kate," he said. "I'm looking for our literature brochures on horseback riding stables."

His name tag identified him as Dave Connor. He was a glassy-eyed, burly guy with a bushy mustache. His khaki uniform buttonholes stretched ever so slightly around his middle.

"Someone's on the phone," he said. "Would you find them for me?"

Interruptions were part of the job at the front counter, and Kate Barton was good at her job. Within seconds she produced a stack of brochures.

Connor stopped himself mid-stride on his return to the phone call and turned to Eleanor, scowled, and asked, "Have you been helped?"

"Thanks, Kate helped me. I'm Eleanor Wooley from the *Tribune*." She reached across the counter to shake his hand.

"Sorry," he said. "After Covid, I don't shake hands."

"I understand." She withdrew her hand. "I'm covering the story on the woman they pulled from the river yesterday. She hasn't been identified, but since she was discovered in designated wilderness, we hoped she might have taken out a wilderness permit."

"More times than not," he said, "folks don't think they need a permit. Or when they decide to hop out of their vehicle and take a hike, they're too far from the ranger station to conveniently return for a permit."

She slipped her notepad into her back pocket. "So I hear."

"You might want to call our public relations officer. He gets in at eight."

"Thank you." Eleanor gave Kate a knowing glance, not unlike the knowing glance between the diver and Adelia. "I will."

* * *

Eleanor pulled up to the curb in front of the old newspaper building in the center of Gold Strike's historic downtown and cranked her wheel to the curb because the parking patrol loved to ticket her when she didn't. Her cell phone rang. Easton's name flashed on her screen.

"Hey."

"How's your morning so far?"

"I'm good."

"You at work?"

"Just parked. I stopped by the Ranger Station to see if the victim had taken out a wilderness permit in the last few days."

"How'd that go?"

"No luck."

"People usually don't bother."

"Forest Service said the same thing. Twice."

"Lee—"

In the background Easton's television was blasting the morning news. MSNBC, another obsession they shared.

"—let's put something on our calendar. Go somewhere we can chill out."

"You have someplace in mind?"

"Not on the phone. Lunch at Manuel's. Noon. We'll brainstorm."

Manuel's was a few doors up Main Street from the newspaper building, a popular restaurant with an outdoor patio landscaped with bougainvillea. The profusion of papery orange blossoms contributed to the ambience of the place.

"Now I'm craving flan," she said.

"I'm craving you."

"Settle for salsa?"

He laughed. "I like it mild."

"I like you, anyway."

"See you soon."

She ended the call, smiling but tense. Sexual innuendo made her nervous.

* * *

The AP wire service headline grabbed Eleanor's attention.

Reno, Nevada. *22-year-old woman arrested for freeing federal wild horses from government corrals.*

Eleanor recalled the day less than a year ago when she and Easton had ridden onto private property and freed a corral-full of wild horses doomed for slaughter. Slaughter in the US is not illegal, even though the BLM forbids wild horse adoptees to sell mustangs for slaughter or transport them out of the country for that purpose; however, because the BLM's follow up is insufficient to nonexistent and the federal government annually refuses to fund slaughter facilities, horses are nonetheless hauled to Canada and Mexico to get the job done, and kill buyers, including the man who owned this property, did so with impunity. Eleanor and Easton had unpenned the horses and returned to camp and made love for the first time. They fell asleep inside their tent and were awakened by two armed ne'er-do-wells searching for the thieves who'd stolen their mustangs. She was pretty sure one of them at least was the kill buyer whose horses they'd freed, but thanks to Easton's alibi and Eleanor's Highway Patrol press pass, the men left.

However, what she and Easton had done *was* illegal, and Easton might have warned her ahead of time about his plan to unpen wild horses before she'd become an accomplice, even though, given a choice, she'd do it again. That said, well-intentioned people can make things worse. Those same horses had likely been rounded up again, and their actions could've given the BLM a reason to ban wild horse advocates from observing roundups and holding corrals, essentials for documenting abuse.

Mac interrupted her thoughts, shouting across the newsroom, "Eleanor, what've you found out about the drowned woman?"

She didn't have much to offer. "The coroner hasn't confirmed she drowned or released her ID," she shouted back. "She did not take out a wilderness permit, even though she was found in designated wilderness."

He peered over his reading glasses. "You usually have a theory."

"When a wildfire breaks out and shortly thereafter a dead woman shows up in the adjacent river, the coincidence makes me suspicious foul play's involved, but the Sheriff isn't admitting to that. A wildfire in May and a drowning despite numerous public service warnings to stay away from high water feels too coincidental not to be connected."

He nodded. "Search and Rescue called."

"I called them twice. They didn't return my calls."

"They found a fly rod on the other side of the river, upstream from the recovery site."

"The river's too turbulent to fish. What would that mean?"

"Fly rods are expensive. An angler wouldn't leave his rod behind."

"Why would it be there?"

"Thought you might figure out a reason."

Right now, she was distracted. "I'm drawing a blank."

"What's wrong?" Mac leaned back in his chair. "You're not all here."

"A wire story I just read. A woman outside of Reno was arrested for trying to free some wild horses from a federal holding corral."

"Where?"

"Nevada."

"It might be a story if she were local."

"It's a disturbing story and Reno's not that far away."

"Why disturbing?"

She waited a beat and inside that beat weighed telling him. "I did the same thing she did. Freed some BLM mustangs from a kill pen."

Mac took off his glasses.

"Stop staring at me," she said. "I didn't get caught."

He picked up yesterday's newspaper from his desk and snapped it open so it hid his face. His reading glasses were on his desk. The half-page photo she'd taken of McKenzie tearing around the arena, flag aloft, filled the top half of the front page.

Mac turned the page and snapped the newspaper a second time. "It'd be a story if you were arrested," he said. "You could write it from prison as your last piece before I fired you."

6

EASTON SAT OUTSIDE ON MANUEL'S patio, drinking coffee. Eleanor saw him and her angst dissolved; his mere presence created a buffer zone of calm. Dodging the slings and arrows of life kept her agile, she told herself, but with Easton she was learning to live without being forced to the edge. And their chemistry held. They would slip into his bed or hers and hold each other as their pleasant feelings grew more pleasant and every move was rhythmic. Their skin slid across each other's. Love came easily.

"What are you smiling about?" Easton asked.

She scooted around into the bench seat across from him. "You."

He leaned over and kissed her, and she reached for the can of Coke and the glass of ice he'd ordered, flipped the tab, and waited out the sizzling dun foam of the sparkling liquid. She bent down and sipped the overflow.

"What'll you two have?" Enrique stood at their table, ready to file their order to memory.

"Chicken tostada," said Eleanor. "And a side of guacamole."

He turned to Easton.

"Enchilada and chili relleno plate. Refill on the coffee."

Enrique disappeared behind the swinging door to the kitchen.

"When was the last time you went fly fishing?" she asked.

"Last fall I went up the middle fork of the Stanislaus with a buddy of mine."

"Can you teach me?"

"I can teach you how to tie on a fly and cast. Catching a fish is between the two of you."

"Can I learn in a weekend?"

"Nope. Fly fishing is a way of life." He sipped his coffee.

She told him the Sheriff found a fly rod across the river from where the body was found and how Mac made it sound significant.

"Was it on the bank or in the water?"

"He didn't say."

"If it's on the bank, someone left it there, and rods are pricey. No one's going to leave it unless they're scared shitless. If it's mangled in the brush or water, that's different. It could be an angler's mistake, washed down by winter storms."

She asked him why a person wouldn't be afraid to cross a dangerous spillway to fish but would get scared off and leave their rod.

"Might not have crossed the spillway. There's a road up mountain that takes you to the other side. But it's bad this time of year."

A blossom dropped from the bougainvillea onto her placemat. She took it as a sign Easton was on to something.

"I have two rods," he said. "You can use the good one and we'll go up to my favorite fishing hole for our getaway. How's that sound?"

"Sounds great."

"We'll take the horses," he said. "A two-person tent and sleeping bags. Make a thing out of it." He looked down at his tepid coffee. "I have a bit of bad news. My horse has been chewing your mare's tail."

"Are you kidding me?" Jessie's tail was one of her most beautiful physical attributes. Dark red, nearly reaching the ground. "How much of her tail?"

"A visible hank on the outside. I didn't notice until I caught him at it. She seemed to like it."

"Don't blame Jessie. Will it grow back?"

"It takes a while."

She pulled her phone out of her back jeans pocket and googled *will horses tails grow back* as Enrique placed their plates of food on the table.

"Careful," he warned. "They're hot."

Her stomach growled.

"Thanks, Enrique."

Eleanor turned her phone to face Easton. "It takes four to five years. Vaseline and cayenne pepper on the tail are good deterrents to further nibbling."

"I already moved her back to the paddock with Fred."

She dug into the tostada, hungrier than she'd realized.

"A woman was arrested recently, for trying to free mustangs." She took a drink of Coke.

Easton looked up from his enchilada, his fork in the air. "Are you trying to get even?"

"No, but my instinct to protect you has vanished. She tried to release some wild horses from a BLM corral outside of Reno and was caught in the act."

He put the forkful of meat and beans and cheese into his mouth and chewed slowly.

"Thought you should know."

"Are you worried?"

"No. I want to interview the woman. Mac turned me down and I told him I'd done the same thing."

"Why'd you do that?"

"To push his buttons. He irritates me when he turns down my story ideas without giving them two seconds of thought."

"What'd he say?"

"If I get caught, he'll fire me." She took another bite of tostada and washed it down with the Coke. "Want to hear about my weekend?"

"I'd like to digest my food a bit longer," he said.

"Seriously?"

"Not everyone can stomach dead bodies as part of their work routine."

"Let's talk about your fishing hole."

He removed his Oakland As ball cap, tossed it on the seat, and ran his fingers through his hair to rough up the pressed hair line.

"It's sacred," he said.

When a cowboy who made a living raising horses and cattle referred to a favorite fishing hole as "sacred," the effect was endearing.

"My pop took me there when I was a boy," he said.

"You call your dad 'pop'?"

"Yep. What do you call yours?"

"Dad." She missed her parents. Her mom had died of breast cancer, and she hadn't seen her dad since Thanksgiving.

"Pop taught me to dig up insects for bait."

"My dad," she said, "taught me to thread worms on a hook."

"That so?" he said.

"Yes, and to clean trout."

Easton threw back the napkin that lined the basket and grabbed a warm flour tortilla. He folded it over and swept it around his platter until every speck of red sauce was gone. He ate the tortilla and pushed back his plate.

He patted his stomach, still flat but apparently full. "So, tell me what happened."

"We lake-trolled, and I caught a few fish."

"I mean this weekend."

Eleanor explained how the fire had charred the entire mountainside and stopped yards from the river, where an inmate from the fire crew spotted the woman's red jacket.

"By the time I arrived, Search and Rescue had recovered the body."

"Did you see her?"

"No, they'd already taken her to the morgue."

"An inmate found the body?"

"He had to take a leak and went to the river to do his business. The victim's jacket had an air bubble that broke the surface, and he spotted it."

Easton rubbed his chin. "Think there's a connection?"

"If there is, I can't get my head around it. The diver who pulled her out suggested she might have taken out a permit because she was found in designated wilderness, but, like I told you this morning, the Forest Service doesn't have a record of anyone taking out a permit in that area."

He stared at his coffee. "Could mean she might not have intentionally gone to that wilderness."

"Which complicates things."

"I'd go back to your editor and find out what kind of rod and what condition they found it in."

"Because?"

"Because no one's intentionally going to leave a high-end Winston or a Sage that's in good condition."

"Wouldn't most anglers know better than to fish a river at this flow?"

"You'd think, but people screw up all the time. Find out if it's in one piece, what brand, if the reel's attached, what brand of reel, what kind of shape the line's in. That might tell you something about the angler." He shook his head. "The town's going to freak if they think too long on a dead woman and ash in their drinking water."

* * *

Eleanor and Easton left the restaurant, full and satisfied, and walked down the street to the old newspaper building. Easton opened the heavy glass door and kissed her goodbye. While climbing the stairs, she mentally organized her afternoon phone calls, and by the time she reached the top step, she realized she'd forgotten to tell him about fainting in the forest. Maybe that was a good thing. She didn't want to ruin his fantasy of her as the buffalo girl who runs through the gauntlet of danger.

7

THE SHERIFF'S OFFICE HAD IDENTIFIED the body as twenty-year-old Marisol Teresa Rodriguez. She'd grown up in Gold Strike County and attended Sierra Community College, majoring in biology and serving on student council. She was reported last seen on campus in the college cafeteria, where she'd told friends she was going to Yosemite for a day trip and hiking. No one from Yosemite reported seeing her. Eleanor called Sheriff Duncan for new information.

"How's that pup?" he asked.

"Great."

Granite, the runt of Duncan's litter of Aussies, came into Eleanor's life a year ago. Duncan had wanted to give her the dog at no cost, but to avoid a conflict of interest, she'd paid one hundred dollars, all she could afford, with the Sheriff's guarantee he wouldn't dock the Aussie's tail. Thanks to the Sheriff's influence, Dolores had made an exception to the mobile park's *no pets* rule.

"He's a lucky boy." Duncan cleared his throat. "What's up?"

"I read the Sheriff's Office Facebook post on Marisol Rodriguez. Do you know the cause of death?"

"We don't have the complete forensics report, so no."

"Can I assume it's death by drowning?"

"Never assume anything you can't prove, Eleanor."

"Have you linked Marisol's death to the fire?"

"We're investigating all angles."

"Would you elaborate on which angles?"

"I can't get specific while an investigation is ongoing, and you know that."

What she knew was generic questions resulted in stock answers, and specific questions resulted in pretty much the same. "What about the fishing rod you found at the river?"

He didn't respond, which meant he didn't want to confirm they'd found a rod, or he didn't know about the rod and wanted her to feed him all the information she had.

"What about the rod?"

"How can I find out what brand and what condition it's in? If it's in good condition, someone may have accidentally abandoned it after witnessing something."

"I can't go there with you. If you hear anything more, you'll let me know." He tsked. "I have a phone call I have to answer. Next time you come in, bring the pup."

* * *

By noon on Friday, Eleanor looked forward to a weekend with Easton at his sacred fishing hole. As soon as she dropped off Granite at the dog sitter's, the void was palpable. Without him grounding her by holding down space in the back seat, she felt a hole in her insides and needed caffeine to fill the void. She turned at the entrance to the drive-thru coffee shack and drove up to the speaker.

"May I take your order?"

Eleanor leaned out her car window and placed her order for a large black coffee. When she drove up to the serving window, McKenzie Wilson stood behind the counter holding her hot drink. She smiled when she saw Eleanor. "Hi, Ms. Wooley."

"Good to see you, McKenzie. You're here early on a Saturday." Eleanor glanced in her side mirror to make sure no one was behind her. "How are you?"

"Honestly, a little bummed. Last weekend's rodeo was supposed to be my pinnacle of recognition," she said. "The most important day of my life. Instead, a horse died because of a couple of idiots and cast a shadow over the entire day—"

"That was terrible for sure, but you shined right through the sadness."

"Thanks, Ms. Wooley." She didn't sound convinced.

Eleanor took a sip of the too-hot coffee and removed the lid so it would cool faster.

"I hope you don't take this wrong, but I saw you walking down Main Street earlier this week with Easton Jode. My dad makes his saddles and some years we help him take the cows in and out up mountain."

"I keep my horses at his ranch." She couldn't help smiling. "I'm on my way to his ranch as we speak."

"Small world."

"Small town, for sure. But nothing small about your performance, McKenzie. Your ride was epic. That's what people will take away from that day. You and your horse brought tears to my eyes, and I don't cry much."

McKenzie straightened her shoulders. "Thank you for saying that."

"Because it's true. How'd you like the front-page photo of you and your horse?"

"It was awesome. Scotch was beautiful."

"I can save you a few copies?"

She laughed. "All our friends saved the front page and sent it to us."

"I have the original photo if you want it."

"That's something. I'll let my mom know."

She handed McKenzie a five and told her to keep the change.

"Thank you, Ms. Wooley." She grinned.

"You know anything about how to get a horse's tail to grow back? Easton's horse ate a big chunk of my horse's tail. They say it takes four years."

"Get some Mane Tail Groom. Three inches a month. I use it on Scotch for volume."

More than a flicker of hope rose in Eleanor. She loved this girl who knew so much about horses and seemed genuinely happy to see her. She was a special kid who worked hard in school, played soccer and basketball, held a job, and was involved in a myriad of school and community activities. She planned to go to college to become a nurse. She was lovely and deserving. A thriving young person endemic to this place. The type of kid even a lefty transplant like Eleanor wanted to befriend. McKenzie was determined to *become* the best by scouring her deepest reserves to *do* her best. And when she rode that buckskin horse of hers, Butterscotch, horse and rider were two shooting stars on a clear summer night, her white straw hat pushed low on her head, her dark brown hair curled and flowing, green silk scarf fluttering, rhinestone shirt and black wranglers molded to a lean body, tooled green boots shoved deep in the stirrup, heels down. How could you not love a kid who streaked by onlookers in a primal force of beauty and courage? She was a Western cowgirl goddess. If Eleanor was honest, McKenzie embodied a culture that had drawn her from the Pacific Central Coast to this slow and steady paced western countryside.

"Ms. Wooley."

Eleanor snapped out of her reverie. McKenzie leaned out the serving window, waving. She backed up the Blazer, embarrassed by the exhaust.

"I read your story. They identified the girl found in the river."

"Did you know her?"

"I know *of* her, and I have friends who knew her. Did she drown?"

Eleanor studied McKenzie's face, her eyes so steady, her young face so clear, waiting for Eleanor's response. She crafted an answer that was honest but not terrifying.

"The Sheriff's Office hasn't finished its report, but we'll know soon and once the medical examiner's report is in, we'll post the information in the paper."

"But the river. Everyone knows better than to go anywhere near the rivers right now."

"Keep that thought, McKenzie. I don't have the facts yet, but when I do, I'll let you know."

"I'd appreciate that, Ms. Wooley."

She was about to say *you can call me Eleanor*, but McKenzie felt at ease addressing her formally, and she wasn't going to mess with a teenage girl's comfort zone.

8

AT THE FIRST RAY OF morning light, Easton threw a backpack of camping gear into the truck bed, and they took off, driving across the cattleguard slowly to keep the horses calm as they turned sharply onto the rock road. They clinked coffee cups, sipped, and chatted as they drove through the ranchlands, which were, topographically speaking, prairie. Small compared to the Tallgrass Prairie in Oklahoma (nearly fifty thousand acres compared to Gold Strike's seven thousand), but prairie nevertheless with its vast fuzzed face of cheatgrass and thistle, erupting in single hillocks that broaden and flatten then shoot straight up to vertical tables of ancient lava flow. The flows seemed to Eleanor like welcoming arms as you entered the foothills and climbed to the first whiff of pine in the middle forest, and after miles of curves, arrived in pristine high-country meadow and snow-capped escarpments.

Easton slowed and turned off at the road to the Sierra pack station. The rig jounced slowly along the badly rutted road parallel to the main river and campgrounds. Trees had split and fallen everywhere, testifying to the past winter's extreme weather. A Douglas fir lay across the road ahead. A crew had cut through the tree's diameter so cars could keep driving parallel to the drowned campsites at the swollen river's edge.

The wildflowers at this elevation had yet to bloom. The meadow was a bright green marsh. The corrals came into view. They were empty. The snows had been so severe and late in the season the pack station had delayed bringing its horses up from lowland pastures, which they typically did during the first week of May. Tie rails stretched for a good way and a platform had been built where people would stand and wait to mount their rented steeds before heading out for a few hours or days toward a high-country adventure. In a couple of weeks the place would be bustling with activity. For now, it was deserted.

Easton pulled up close to the corral and shut down the truck in front of the main buildings, a traditional rustic lodge with a grocery store, lobby, restaurant, and bar. The buildings were board and batten, painted brown with white trim. From Eleanor's perspective the station contributed a rare aesthetic to the high-country landscape.

A woman pushed out of the screen door to the building labeled OFFICE and stood on the wraparound porch, hands on hips.

"Jode!" She waved an arm above her head and walked down the steps and into the dirt yard toward them.

"Hey there, Annie," Easton said.

Annie, a hardy woman whose long gray-brown braid reached the small of her back, enveloped Easton in a hug. She leaned forward, grasping Eleanor's hand with both of hers. Her hands were calloused, her nails short and filled with dirt.

"I'm Eleanor."

"Good to meet you, Eleanor. I'm Annie. I manage the resort and pack station." She squinted at Easton. "I can put you two up. I can make up the beds. The kitchen's open. How long are you here for?"

"We're riding up mountain for a night. This is Eleanor's first time. She has a real job back in town working for the newspaper, so I have to get her back by Monday morning."

Annie eyed her with a mix of awe and skepticism. "Yeah? You wrote that story about the deceased young woman. I read your byline. A shame that had to happen. A fire and a body in the same vicinity." She rubbed her face. "I knew that girl. Marisol, she had a few problems in high school and went on to do real good at the college.

"Annie's only here in the warm months," said Easton.

"Don't be giving away my secrets," she said. "All I want from you is a fishing report when you get back. Someone caught a grayling up top."

"No kiddin'."

"Never saw the darn fish, so who knows if it's true." She rolled her eyes. "If you change your mind and don't want to sleep on hard ground, we have plenty of cabins. We're bringing up horses before pack season officially starts in two weeks and the kids get out of school."

"Tempting," Eleanor said.

"You the only one up here, Annie?"

"Owners are in an' out. We have a few girls coming today to shine things up. Wilson is fixing our saddles."

Easton turned to Eleanor. "That's McKenzie's dad. Jed Wilson."

"You know McKenzie?" Annie asked Eleanor.

"I did the Rodeo Queen story on her and her horse, Scotch. She works the drive-thru coffee shack and I'm a regular."

"Next time you drive through that coffee shack tell McKenzie there's a job up mountain if she gets tired of town. We'd love to have her around. Tell her Annie, her self-appointed godmother, misses her something terrible."

"You're everybody's self-appointed godmother."

"No, not true," Annie said. "Okay, you two. You have all the supplies you need, I'm sure, knowing Easton, but we have soda, candy, and energy bars. General store opens in an hour and the restaurant's serving lunch and dinner."

"We ate," said Easton.

"A Coke sounds good." Eleanor glanced up at Easton. "I'm a little queasy from the road."

"Let me grab you one. Follow me."

She followed Annie up the wooden steps and along the plank porch to the small market. The floors were beat up hardwood from the years of scuffing boot heels. Annie made a beeline to the tall refrigerator. "Diet or regular?"

"Regular. Thanks."

Eleanor pulled back the tab and sipped the brown foam. Easton shouted from outside. "Need some advice out here."

When they heard Easton yelling, they hurried out to the porch.

"Where do you want me to park the rig? I can drive up the road out the gate if that's better."

"You're good right there, Jode. Makes it look like horse people hang around here. You still ride Chester?"

"I do."

Easton swung aside the trailer door and brought out Chester.

Annie rubbed his neck. The horse seemed to know her. "He's still a beauty."

"How long's it been since you've been up here, Easton?" Eleanor asked.

Easton looked to Annie for the answer, then shrugged. "Since before Carol died," said Easton. "Five years."

"More like a century." Annie cupped Easton's face and squeezed his cheeks. "Eleanor, I'm very happy this man's found you. He's had a rough go keeping that ranch together. That your horse in there?"

"Jessie, short for Majestic. Her first time up here."

Easton brought Jessie out and handed the rope to Eleanor, who felt like a puffed-up greenhorn in front of this rancher and part-time mountain woman.

"She's a pretty horse," Annie said. "Like her mama. You let me know when you get back and make Easton sit down with us and have a meal together. You keep your rig here. That way, I'll know when you're back. You need anything?"

"We're good," said Easton.

"Then, I'm going back to organizing. Before you know it, we won't have one campsite or cabin that's not taken up. Great to see you Jode, and especially you, Eleanor."

She held out her arms and took both of Eleanor's shoulders, gave her a long comfortable gaze, likely evaluating whether she'd break this man's heart or heal it. Then, Annie turned, walked up the steps of the office-store-restaurant-bar, and disappeared behind the screen door, which closed with a dull thud.

* * *

Eleanor had never ridden in this part of the mountains, and it felt as if they were in a state of grace heading toward the Source. In the distance the glaciated peaks were snowcapped. Surrounding them were stunted pines growing from the seams of massive granite boulders that towered above them. She urged Jessie into a trot. Easton and Chester loped ahead until they came to blasted rock and slowed to climb. The top was sandy, and they walked awhile until a turnoff down the mountain. Eleanor leaned back in her saddle and gave Jessie a loose rein. Halfway down, a patch of blue sapphire glistened between the trees: the fishing hole, which was more like a very small lake. The sun warmed her back. She reached toward the sky and sniffed the sweet air.

"What do you think?" asked Easton.

"Paradise."

He clucked his horse forward and she followed single file along the shore into a grove of cedar where soft, thick duff covered the ground.

"If you look beyond the cedar, you can see a meadow where the Me-Wuk used to summer by the river."

Cr-aack. Cr-aack.

Jessie skittered sideways, and Eleanor moved with her.

"What was that?" She kept her voice down.

"Beer can target practice," Easton said. "It's not deer season, so maybe poachers."

"Are they nearby?"

"I'd say a mile away. Probably two or three."

"They sound closer."

"The air's thin, sound carries."

She dismounted and walked to the lake to test the water. "Icy." She dried her hand on her jeans.

"The fish are cold, too." He pushed back his hat. "Probably not great fishing right now."

She sat on the warm granite shelf, the backs of her legs absorbing the heat. Come darkness, the rock would distribute the sun's warmth long past its sink to the west. Easton sat down next to her.

"Your fishing hole is more like a small lake," she said, staring at the reflection that mirrored the pine and fir that grew close to the shoreline. "It's beautiful."

He picked up her hand and kissed it. "Glad you like it."

"I like Annie, too," Eleanor said. "What did you mean she only works in the warm months?"

"She's a townie. During the school year she works for juvenile hall and tries to find homes for troubled kids. In the summer she runs an outdoor program for at-risk youth." He plucked a blade of grass and stuck it between his teeth. "It's changed up here, like everywhere. Used be every kid hunted. Now, lots of them haven't even been in the woods much less the high country. She thinks kids who experience nature are going to find something in themselves they didn't know they had. She was Bart's counselor until he turned nineteen."

Bart Hargrove was Easton's nearly-adult, illegitimate son. Eleanor didn't like him.

"That's how you know her?"

"Annie and I go way back." He stood up with a grunt and brushed his hands on his jeans. "That is how I connected with Bart, though." He brushed his hands on his jeans.

While he put up portable fencing for their horses, Eleanor dwelled on the conversation that ended with Bart, which meant the air between her and Easton was ever so slightly tainted. Bart had that effect.

She staked the tent, laid out mats and the two sleeping bags. He poked his head in the tent and watched her zip them together. She looked up and smiled. "Want to continue that conversation?"

"Nope. I regret bringing it up in the first place." He grabbed the black cylinder that stored the fly rod and pulled out four delicate pieces. He lined up the dots on the outside and pulled out a reel and fit it to the rod and screwed it down. He stood to thread the line through the eyes, and the entire time she studied the length of him. He was six feet and lean up to his shoulders where ranch work had thickened his chest and arms. He named each piece of tackle: *Leader. Tippet.*

"Now for the fly." He picked up a flat plastic container. "I don't know what they're eating but we're going with an Adams." He plucked a light brown fly and threaded the line into the fly's tiny pinhole, twisted the tag end around the line—One, two, three, four, five times—and poked the end into the first loop, then slid the twists into a neat knot.

"Nothing to it." He cut the extra line, spit on the knot, and rubbed in his saliva. "Let's see if they're biting."

He tossed back the rod, unraveling the spider's silk and flipped the line forward. The fly dropped on the water's surface and the line lay down in front of him.

Eleanor flashed back to Leonard Parker, the Anishinaabe wilderness guide who'd led her to the Jarbidge River in search of Rette. He could fly fish.

"Normally," Easton said, reeling in the line, "about now, I'd cast again, but it's your turn."

"Can't I just watch? You're beautiful when you fish."

He handed her the rod and instructed her to hold it close to the butt end. He stood behind her, his breath on her neck. He held her wrist. "Back, forward."

"How am I supposed to concentrate?" She tried to turn toward him, but he held her still, and she could smell his day's musky sweat.

"Bring the line back, wait a beat, and swing it forward. Ten o'clock, two o'clock. Be intuitive, like you are with a horse. You've got natural rhythm. Use it." He kissed her neck.

She pointed the rod at the water, about to bring back her arm.

"Whoa."

"What?"

"Strip some line from the reel so your fly can travel."

She pulled the line from the reel until it coiled at her ankles. *Pull back*. The fly whizzed toward her. She closed her eyes, *beat*. She threw her arm forward. The fly landed a ways out and disappeared beneath the surface. She pulled. The rod bent.

"I have a snag."

"Maybe the shelf."

"How do you snag a shelf?"

"Driftwood, maybe."

She tugged the line free, and the fly zipped through the air and dropped behind her in a clump of purple penstemon that grew from the granite.

"Let's try again," he said.

She liked the dimple in his left cheek when he smiled.

"This one's a little ragged." She put her palm to his unshaven face and snuck a quick kiss before trying the routine again. The fly whipped behind her, *beat*, and she sailed it forward.

"Nice," said Easton. "Beautiful presentation."

The fly dunked and her rod jerked. *Another snag*. The reel clicked as the line went out, and she yelled, "I got one."

A fish leapt into the air, twisting.

"It's a brown," Easton said.

"It's heavy."

"It's big." Easton walked down the sloped rock to the lake's edge, his riding boots slippery. He leaned over the water with the net as she reeled in the zig-zagging fish, its dorsal fin breaking water. *Splash. Splash*. She backed up the ledge and slipped on loose gravel, landing butt first. Easton dropped the net to help as the trout swam away with the fly, and the rod began to slide down the granite toward the water. Eleanor scrambled down the rock and gripped the cork before the rod submerged. She reeled in the line and when the brown was close, yanked the rod. The fish went airborne for two stunning seconds before it smacked Easton in the face and skipped the hook, flip-flopping down the rock into the lake and away.

Easton sat on the slanting rock at the edge of the lake, quiet. She thought he might be in a bit of shock from the fish hitting him in the face. It was a big fish. She sat beside him, holding the rod. His shoulders shook. He couldn't talk. He slapped his knee and laughed.

"This is— *ha, ha, ha*— this is —*ah, ha, ha*— a damn good fish story."

She giggled. "Better if we'd caught the darn thing."

He wiped his eyes on his shirttail. "This way we don't need to decide. *Ha, ha* "—

"Decide what?"

"Whether to release her or kill her."

Kill her? Why did he have to say those words? Especially now.

9

THE WALL BETWEEN THEM PERSISTED past their dinner of campfire beans. It continued as she removed her jeans—which she did slowly while sitting on the sleeping bag, her back to him, one sock, then another, one pant leg, the other. She folded her jeans and placed them neatly by her head, so she could grab them quickly. She removed her shirt and was down to a tank top and panties when she climbed into the bag, not touching him. She leaned into the zipper, which was cold against her side and laid there with the bag tucked to her chin, staring up at the same thing he stared at—a small battery-powered lantern hanging from the plastic hook in the center of the tent.

"I'm scared," she finally admitted.

He turned onto his side and placed an arm gently across her hips. "Scared of what?"

His eyes were warm and transparent, and she saw clear to the bottom where she knew his kindness dwelled.

"Of you."

"Me?" He reacted like a boy accused of stealing candy.

"I was, until now."

"Seriously?" He looked worried. "Why are you afraid of me?"

"That thing you said after the fish got away."

"What did I say?"

"'*This way we don't need to decide whether to release her or kill her.*'"

"I said 'her'?"

"You did. And you said 'kill.' Not 'release or eat' or 'release or keep.' It made me think—" dare she say, "—there's a serial killer out there and it could be anyone."

"You think I'm a killer?"

"No."

"She says with hesitation."

"The thought crossed my mind."

"Do I look like a serial killer?"

"What does a serial killer look like, Easton? They're serial killers because they get away with it, and they get away with it because they look ordinary. They fake it. Or they compartmentalize their lives and the one we see resembles normalcy."

"You've been thinking about this."

"I have."

"Since when?"

"I'm not sure."

"Were you thinking this at lunch?"

"Subconsciously maybe. The fear was palpable when I dropped off Granite and realized I was heading into the wilderness, like Marisol."

"I'm sorry." He looked glum.

"I forgive you, even though you didn't do anything. One thing."

"Yeah?"

"Sexual innuendo makes me really nervous."

"The hot sauce?"

"It's hard for me to come up with a clever response."

"I won't do it again," he promised. "But you made me laugh."

She scratched her scalp. "I'm so hypersensitive right now. The ranger who was in the Forest Service lobby when I was checking on permits, he creeped me out. I got the impression he was purposely shutting down the woman I was talking to before she said something revealing."

"Did you get his name?"

"Dave Connor. Kate, the volunteer at the front desk, was trying to help me but clammed up as soon as he came in from the back and interrupted our conversation. She told me people don't think of taking out a permit until they get to the wilderness and then it's too late—they're too far from the ranger station. She was about to tell me something else when Dave comes in, like he'd been listening, and he interrupts at just that moment looking for horse stable brochures and he says the same thing in almost the same exact words. *People don't think of taking out permits until it's too late.* And then you said the same thing."

"Remember what else I said?"

"Maybe she didn't take out a permit because she wasn't intentionally in the area."

"Maybe someone killed her and moved her body," said Easton.

"Scary point."

"And you saw the pack station. They haven't even brought in the horses." He did that thing, running his hands through his hair until it stood in thick peaks. "Why would he be looking for brochures?"

"Some people plan their summer vacation?"

"Maybe."

"I get this nagging feeling," Eleanor said. "Mac said his buddy at SAR told him they found the fishing pole across the river from where they found the body— "

"Fly rod."

"Fly rod. As if someone witnessed something and ran."

"And here *we* are." His hands were under his cheek, palms pressed together. He looked boyish again, his eyes darting from her chin, fore-head, nose, mouth, looking for some sign of acceptance.

"You're smiling," he said. "Does that mean you're not afraid of me anymore?"

"Not as much."

"I had a thought, not to scare you."

She took a deep breath. "Tell me."

"Rangers have access to information, like the whereabouts of a per-son if they decide to take out a permit to camp in a specific wilderness."

"Egad. Good reason for not taking out a permit."

"Or someone might have known where Marisol would be camping, stalked her, killed her, and moved her body to the river to wash off the evidence."

"I wish we'd brought Granite," she said. "He takes me out of my head and my head is bursting with bad."

"I've lived in these mountains a long time." He was on his elbow now, pushing a strand of hair off her forehead. His warm palm on her chest brought a sigh. "People start out in one place, intending to go to a specific destination with a specific goal, and they wind up in an entirely different situation."

Like her searching for Rette nearly a year ago, where "different" was putting it mildly. The experience had changed her in ways she hadn't finished processing. Some good, for sure. She'd been touched by that elusive spirit of nature. Others, not so good, like when it came to trust.

"You know the dinnertime story I told about this guy I saw who lives in a shack down mountain from the trailer court."

"Yeah?" An expression of protectiveness rippled across his face.

"After our phone call cut out, I realized I'd taken the wrong path and wound up completely turned around." She told him, again, about the sudden appearance of the bear cub, and how Granite had chased it downhill. "There was a shack, and a man came outside to check on his dog. I ducked, and when I looked up he wasn't there, so I bushwhacked up mountain to the fire trail."

"First, glad you beat it out of there before the mama showed up. Second, explain again why you didn't tell me about this guy?"

Answering his question more fully required no small amount of courage. She cleared her throat.

"I was afraid. If I told you, you'd pressure me to move in with you for safety reasons."

Easton placed his hands behind his head and stared at the tent ceiling. "Want to know my take on our topic of living together?"

"I think so."

"If we end up living together, and I hope we do, sweet pea, it's going to be natural. One morning in the middle of feeding the horses or bringing them in from the trail, we're going to realize we've been living together for quite a while and can't pinpoint when the shift began."

Good answer.

Eleanor told him then more details of that disorienting afternoon—the fainting and waking up with Granite pressed to her side. When she turned on her side to check his response, he'd fallen asleep.

No. She crossed a leg over his hips and pulled herself onto him. Tugged her shirt over her head. Shook her hair from its messy ponytail so it spilled over her breasts. He was awake now. She closed her eyes, everything about her ready for him.

10

He handed her black coffee in a tin mug. She sat up, her tank top askew, a breast falling out.

"Morning, beautiful," he said. "Instant oatmeal okay?"

After a good night's sleep beside the man she loved, the fear was gone without any residual. Just a sense they'd left something unsaid that she couldn't put her finger on.

He returned with the oatmeal, and she pulled back the sleeping bag to make room for him. He kicked off his boots and removed his jeans, slipping into the bag next to her.

"Tell me about this place," she said. "What's your first memory?"

"I was up here before my first memory. My mom and pop rode up here, Mom carrying me in a sling. They'd pack a mule or two and camp for a month to get out of the heat. One reason she breastfed me for so long. Mom would paint landscapes, and my dad would fish and hunt. My first memory is catching a fish right out there where you slapped me with that brown. I didn't let them eat it. I made them promise I could take it home. I brought it everywhere, including kindergarten, where it lived in my desk until the room stank. My father made me a deal. If I turned it over to him, he'd take it to the taxidermist and get it mounted. Deal. He took it to the taxidermist with instructions to keep it simple. A taxidermized fish that I could keep at the foot of my bed with Paddington Bear."

She laughed, but her laughter stopped abruptly when Easton's face turned serious.

"Another time I took apart the family's wall clock. Pop didn't like that and took a belt to my butt."

She imagined the sting of leather, his undeserving little boy butt, bright red with welts. Eleanor's father had never raised a hand to her. He barely hugged her. She wondered what was worse and leaned forward to kiss Easton good morning, smelling the faintest whiff of trout.

"You're laughing." His eyes twinkled.

She put down her coffee to keep it from spilling and laughed some more.

"This is our magic place," he said.

"Everywhere I go with you is magic," she said.

"This place really is. The Me-Wuk hung out here in the old days."

"The Me-Wuk hung out everywhere in this county."

"They did. The river was their lifeblood. The trout were all native. The river's free-flowing water so pure that people drank from it and never worried about *giardia*. I wouldn't take the chance today unless I was dying of thirst."

Dying. She remembered what bothered her during last night's talk.

"What did you mean when you said people start out with one destination and end up in an entirely different predicament. Were you referring to me or Marisol Rodriguez?"

"Neither. I was just saying wilderness can kill you, no matter how experienced you are."

She nestled her head into his shoulder, and he pulled her closer.

"You good?" he asked.

"I'm good."

"If the county had succeeded twenty years ago in damming the Bear like they wanted to, this whole area for miles up and down the river would be flooded, and we'd be underwater."

"That would be a travesty. Maybe the developers figure the old enviros have died out and a new generation is in power without a memory of the past."

"Maybe. My gut tells me Peckham County, our neighbor to the west, is up to something."

She rose on an elbow and looked down at his face. "Like what?"

"Peckham utility district pays me for an easement to run power lines across my ranch. I got a letter they want my permission to improve the lines and deliver more power which means they need a new source to generate the power."

She hadn't seen power lines and towers on their rides.

"Next time we ride at the ranch, I'll show you."

A warmth spread through her when Easton spoke of their future. She touched his chest. He covered her hand with his.

"Those power developer dudes," he said, "are the long Covid of the waterways." He kissed her hand and flung back the sleeping bag. "They go into remission but never die."

* * *

Even the long cones hanging from the tips of sugar pines reflected sharply in the morning glass of the lake.

The stillness invited her to step into the water, to feel the cold inching to her thighs, her waist, up her back, until she dunked and the cold shot from her scalp to her vagus nerve, restoring her entire system and producing a sense of clarity and well-being.

"You look lost in thought." He crouched beside her and presented her with a second cup of coffee, the white puff of steam painting the cold morning air.

"I was contemplating a dunk," she said.

"From the look on your face, a dunk doesn't look like much fun."

"Everything up to the dunk including thinking about it is worth the after effect and bragging rights." She sipped the coffee, careful of the hot metal rim, and he put a gentle hand on her back. "I know that," she said, "yet—"

He pulled an acorn from his T-shirt pocket and handed it to her. The brown nut was shiny and smooth. Its cap felt rough on her fingertips.

"Acorns in these mountains are like snow in the arctic. Many varieties."

She hugged the acorn to her chest. "I cherish it."

"A mountain man's rose." He stood and held out a hand.

She grabbed on and let him hoist her to standing. She watched his surprise as she peeled off her clothes, stepped to the freezing water, screamed, and kept going. Easton tore off his shirt, kicked off his boots and jeans and underwear, and dove, surfacing with a shake of his head, breathless and exhilarated.

* * *

They lay naked and wet on the clean granite shelf. The rock had cooled overnight, but the sun and breezeless, mountain air quickly soaked up their moisture. They'd become as calm as the morning, not an oak leaf fluttering, not a blade of grass moving.

"It's so still," she said.

"Time we got going."

"I think we're meant to stay." She dried her foot with a sock. "It's so peaceful."

"Leaving before the wind shows up on the water's surface is good luck. I want to show you something first."

She followed him along the granite shore and up a shelf overlooking the water, where he stopped and pointed to an indentation in the rock.

"These are *chaw'se*," he said. "Grinding rock. The Me-Wuk created them by grinding acorns into meal generation after generation." He waved his hand over the land. "Everything you'd want and need until the snow came." He gazed upward toward the meadow beyond the cedar grove where the horses made soft nickering sounds and swished their tails at flies.

* * *

Eleanor swayed with Jessie's stride as they rode down mountain and leveled out. She ducked as they approached the low limb of an old mother oak. Beneath its canopy, hundreds of the biggest, shiniest acorns she'd ever seen were scattered across the ground, two acorns deep, waiting for a harvest that wouldn't come. That saddened her. The Me-Wuk still gathered acorns every fall, but she doubted the people would gather these. Since the discovery of gold in 1849, hordes of insatiable white men had invaded the land like armies of ants. With self-righteous zeal, they murdered Me-Wuk men, women, and children and drove them out of their summer camps, stealing their land with the state government's encouragement. By 1854, the State had paid volunteer militias nearly one million dollars for their atrocities, and the heinous goal of "extermination" wasn't over. At least one band of Me-Wuk today claims that in 1856 the Governor of California issued a bounty of twenty-five cents per Indian scalp; four years later the bounty was upped to five dollars a scalp.

The acorns at the mother tree's girth held so much potential and such loss that she ached as her horse stepped on the perfect seeds and their shells popped under hoof like crushed bone.

* * *

By the time they reached the pack station they were hungry. Annie was inside the restaurant setting tables and barking orders to the cook. Easton and Eleanor clomped up the porch steps and opened the screen.

"There you are." Annie threw up her hands. "I was starting to wonder. Take a seat. Anywhere."

No one else was in the room and Easton took the window seat that looked out the front porch to the meadow.

"Wonder about what?" he asked.

"If you decided to forget work and stay up there another night," she said. "That place is like that. Makes a person question her paradigm."

Eleanor was liking her paradigm these days: her dog, her horse, her boyfriend, her work. The only thing that disturbed her contentment was this shadow that lay over the town since Marisol had been killed, and that shadow felt aggressive, as if nothing was holding it back.

"It's a special place for sure," Eleanor said. "We dunked in the water. We caught a fish. A brown. It got away. We heard gunshots when we first got there."

"Idiots," Annie said. "How many shots? One shot, it's a poacher. More than one, it's likely a drunk doing target practice."

"Two shots," said Eleanor. "I haven't thought about it until now, but last night, I had the creeps."

"I can vouch for that," said Easton, turning sideways in his chair and stretching his legs in front of him. They looked at each other, unwilling to share her short-lived fear of Easton-the-wolf-in-sheep's-clothing.

"A lot of different energies floating around and converging up there," said Annie. "Site of a massacre, so, naturally, spirits dwell and past, present, and future are one. Your fear could be getting in touch with something ahead."

Easton plucked a menu from between the napkin holder and the condiment tray. "I think we need to eat," is all he said.

* * *

On the drive home from the ranch, Eleanor pulled up to the yellow coffee shack believing the caffeine would buffer the emptiness she felt when leaving Easton after spending time with him, which felt more intense even than dropping off Granite at the dog sitter's. Her chest ached where the invisible tendrils that had grown between them were severed when she departed.

"May I take your order?"

Eleanor leaned out her car window toward the speaker and greeted McKenzie. "It's Eleanor. Frappuccino Grande."

"Hi, Ms. Wooley. With whip?"

Why not. The extra sugar might kick her out of her funk. She could've spent the night with Easton at the ranch, except she had to pick up Granite and tomorrow was Monday, and she had to mentally prepare for following up on Marisol's death and the weekend crime report.

She drove forward and shut off her engine. McKenzie appeared at the service window, holding out the cold icy beverage.

"How was your weekend, Ms. Wooley?" Her voice was sympathetic, as if she knew Eleanor was blue.

"Great. My friend Easton Jode and I rode on horseback up to his old fishing hole and camped out."

"Did you catch a fish?"

"I did. And it got away." She smiled, recalling the fish. "I swung the darn thing into Easton face."

She remembered the special request. "Annie at the pack station told me to say hi to you."

McKenzie rolled her eyes. "I bet she told you she's my godmother."

"She did."

"And I bet she told you she wants me to work up there."

"That, too."

McKenzie's face turned serious. "Do they know yet if Marisol was murdered?"

"They haven't released that information. If you want, you can give me your contact and I'll call or text when I find out."

As McKenzie recited her cell number, Eleanor tapped it into her phone, pressed send, then hung up. "Now you have my number, too." She checked her mirror. No cars behind her. "How was your weekend?"

"I moved some cows."

"Moving cows sounds fun, as long as you have a horse." Eleanor dipped her finger into the whipped cream, her spirits lifted at the first taste of sugar.

"Yup, I got a mighty fine horse. Maybe you'd like to help out sometime."

"I'd like that, McKenzie. I'd like that a lot."

* * *

You'd think Eleanor had gone to Jupiter and back from Granite's carrying on. Whining, wagging his body, rolling over on his back. She paid the sitter and led him to the Bronco's back seat. He jumped in and immediately squeezed through the space between the bucket seats and started licking her face.

"Granite," she said as sternly as possible, feeding him through the gap into the back seat. She pointed her finger. "Stay."

That night he slept on her bed, and his weight against the back of her legs felt good.

11

Two mugs sat beside her computer where she'd left them last week, both bearing a thick, dark brown ring and an inch of old coffee. Her desk was cold gray metal, her chair an outdated swivel with stained upholstery. Eleanor looked around the newsroom, reaffirming what she already knew: A newsroom was, aesthetically, the least attractive of office spaces. She placed the acorn Easton had given her on the windowsill.

Press releases cluttered her desk. Books lay on the edge. *The Wild Horse Conspiracy* by Craig Downer, with yellow sticky tabs poking out. Her hard copy of the *AP Stylebook* covered in dust. *Ghost Town* by Ezra Dane, overdue from the community college library. Two KN95 Covid masks were unopened in their plastic covers. She dropped the masks into her bottom drawer, reminding herself to get a fourth vaccination.

She went to the break room and made coffee. The *perk, perk, perk* of Folgers eased her into the day. She poured a cup before the pot was done brewing and took the mug to her desk, where she opened her computer and checked wire service updates.

AP Moraga Plateau, CA. *Forty-two wild horses died during a series of roundups from the Moraga Plateau. Operations began yesterday with temperatures expected to reach 110.*

The caffeine hit her brain stem, released dopamine, and provided her first inspired word of the morning: *Fuck.*

ONE OBSERVER REPORTED, *"AN 8-YEAR-OLD mare in the back pen of the trap tried jumping the panel, fracturing her neck, and was euthanized."*

Eleanor thought of the injured rodeo horse that had been put down for the same reason. Since that incident, she'd learned a vet couldn't be certain a horse suffered a neck fracture until they were X-rayed.

THE MARE IS ONE OF *many wild horses euthanized for non-life-threatening conditions or dead from roundup-related causes. Several died in transport before arriving at off-range corrals, raising concerns about the stress they are enduring during the roundup.*

THE BLM NOW HAS MORE *than sixty thousand wild horses in captivity, nearly as many as remain in their "federally protected herd management areas."*

A SPOKESMAN FOR THE HORSES *said, "Wild horses are not the problem. The problem is management."*

* * *

"God damn it," said Eleanor.
"What's going on?" asked Mac.
"I'm pissed."
"No. You're a reporter. Start over."
She picked up her laptop and walked it over to Mac's desk. "Just look at this wrangler on horseback rounding up a mustang the helicopter missed." She tapped the video. "See him kicking the poor horse in the head? That horse died in transport to the fucking government corrals."

"Those cowboys are in the wrong business," Mac said. "They should get work as cops."

"Not funny. I want to do the story."

"It's already been written, right here. It's not local and you're biased. Pissed, if I heard right."

"Gold Strike is full of horse people who would share my feelings."

"Which are?"

"We love horses and want them protected, not abused."

"People in Gold Strike don't necessarily care about horses they don't own, especially if those same creatures are treading on pasture they could otherwise graze cattle."

"One, I think people here would do almost anything to save horses. And two, they'll care because the government is fucking this up, and often, they don't like government."

"Three?"

"The helicopter roundups are costing the everyday taxpayers a fortune, they're abusive, and not solving the problem."

"Here's the problem," said Mac. "We don't have wild horses in this county, and I'm damn sure ranchers want to keep it that way."

Eleanor inhaled deeply and lowered her voice. "It's a great photo op."

"We'll pick up the AP story. You stick to local news."

She carried her laptop back to her desk, angry, until the email notification from the Gold Strike County Medical Examiner popped up on her screen. She opened the file on Marisol Rodriguez and scanned the report. For "Cause of Death," *asphyxia* had been entered. In other words, Marisol had been strangled. Forensics had found no evidence of water in her lungs. She hadn't drowned.

The ME also reported a single blunt-force trauma to the parietal region of the head. The blow could've been river rocks, but if that were the case, a single blow would be unlikely. Debris was found in her pharynx that was determined to be *Cornus florida*. She googled the term. *Cornus florida* was the scientific name for dogwood. A chill ran up her spine and tightened her scalp. She googled "dogwood" and religious sites came up. According to one site, Jesus's cross was built from dogwood, and after the crucifixion God put a curse on the tree. From there on out it would be small and weak and useless for timber, which was certainly true of the dogwoods in her own backyard forest.

* * *

Sheriff Duncan picked up on the first ring.

"It's Eleanor."

"What can I do for you?"

He didn't ask about the pup, so she got to the point.

"I received the coroner's report. Marisol Rodriguez was strangled."

"She died of asphyxia," he said. "Strangulation would imply someone or something strangled her. We don't know that."

"No water found in her lungs, so she didn't drown, is that correct?"

"No water found in her lungs, correct."

"And dogwood blossoms found in her throat?"

"Yes."

"Do you suspect foul play?"

"The case is under investigation. That's all I can tell you at this point."

"Do you have a person of interest?"

"What did I just say?"

"You're being rhetorical, correct?"

No answer.

"I did check the Forest Service for names of people who took out wilderness permits," she said. "Did your detective cover that angle?"

"What'd you find out?"

"The section of river where Marisol was recovered is designated wilderness. You're supposed to take out a permit to camp in designated wilderness. The Forest Service doesn't have a record of Marisol Rodriguez taking out a permit."

He didn't respond. She figured right now he was thinking.

"Sheriff Duncan, for the record, what is your official statement on Marisol Rodriguez's cause of death?"

He cleared his throat. "Last Sunday, the Gold Strike Sheriff's Office recovered Marisol Rodriguez's body from the Little Bear River, and today we can confirm her death was caused by asphyxiation."

"Does that exclude the possibility of drowning?"

"The medical examiner concluded there was no evidence of water in her lungs."

"Which means you are ruling out death by drowning?"

He sighed. "Yes."

"And the blunt force trauma to the head?"

"We can't say the cause, but we're continuing to investigate the case, and we ask anyone with information to call our office. That includes you, Eleanor. I have a call on the other line." *Click.*

12

THIS WAS A SCHOOL DAY so Eleanor texted McKenzie Wilson, as promised, and asked her to call when she had a chance.

At ten-twenty a.m. McKenzie's name showed on Eleanor's cell.

"Hi Ms. Wooley. I'm between classes and walking while we talk if I sound rushed."

"Thanks for returning my call, McKenzie. I said I'd let you know when I heard the official news about Marisol. The coroner released the report this morning. They determined that Marisol died from asphyxiation."

"What does that mean?"

"She didn't drown."

"You mean after she was dead, he threw her in the river. Why?"

"We don't know. And we don't know the gender of her killer, either."

"Was the killer trying to hide the body or wash away evidence?"

"Don't know that either." She sounded like Sheriff Duncan.

McKenzie was silent.

"Do you have a contact for one of Marisol's girlfriends?"

"Why? Do you think one of her friends killed her?"

"Not at all. A girlfriend might know what Marisol had been planning that day and where she might have been when she encountered her killer."

"That's so awful to imagine."

"It is, McKenzie, and you and your friends need to be hyper-aware of your surroundings when you go out."

"Rosie Taft. She hung around with Marisol. Rosie was a senior at my high school when I was a sophomore and now she's a second year at Sierra. I'll text you her contact."

Eleanor tapped the contact box McKenzie had texted, and Rosie picked up on the first ring. She confirmed Marisol had told her she planned a solo campout that weekend at Lake Eleanor in Yosemite.

"Eleanor," Mac shouted. "I need your story."

She inserted her AirPods, tapped Spotify, and turned up the volume on "Tennessee Whiskey."

GOLD STRIKE COUNTY CORONER TODAY released the cause of death for 25-year-old Marisol Rodriguez as asphyxiation. Rodriguez was found dead in the Little Bear River on Sunday—Mother's Day— leaving her family, friends, and the Gold Strike community grieving the tragic loss of a young life.

HER BODY WAS DISCOVERED IN the Little Bear River just above the Browns Ferry Reservoir inlet.

ACCORDING TO GOLD STRIKE COUNTY Sheriff John Duncan, "The medical examiner concluded there was no evidence of water in her lungs."

THE MEDICAL EXAMINER ALSO REPORTED evidence of blunt force trauma to the head, without stating a cause.

DUNCAN WOULD NOT COMMENT ON the possibility of foul play in Rodriguez's death.

"THE SHERIFF'S OFFICE IS CONTINUING to investigate the case," he said. "We ask anyone with information to call our office."

A FRIEND OF RODRIGUEZ TOLD the Gold Strike Tribune that

Rodriguez had planned to spend her weekend camping at Lake Eleanor in the Yosemite wilderness. No one has reported seeing her in that vicinity.

HER BODY WAS DISCOVERED EARLY Sunday by an inmate with the state prison fire crew who was working on the nearby Brown's Ferry wildfire. He noticed Ms. Rodriguez's red jacket on the surface of the turbulent river, her body lodged against a fallen tree. A Gold Strike Search and Rescue diver pulled the body from the river with the assistance of United States Forest Service fire personnel and Gold Strike Sheriff Deputies. Rodriguez was pronounced dead at the scene.

IN THE MONTHS PRECEDING HER untimely and tragic death, Ms. Rodriguez, a 4.0 GPA honors student at Sierra Community College, was preparing to transfer to a University of California campus in fall to pursue a bachelor's degree in Natural Resource Management.

Eleanor walked the two blocks to the Alano Club for lunch. Considering the longing effect of Chris Stapleton on the subject of whiskey, an AA meeting was a good idea.

Charlotte, one of the regular meeting attendees, stood behind the counter, flipping burgers. She had three years of sobriety, and manning the grill was her service commitment.

Eleanor slipped onto a stool at the counter. She ordered a cheeseburger and Coke for five bucks.

"You look pissed," Charlotte said.

"A little." At Mac for snuffing the story she wanted to write, at the BLM for causing the issue, at Sheriff Duncan for directing his irritability at her. All the tangible objects she could blame. What really bothered her dwelled within an inarticulate fog she couldn't navigate.

Charlotte placed a paper plate with a glistening patty plopped on one side of a bun and lettuce, tomato, and pickle on the other. She pushed the plastic squeeze bottle of ketchup closer to Eleanor and watched her wolf down the burger. Eleanor asked for mayonnaise.

"I read your story," said Charlotte.

Eleanor nodded as she bit into the burger. Ketchup and beads of juicy grease fell to the paper plate.

"I got a bad feeling there's a predator out there looking for his next young woman."

Eleanor put down the last bite and wiped her lips with a small white paper napkin. "Why's that?"

Charlotte held up her phone. The online version of Eleanor's story flashed on the screen. "She was found in the river, but she didn't drown? And the fire right there? Catastrophe on top of catastrophe in the same place at the same time is just plain weird."

"I don't disagree."

"And the woman was in her twenties, like me. Attractive."

"Like you."

Charlotte's version of a smile was guarded. "Thanks, but I'm thinking of that guy in New York City they busted for killing seven women. All young."

"Over the span of two decades."

"I'm not waiting around. Those fucking cops better get their fucking act together and catch this fucking pervert."

"I hear you." Eleanor recalled the stress in the Sheriff's attitude. "My take, they're working overtime on this one."

Someone entered the building. He walked behind her, past the grill and down the hall to a meeting that would begin in five minutes. Two women walked in next and remarked on the lingering scents of onion and grilled beef.

"That was delicious," said Eleanor. "Thanks."

"If you want another, let me know now or you're shit out of luck. I close the grill in an hour."

Eleanor dropped her napkin on the paper plate and tossed it in the trash. She entered the meeting room and sat down. Moments later, Charlotte stuck her head in the doorway.

"I'm taking burger orders," she said. "Five bucks per, all proceeds to the club. Last chance. Kitchen closes in an hour."

The two women who'd passed her in the front room raised their hands.

As Eleanor sat still for that hour, she winnowed down her long list of must-dos to one item: She needed to see Easton.

13

LOVE WAS UNSETTLING. IT TOOK the power out of daily routines and relegated a lot of things Eleanor thought she should do to "unnecessary." She did have to pick up Granite from the groomers, and she had to get gas. Then, she'd help Easton with the mare.

She found him in the barn. The stall had been lined with fresh straw, and he knelt on the straw beside the mare who lay on her side in labor.

"How can I help?" she asked.

"Glad you're here, babe," he said. "You can bring those clean towels over here."

She lifted the towels off the stall door, held them to her chest, and knelt in the hay near Easton. Granite walked into the stall as if a dog being present when a horse was giving birth was normal.

Eleanor pointed to the stall gate. "Out."

He slunk out and lay down just outside the gate.

All her adult life Eleanor had heard about people who'd observed a live birth remark in awe at the transformation of the female body when delivering a newborn—horse or human. But it was one thing to hear about foaling and another to witness. The foal's front hooves pushed out of the mother's vulva. Then the head covered in a white birth sac. Easton broke the membrane near the nose, and the foal received its first contact with fresh air. The shoulders came next.

"This is the hardest part, given the width."

The mare contracted and the shoulders came through. The rest of the foal slipped onto the straw. The mare raised her head, sniffed the baby, and lay back on the straw, exhausted.

"Mama's resting," said Easton. "Which is good. The longer she's down the more blood flows to the foal. You want to dry her baby with one of those towels."

Eleanor did and soon the foal, a filly, struggled to stand on all fours.

Later, that night in bed, the two of them went over the birth. They bandied names.

"We seem to do a lot of naming," she said.

"Names mark a special place in time. They hold a lot of power. Glad we're naming together."

He lay back with one arm under his head and she ran her palm along the fine hair on his broad chest and down his slim belly that flinched at her touch. She kissed him.

Later, as they lay there, she said, "Perfection," and a tinge of sadness followed because perfection didn't last.

* * *

Next morning a press release from the Rancheria sat on her desk. It announced the California Indian Market two weeks from now. Eleanor called the Rancheria, gazing out the second story plate glass window at the town's Western shop façades and flat rooftops. A woman on the other end of the call gave her the contact information for an artist, Renee Standin, who lived at the Rancheria. Eleanor called the number and made an appointment to interview Renee that afternoon for a short event feature.

She drove through the countryside with her window down. The wavy two-lane road was bounded on both sides by barbed wire, and the far-reaching pastureland bore patches of purple lupin and golden poppy. Granite rode in the backseat with his head out the window as they passed acre upon acre of undulating, emerald-green prairie, some of the best pasture in the state.

Eleanor pulled to the side of the road and stepped out of the car. Dry heat rose from the asphalt. The silence was hollow. Not even a bird or rustle of grass. For miles the land was flat, fringed with hillocks and no sign of human activity. She photographed the panorama and got back in her Blazer.

Ahead, a line of cattle crossed the road. She pulled up to a stop and shut off the engine. Quiet again. A woman on horseback was in the middle of the road controlling the herd as the cattle crossed. A wide-brimmed hat shaded her face, a long braid fell down her back, a big blue scarf surrounded her neck, and she wore full chaps. McKenzie Wilson. Her focus was trained on the livestock as they crossed the road, and she paid no attention to the red and white vehicle, or its driver, stopped in the middle of the road.

McKenzie slapped her hip to drive the cows. One of the cows broke from the line and turned back. McKenzie kicked and Scotch dug in. Her arms were like wings, chasing down the cow. Eleanor stepped out of her car hastily and zoomed in as McKenzie threw her rope and caught the cow around the neck, tightening it as she rode, slowing the cow to a stop and turning it around. As she and the cow neared, she glanced at Eleanor, acknowledged her with a subtle nod, and drove the cows home.

Eleanor was late for her interview at the Rancheria. As she drove down the twisted road to the river canyon, she felt carsick from the curves. She pulled onto a turnout, opened the car door and heaved onto the asphalt. She leaned back in a light sweat and stared out her windshield. *1906* had been stamped into the cement pillar of the one-lane bridge ahead that spanned the middle fork of the Little Bear.

She drove forward onto the road, and as she crossed the one-lane bridge, she slowed to check out the river. This was the rocky, dry end of the watershed, pocked with chaparral, live oak, and bull pine. But the water flowed high, and this year the river rocks wouldn't show their skullcaps until August.

She climbed out of the canyon and, finally, turned off at the wood sign "Rancheria" and followed the arrow. Straight ahead and to the right was the Roundhouse. The Roundhouse was a place of tribal ceremonies and off limits to outsiders. Eleanor pulled in beside a dusty black Dodge Ram with Nevada license plates.

She tied Granite to a shaded bench on the Tribal Headquarters porch. The receptionist directed her to Renee Standin's office two doors down the hall.

Renee waved her in. "Sit anywhere."

She wore her hair in a loose bun. Long red and yellow beaded earrings hung from her ears and draped the tops of her shoulders. The button-down white shirt was striking. She wore a wide silver bracelet on one wrist, a turquoise Apple watch on the other.

Framed diplomas hung on the wall behind her. A bachelor's degree in Hydrology and Water Sciences from Stanford and a PhD in Earth and Planetary Sciences from the University of California, Santa Cruz.

"You're a slug," said Eleanor.

The banana slug, which is the university's mascot, is notably a bright yellow, fat mollusk that can grow up to nine inches long. It thrives in the Pacific Coast redwoods, and its trail of slime numbs the tongues of its predators.

"Takes one to know one," said Renee.

"And you're a hydrologist," said Eleanor.

"That, too."

"For the Rancheria?"'

"For the Forest Service. I'm in charge of water issues. My office is in town, but they let me work here."

Eleanor felt the synchronicity but didn't go there. She stayed focused on the California Indian Market, the reason she was here.

"Tell me about your artwork."

Renee undid the top button of her shirt, revealing a complicated necklace of delicately curled silver oak leaves and acorns on a double strand, each leaf inlaid with a dot of abalone.

"That's beautiful. How do you create such beautiful art and hold a full-time career?"

"I couldn't do my job if I didn't do my art."

Eleanor asked if they could go outside and take photos. As they crossed the road, she mentioned the rumors of a renewed dam project up mountain on the middle fork of the Bear River.

"That project was turned down two decades ago. My people and the residents soundly rejected that project."

"A reliable source thinks it's resurfaced."

"Rumor's not much to go on."

"He's a rancher who received a letter from a neighboring county notifying him they're upgrading the grid that crosses his ranch. He thinks they're scheming on a dam to provide the grid power. Have you heard anything?"

"This is the first."

"If it were true, how would a dam on the Bear affect your community?"

"The river is a way of life. It's our source of drinking water. Our wells. We fish from that river. That river is a special place for our people. We gathered acorns and ground them by the river."

Eleanor recalled the old oak and the clean dirt beneath laden with acorns.

"And redbud for our baskets."

Eleanor had seen the bright pink of the redbud, too. "Did you work on that project?"

"It was before my time, but I've studied our comments to the environmental report. The dam project research on the planners' side was notably insufficient. They didn't consider the porosity of the rock they'd anchor the dam to or the topography's ability to hold enough water to make the dam economically feasible. Bad for everyone."

"I've recently ridden very near there on horseback with my rancher friend."

Renee's face softened and she smiled. "I used to camp up there when I was a girl. In summer, up and down that river. I want you to meet someone. Do you have time?"

Yes, she had time.

"Bring your dog. He doesn't need to be on a leash."

On foot they trekked up a gravel road, passing small wooden homes, until they came to a red log cabin at the end of the road. The cabin's yard was carpeted with a thin layer of wood shavings on which stood numerous large carvings. Bear on all fours. Bear standing on hind legs. Eagle with salmon in its talons. Three wooden busts of American Indian men in war paint. The one with red and black polka dots on his full cheeks and two wooden feathers sticking out of his bandana seemed to watch her.

The two women walked across the yard and passed through the cabin's entryway of vertical plastic strips to keep out the cold. An old man ate soup by the woodstove. His white braid tapered down his thick back.

"This is my grandfather, Lawrence Standin." She pulled up a wooden back chair and sat beside him. "Grandpa, this is Eleanor from the newspaper. She's doing a story on the market."

He held out his hand and they shook. "Nice dog."

"That's Granite," said Eleanor.

The old man motioned for her to sit on the couch, which she did, and was consumed by the sagging cushions.

"Tell him what you told me about the dam," Renee said.

The old man listened with a calm befitting a lifetime of being taken from.

"The white man's plans get cold," he said, "but they're never gone. Too many greenbacks."

"But you filed your comments the last time."

"Sure we did, and it's documented in the Environmental Impact Report," said Renee. "The thing is we don't divulge to outsiders why a place is sacred. If the public knew where we gathered in the old days they'd vandalize and steal artifacts."

"I understand. A conundrum."

"But he could take some stakeholders there to help them understand the true power of that place."

"That would be great," said Eleanor. "I've taken that trip on horseback. It's rough."

"He's strong."

Lawrence flexed.

"Before you leave, come to the Roundhouse with us, Eleanor."

* * *

Eleanor heard a man praying. She followed Renee and Lawrence, ducking under the doorframe into the earthen room. The praying stopped and orange flames licked the dark from the center of the room. The man threw a log on the fire, and sparks flew up like fireflies.

Renee motioned for Eleanor to come sit by her in front of the fire. Lawrence sat in a chair. The man by the fire threw on more wood. More sparks. The flames illuminated his face.

Leonard Parker.

14

"Nell W." Leonard sat in lotus position, his knees touching the tamped ground. "I knew our paths would cross again."

In the light of the small bonfire, he looked the same as he had the last time she'd seen him. Same wide shoulders in a slouchy red T-shirt, blue jeans. He poked the fire. Same silver cuff he wore when she was searching for Rette. His long, loose braid reached his waist.

Eleanor didn't know much about Leonard. He'd given her the first concrete evidence in her search for Rette. He'd showed up when she needed a guide, fished for her dinner, made her feel safe, then abandoned her on the Jarbidge River in the middle of one of the most remote wildernesses in the country. He wasn't her friend. He surfaced with an obscure phone call, making amends, offering an explanation, telling her he'd purchased eleven horses, then hanging up with nothing for her to go on but a blocked phone number.

"What are you doing here?" she asked.

"Work. You?"

"Gathering information."

"You got any information about the town rodeo? Some of your people didn't like what they saw."

"I covered that rodeo for the newspaper. I was standing at the fence rail during the Wild Horse event when one of the horses crashed into the rail and dropped. I watched them put the poor guy down."

"We're investigating the livestock company that supplied those animals. Know anything, I'd appreciate you sending it my way."

"I'll send my photos. I almost investigated the incident."

"Not an investigative paper. Isn't that what you say, Nell W.?"

"That's what my editor says."

"For the record, that company has a bad reputation and some bad seed. One of their wranglers tortured a mustang during a roundup in Nevada. Exhausted the horse from running it in the heat. Brought her to the ground and started kicking her in the face. We have it on video."

"I read about that."

"The mare died in transport to the BLM pens."

"That's terrible. I *almost* died after you led me to the river and left me there. Why'd you disappear, Leonard?"

"Why'd you not tell me what happened to your missing friend?"

"I think you know what happened to my friend. I think you know what happened to the eleven stolen horses. One of those horses saved my life after you left me to fend for myself against starvation, mountain lion, and bad spirits."

"Which horse?"

"The gelding with one white stocking and a small scar on his forehead. His name is Good Horse Bob."

"His name is Mishko. He's a loner."

"That would be him." Her voice rose from talking about Good Horse Bob.

Renee had been quiet, but Eleanor's excitement spurred her to ask how they knew each other. Eleanor started to explain when a whiff of weed hit her nose. Renee passed a joint. Eleanor waved it off. Renee walked the burner to Leonard. Eleanor closed her eyes and remembered when Gold Strike Search and Rescue had given up their search for Rette, but Eleanor would stop at nothing and her tenacity drew her to Nevada, where she imagined Rette might go; eventually the tables turned, and Eleanor became the victim who needed saving.

Leonard sucked in the smoke and held his breath. "The rancher boyfriend." He let out a stream of smoke. "You together?"

"We are. He doesn't like you."

Renee laughed. Grandfather snored, his head bent over his chest. Eleanor's back hurt from sitting on the ground. "How did you and Leonard meet?"

"Stanford," said Renee.

Leonard tossed sage into the fire. "Pow wow."

Renee sat down by Leonard, their shoulders nearly touching. Sparks flew up from the pit as if their energy had stoked the fire. They spoke tenderly in that intimate shorthand of lovers.

* * *

Eleanor drove down the canyon and reached the one hairpin. At its apex the westering sun cast a pink glow on the canyon walls. She drove slowly, savoring the light until she approached the one-lane bridge. On the far side of the oak where she'd barfed, a woman with stringy, graying blond hair sat slump-shouldered on a rock. Eleanor rolled down the window as she neared.

"Do you need help?" Eleanor asked.

The woman pointed to the river below. Eleanor got out of the Blazer and crossed the road and saw a large animal lying prone under the bridge. It was a coyote, and she assumed the animal had been hit by a car and crawled off the road to die in the shade of the bridge. Someone had placed poppies on its fur.

The woman under the oak had that thin-jawed look of addiction. Meth was the cheap drug of choice in the foothills, and the drug ate its consumers from the inside. She was old before her time. Her clothes sagged on her frame and her black and white Keds were missing their laces.

"I need a ride to town," she said.

Granite growled when the woman got into the passenger seat. Eleanor reprimanded him with a loud "No" and made conversation to distract the carsickness she'd suffered on the way in.

"What happened to the coyote?"

"That poor coyote was shot." The woman's eyes were bloodshot, and Eleanor couldn't tell if she was high or they were red from crying. "A female with pups from the looks of it. I gotta find them."

"That's sad."

"Makes me want to string up the asshole who finds pleasure in killin' beautiful things."

"Seems to be a lot of that going around," Eleanor said.

"You mean the woman they found upriver?" She put up her hand to shield her eyes from the sun as she looked over at Eleanor. Something flicked in and out of her mouth.

"Yes, the woman."

"I was there."

"You were where?"

"At the river. The night before. It was sundown after the mosquitoes. First, I thought it was a bear crashing down mountain. Then the flash of red and I can't believe what I'm seeing. Hooded blob like a zombie carrying a woman down mountain and pacing up the river a ways and back down and decides right there's the spot and dumps her practically in front of me."

Eleanor didn't believe her. "Where were you?"

"Opposite side of the river."

"You saw the killer throw Marisol Rodriguez in the river?"

"I wish I hadn't."

"Was she alive?"

"She wasn't moving, and I didn't stick around to find out."

"Did you tell the sheriff?"

"Hell no. All they'd do is lock me up for crazy."

"Why were you there?"

"Fishing for dinner. Brookies like the inlet that time of night."

"Did you see the fire?"

"I heard about the fire."

"Could you find that spot again?"

"You couldn't pay me to go back up there. That place is evil now. My pole's still there. Proof I'm telling the truth. Not that I care. I care about this coyote's pups. Could you drop me at Walmart for some pup formula?"

She did that flicking thing again.

"Do you happen to know the brand?"

"Milk replacement for puppies but it'll work for coyotes."

"I mean the fishing rod. Do you know the make?"

"It had green string."

As Eleanor drove back to town the woman made that flicking noise. She glanced at the woman and realized she'd been flicking her false teeth in and out.

"Are you comfortable giving me your name?" asked Eleanor.

"I'd rather not. I don't care if you know, but you never know who's listening."

Eleanor pulled up to the curb in front of Walmart and put the Blazer in neutral. A few people walked out of the building pushing big shopping carts into the parking lot. A steady flow entered the air-conditioned building, and Eleanor was certain—because she was guilty of this herself—at least a few of the so-called shoppers were actually in that spacious store seeking a cheap way to cool down on a blazing saddles afternoon.

"I'll get out here."

"How can I find you?"

She opened the car door and stuck out a leg. "I guess you'll bump into me when God wants you to." She turned back and said to Eleanor, "That coyote mama was a warning. I'm next. They're waiting for the perfect time to take me. I've been abducted once before by extraterrestrials."

"I wouldn't tell the sheriff about the extraterrestrials—"

"I'm not talking to no sheriff."

"What if they —"

"That's not who I'm worried about."

"Who are you worried about?"

"That thing they say about lightning not hitting the same place twice ain't true. It hits once and you're an attractor, and now I'm a walking lightning rod and their radar is on me."

"They?"

"It's a movement."

"What kind of movement?"

"A plague of darkness moving over the land, consuming the light."

"I'd keep that to yourself as well if the sheriff does pick you up. Now, before you go, is there anything else you remember about the person carrying the woman? White? Male or female?"

"Strong is all. Carrying a dead weight." The woman backed away from the car, about to shut the passenger door.

"The fishing rod. What color?"

"Brown, I guess. Long. I kept getting it caught in the tree. There's some string and my hook still up there where I broke the line."

"What kind of tree?"

"You ask too many damn questions. Do you have any cash?" She flicked her false teeth.

Eleanor dug into her backpack and found a twenty and offered it to the woman's outstretched palm. The woman snatched the bill and stuffed it in her back pocket as if she were entitled.

"Good luck with the pups," said Eleanor.

The woman shut the car door and disappeared inside the store.

15

THE POSSIBILITY OF ORPHANED COYOTE pups consumed Eleanor's thoughts. She hoped the woman succeeded in finding them because most old timers of Gold Strike hated coyotes. Coyotes preyed on their livestock and ate their pets. A cat who didn't come home was likely a meal. A small dog in an unfenced backyard dragged away in front of their owner's eyes was an oft-repeated cautionary tale. Kids grew up shooting coyotes, along with snakes, squirrels, birds, anything wild, and did so without much thought. These were small violences compared to wars and acts of terror and outlawing maternal health care, but without guidance, this mindless trajectory evolved into a lack of compassion for suffering. Her best friend Rette, a math teacher, had worried about this and had done her best to teach empathy and tolerance in her classroom.

Eleanor's phone pinged and she pulled over to read a text message.

This is my thirty-day notice. I'll be moved by the end of the month. When I move, I'll expect my security deposit back.

"Goddamn it." She didn't need one more problem. Renting Rette's house covered the mortgage and insurance payments. That way, if Rette ever returned, she'd have a place to live. Eleanor had spent the tenant's security deposit hiring handymen to clean rain gutters, fix a cracked window, and replace a broken wall furnace.

She made a hasty rolling stop at the next intersection but the driver with a pickup-truck load of hay had already started a left-hand turn in front of her. She slammed on her brakes. The driver rolled down his window and stuck out his elbow. As he turned the corner and his face was within a yard of her face, he looked straight at her, not in a mean way, but in a fed-up-with-people-running-around-like-headless-chickens-way, and said firmly, "Slow down."

She did.

* * *

Eleanor stood calmly in the lobby of the Sheriff's Office while Sally got on her desk phone and told Duncan she was in the lobby.

"He'll see you."

He pointed to the chair across from his desk and told Sally to hold his calls.

"What's up?"

"I met a woman," she said. "She told me she witnessed someone at Brown's Ferry run down the mountain with a body and throw it in the river."

"That's something." He leaned forward. "You believe her?"

"Some of it. She mentioned a red jacket."

He rubbed his chin. "You wrote that detail in your story. She might have read it in the newspaper."

"Maybe. She said that at the time she'd been fishing on the opposite side of the river from where the body was tossed, and after she saw the person basically throw Marisol's body in the river, she split."

"Anyone could say that."

"Leaving her fishing pole on the bank."

Duncan plucked the pen from his breast pocket and pulled the small pad of paper closer. "She brought up the rod?"

"Green line."

His pen remained poised an inch above the paper. "Anything else?"

"She snagged the line in a tree. It could still be there."

"Where?"

"In the tree. Unless you've already collected it."

He pulled a set of keys out of his bottom desk drawer and stood up. "I'll check it out. You want to come?"

She did.

"We'll take my vehicle."

"I have Granite."

"He rides in back."

They drove up mountain in his Ford Escape, siren off, passing Eleanor's mobile home park and the Brown's Ferry reservoir road. Little was said. They continued up the mountain pass to a gated Forest Service road that was closed to the public. Duncan got out, unlocked and swung the gate to the side and drove through. Eleanor volunteered to open the next gate. He declined the offer. A ways down the road, they approached a questionable wooden bridge spanning the river and crossed it. Eleanor gripped the overhead handrail as Duncan continued down mountain into the canyon on what appeared to be a rarely used storm-eroded dirt road. All sizes of branches and debris littered the road. Cut trees with exposed roots stuck out of the bank, looking like they could fall with the next forest breath.

"Hope we get through," he said. "A helluva long way to back out."

After another half an hour of driving in low they sighted the burn scar on the opposite side of the river.

Duncan drove a ways and parked. He got out of the Escape and started walking as if he knew where he was going. She followed until he stopped at a dry, flat spot close to the swift water.

"Right here." He pointed to yellow tape that had been strung around a couple of tree trunks and brush. "Here's where we found the rod." He straddled his legs and stared at the ground. Eleanor looked up and saw the bright green fishing line with a plain hook dangling from the end.

"Up there, just like she said."

"How do we find this woman?"

Eleanor shrugged. "She wouldn't give me her name, but I'm pretty sure she lives by the river. Not up here. She was adamant about getting as far away from this evil spot as she could. I found her at the Rancheria bridge and drove her into town, gave her twenty bucks so she could buy formula and baby bottles for orphaned coyote pups."

"What about the pups?"

"Someone had killed a mother coyote, and the woman was determined to find the den of pups and feed them the formula. I dropped her off at Walmart."

He shoved his hands in his pocket and stared over the river to the charred forest. "All right. I'll get a warrant for the surveillance tapes. It should be out by the time we get there."

* * *

Sheriff Duncan asked the information clerk to find the store manager. A middle-aged man hustled to the front of the store, breathless, and introduced himself.

"How can I help you, Sheriff?"

"I need to check out your video surveillance from earlier today."

"Ah," he clasped his hands. "Can I ask what the issue is?"

Duncan looked at Eleanor, who summarized the situation.

Nodding, he said, "Usually, I need a warrant to show videotape, but in this case it's not necessary. Come with me."

They followed the store manager to his office. He shut the door and played back the surveillance video.

"That's her," said Eleanor.

The time strip said 16:11. The woman stood in line with an armful of items, waiting for the person in front of her to finish checking out. She moved forward, spilled the bottles and formula onto the counter. The clerk rang her up and she handed over the twenty Eleanor had given her.

"Can you bring the clerk in here?"

"Right away." The manager got on the loudspeaker and called the clerk to the office.

Her expectant expression turned anxious when she saw the Sheriff. They replayed the tape.

"Oh, yeah, I remember her. Baby bottles and puppy formula. All kinds of things went through my head," she said.

"What kinds of things?" asked Duncan.

"Like maybe she'd stolen a litter, and she planned to sell the puppies."

"What'd she say when you rang her up?"

"She told me she was born and raised here, which surprised me, partly cause I didn't ask. She said she'd lived here decades before we even had a Walmart, and the town had been going to hell in a handbasket ever since. Hypocrite. I mean, where else in this town can you buy puppy formula?"

"What made you think she stole a litter of puppies?"

"She didn't look like someone who could afford to take care of a dog, much less a litter of puppies. Very disheveled. Dirty clothes. Skin and bone. Maybe an addict."

"Did she say where she was going?"

"Nope. Clearly transient and she stunk to high heaven. I think she had lice."

"Why do you think that?"

"Her hair was greasy, and she kept scratching her head. Her hand shook when she handed me the twenty and I didn't want to touch that money."

When the clerk left, they played the outside surveillance video and watched the woman exit the building and head west toward the road she'd come in on.

They got back in Duncan's vehicle. "You have time to check out the middle fork?"

"Of course." She kept the carsickness to herself and listened to Duncan call in.

"Looking for a woman who left Walmart at sixteen twenty-five possibly headed to the middle fork river in the vicinity of the one-lane bridge. White, middle aged, thin, possibly transient. She may be carrying puppy formula and baby bottles. Possible 5150."

They descended the canyon to the river, and Duncan followed Eleanor's direction and pulled over to the oak. Duncan let Granite out of the back seat and handed his leash to her. The three of them walked across the road to the edge of cliff overlooking the river. The dead coyote lay on her side not far from the water. Eleanor couldn't see signs of blood even though the woman insisted the female had been shot. Overhead, turkey vultures circled, waiting for the carrion to decompose before they landed to feed.

* * *

They didn't find any sign of the woman or a coyote den. Granite was full of joy being in the out-of-doors. Eleanor unleashed him to keep her own balance, and the dog remained close as they hiked upriver until the boulders became too steep to climb without gear.

Duncan drove back to the station where Eleanor had left her car. There, she called Easton. He didn't pick up, but he'd left her a voicemail. He was catching up on bookwork and waiting for a truckload of hay to arrive from Oakdale.

16

It was dark when Eleanor pulled up to the coffee shack drive-thru and the familiar voice of McKenzie Wilson came over the speaker.

"May I take your order?"

"Hey, McKenzie. Iced mocha, please."

"Whip?"

"No whip."

Eleanor drove up and peeked inside the window. McKenzie turned.

"What are you doing working on a school night?"

"The other girl called in sick and asked me to cover. It's okay. My boyfriend's keeping me company. He's right here."

The boyfriend rose from a chair inside the shack and walked over to the takeout window to stand beside McKenzie. He leaned forward and stuck his hand out the window.

"I'm Chad. Nice to meet you." His smile was fulsome. He wore a blue T-shirt with the Sierra Community College firefighting logo. He was attractive, and the vertical worry crease between his eyebrows made him look like a person who cared. She took his hand—a strong hand and a firm shake.

"It's good to meet you, Chad. Eleanor Wooley."

"Heard a lot about you, Ms. Wooley. All good."

She glanced at McKenzie, who beamed, and Eleanor gave her the look of approval, which was too obvious because Chad blushed and ducked back into the coffee shack. McKenzie leaned over the space between their windows.

"You look tired, Eleanor."

"And you just called me by my first name."

"I hope that's okay?"

"Of course." Eleanor placed the drink in the holder on the dash and reached into her wallet for money, which wasn't there because she'd given away her last twenty to the coyote woman.

"Hold on, I need to find my credit card."

"It's on me, today. I get to give away one coffee a day and you're my lucky customer."

"Thanks." Eleanor raised her hand. "Great to meet you, Chad."

"Likewise."

* * *

The temperature had dropped a few degrees from 102 to 99, but the interior of her cottage hadn't. Granite went straight to his water bowl. Eleanor heard him lap water as she tugged the living room pull-cord to high and waited for the ceiling fan to spin its small miracle. She went out front, pulled the sprinkler along the crabgrass closer to the window, and turned on the outside spigot. The sprinkler spit arcs of water that would cool the outside air as it moved through the window screen—a trick she'd learned from Rette.

She stood on her bed to raise the skylight and slid open the bedroom window. Eleanor cursed herself for putting off buying an electric fan, at least one for the bedroom. After a cool shower, she walked through her cottage naked to dry, wondering what motive a person had for killing a woman and disposing of her in the river. A strong person, the coyote woman said, strong enough to carry a body down mountain and heft it into the river. Not someone a lone woman would be comfortable encountering on a wilderness path.

A chill came on as Eleanor leaned against the kitchen counter, dwelling on the day Marisol Rodriguez had become a casualty and the Gold Strike community mourned. It was only because of the fire that a con crew inmate found the body and the town had some closure. She wondered if closure was the killer's intention.

* * *

The next morning, Billy Perlman shouted to Eleanor across the newsroom.

"Would you cover the water district meeting?"

"Those meetings are boring."

"I promised my wife I'd watch the kids so she can go to yoga."

"Can't she go another time?"

"She goes in the morning after dropping the kids at school, but she hurt her back. This is the only time slot for restorative yoga."

Mac looked up from his laptop, over his glasses. "Restorative yoga with the wife. Mine keeps trying to get me to go with her."

"Why don't you?" asked Billy.

"Same reason you don't."

"Yeah, what's that?"

"Once I sit on the ground, I can't get up."

"I can get up," said Billy.

"Stop, both of you. I'll cover the Water Board, but you'll owe me."

Eleanor perused the wire service. AP had run a story about a bill, The Wild Horse and Burro Protection Act, before the House of Representatives. California legislators were demanding the United States Bureau of Land Management require that wranglers hired by the livestock companies they contract for roundups wear helmets fitted with video cams. The obligation to suit up with video cams also applied to the helicopters. They were California legislators, and the cowboy hat was iconic in Gold Strike County. She flagged it for Mac.

Her desk phone rang. She cradled the receiver between her shoulder and cheek.

"*Gold Strike Tribune*," she said.

"Is this Eleanor Wooley?"

"Yes, this is Eleanor."

"I have a tip."

"I'm listening."

"I read your story on Marisol Rodriguez, and her plan to camp. I don't know the poor woman, but I was at Lake Eleanor in Yosemite on Sunday."

As the tipster explained how she went off the trail to pee behind an oak, Eleanor typed. She described the oak as a giant octopus. Eleanor had seen trees like that before. They sent out their limbs parallel to the ground, seeking sunlight. Like the dogwood behind her cottage that climbed pines to bask in slivers of light.

"I saw what I thought at first was a skull and thought a mountain lion had dragged its prey into the bush. I realized it was only a rock. But I'm sure I saw blood. I read your story about Marisol Rodriguez telling her friends she planned to hike in Yosemite, and something clicked."

"Clicked in what way?"

"The blood could be Marisol's. Your article said she died of asphyxiation and blunt force trauma to the head. Her killer might have knocked her out with that rock and left it in the brush."

"Have you notified the Sheriff?"

"I did, right before I called you."

"Would you give me your name in case I need to call you back?"

"I'd rather not."

"I understand, and I appreciate your call."

17

THE AFTERNOON SUN BROILED HER jeans, and her feet hurt because she'd worn her boots to work for a change. As she stood at the Lake Eleanor trailhead to Yosemite National Park, an hour from Gold Strike, she thought grimly about the coincidence of sharing a name with a place where a murder may have taken place. If it were a sign, it was a foreboding one. She was glad she'd brought Granite. Even though dogs weren't allowed in the Yosemite Wilderness, she couldn't leave him in the sweltering cottage or the even hotter Blazer, and his presence made her feel safer.

Eleanor was halfway along the trail to the lake when she saw the unmistakable oak on her left growing on the north side of a granite shelf. Limbs like octopus arms undulated along the ground from the massive trunk. Granite started toward the tree, nose to the ground. Eleanor called him back. If there were a bloody rock on the far side of the trunk, she didn't want to spoil the scene with Granite's paw prints or her own. She snapped a photo and turned back, hiking briskly down to the trailhead.

A Sheriff's patrol car was parked several yards from her Blazer. Two people sat in the car, and Deputy Perelli stepped out on the driver's side. He shook his head when he saw her.

"Wooley, you're the last person I want to see."

"Thanks for that. What took you so long?" she asked.

"This isn't our jurisdiction," he said. "We're in national park jurisdiction within Tuolumne County so needed Tuolumne County Sheriff's to grant us authority to collect the evidence."

"Why aren't they here?"

"You're the reporter. Limited state funding. Hard time attracting qualified personnel. They're short-handed and no exigency exists, so they requested we respond to the area without their physical presence."

"Well I found the tree," she said. "I never went off the trail and came back the way I went."

The other deputy, a woman, Deputy Zim, according to her name pin, said, "We'll follow you."

She led the deputies back up the trail, huffing it to the oak. On the way, Deputy Zim was forthcoming explaining she was Gold Strike's evidence collection team. As they perused the area, Deputy Zim made the first move by running yellow tape around a clump of tick brush and back across the path to the tree.

"Wooley," said Perelli, "you can make yourself useful. Don't let anyone through."

"What do I tell them?"

"Tell them they have to go back. How hard is that?"

"Perelli," she said. "I can see why you haven't made captain."

He scoffed. Apparently, he disliked her less when she insulted him.

Zim stood beneath the oak's canopy, peering at something near the trunk as she pulled on latex gloves. She grabbed a flag from her back pocket and inserted it in the ground. Perelli radioed in for two more deputies, while she enlarged the perimeter of the crime scene, pulling the tape across the trail and around a more distant manzanita. She unfastened a small hatchet from her utility belt and hacked a blaze mark in the big oak. She tore off the bark and let it drop to the ground. She walked to the other side of the oak and selected a stunted conifer that grew from a fissure in the granite. With a pocketknife, she scraped the bark and began to triangulate the evidence, measuring the distance between the two blaze marks. She followed up with her cellphone, presumably taking GPS measurements, which Eleanor knew from experience were much more challenging in forested terrain.

A young couple was hiking up the trailhead. Eleanor readied herself to turn them back. The mom had a fly rod strapped to her daypack and the dad packed the baby on his back in a carrier with a sunshade, a girl judging from her pink beanie. Turns out, they were looking forward to a swim in the lake.

"I'm sorry, you can't go through. Gold Strike Sheriff has secured the area for a possible crime scene."

The mother grimaced. "Oh. That's awful."

The father said, "Can we go around?"

"I advise you to err on the side of safety," Eleanor said. "Plus, more deputies will be arriving shortly and posting themselves along the trail. If you go in, they might not allow you to return."

"Really?" The husband was the skeptic of the two.

"C'mon let's go back." The mother checked her baby, who was starting to fuss. She put a pacifier in the child's mouth, which instantly quieted her. She started back down the path. Her husband followed. Eleanor watched the child frog-leg on the father's back as they returned in the direction they'd come. A warmth tinged with a pinch of envy filled her heart.

* * *

By the time the deputies arrived, Eleanor was parched, and her water bottle was empty. Granite panted in the shade. She listened to Perelli give orders for the officers to station themselves one hundred yards on either end of the trail. They were to maintain a log of who entered and exited the scene while Zim continued to comb the area for disturbed soil and bag evidence.

When Eleanor returned to her office, she called Sheriff Duncan and asked him for an official statement.

"If I give you a statement the entire county is suddenly going to want to hike to the lake."

"Off record, can you tell me what you *think* this means?"

"Off the record, whatever evidence the deputies collect could take several weeks to analyze."

"Sheriff, c'mon. It looks like Deputy Zim found the rock the tipster saw. She was still bagging evidence and flagging the group when the deputies showed up."

The Sheriff didn't answer, and she thought she heard his office door click shut.

"What I can tell you, Eleanor, is we're collecting all circumstantial evidence to put together a lead because whoever ambushed a woman, killed her, moved her body to the river, dumped it, and started a wildfire to draw attention scares the hell out of me. And, also off the record, killing another human that way don't make a sick fuck well."

18

AT FIVE MINUTES TO THREE, Eleanor remembered her promise
to Billy Perlman. The Gold Strike Water Board sat behind a table in a
drab room. Five of them. Four white men and one white woman. The
name plate on the table in front of her said Yvonne Ward. She handed
out a half-page agenda, which Eleanor scanned, stopping at the heading
"New Business."

Item A: Water Expansion Project
Presentation by Jerry Ward of Peckham County

Jerry Ward had to be the project director. His short-sleeved white
shirt and tie exuded a rural attempt at semi-formality, and Eleanor wondered if he was any relation to Yvonne Ward, who sat catty-corner to
him.

He stood to give his PowerPoint presentation. The first slide was
titled "Bear River Dam Project" with a grassy riparian meadow on a
background of snow-capped Sierra Nevada. The next featured a topo
map of the proposed dam site. She recognized the area even though the
map was a drab green and white elevation grid. The watershed. The pack
station. Easton's fishing spot, separated from the upper Bear River by
a steep granite shelf. The widely spaced topo lines marked the meadow
at the foot of the peaks, which rose so high and so quickly the space

between the topo lines was whisker thin. Ward had branded the meadow with a big red star to mark the proposed dam site.

He began his presentation and Eleanor started taking notes.

"The Bear River Dam would fulfill Peckham County's future needs to serve, one, California's burgeoning population and, two, a new tech industry that's moving in from Silicon Valley and would attract more families and planned residential housing developments, creating more jobs and greater infrastructure needs.

"Counties expect to share their resources, and the state requires it," he said, "and we'll go public with our proposal at the next Gold Strike County Supervisor's meeting. But first I need the Gold Strike Water Board's approval."

"Thank you, Jerry," said the Board chair. "We'll take questions now."

Eleanor raised her hand.

"I didn't mean reporters," the chair said. "You can ask your questions after the meeting."

"I'd like my question on the record, please," Eleanor said.

If five sets of eyes could kill, she'd be dead.

"Why wasn't this proposal on your public agenda? This is an extremely controversial issue to Gold Strike residents."

The Board members looked at each other blankly until the chair turned to the others.

"Why wasn't it?" he asked.

"The phrase 'Water Expansion Project' on the agenda covered that," said Yvonne Ward.

Eleanor wrote down the response to let the woman know she, too, was on the record, a different record, the news and record of the *Gold Strike Tribune.*

"A dam project on this exact spot was rejected thirty years ago," Eleanor said. "Why would you bring it back?"

The silence sunk in way past the Board's comfort level.

"Times change," Yvonne said, "and the will of the people change, too."

"Times do change," said Eleanor. "Water companies are removing dams, not building them. They're economically unfeasible, and it makes more sense in this era of climate collapse to protect river ecosystems rather than destroy them."

Yvonne's eyes narrowed. "I read your stories," she said. "You're a liberal and you're not from here. My family has lived in Gold Strike for five generations. You don't belong and you can't understand."

She did understand. Yet another perfect natural landscape was on the cusp of obliteration, and in that moment, she felt as if she *did* belong, more than she ever had.

"Sometimes it takes an outsider," Eleanor said.

All eyes were on her, waiting for her to elaborate. "Outsiders have historically offered an objective reflection of what's wrong with a town."

"Objective, ha," said Yvonne.

"You said, 'Times change, and the will of the people change, too.' I'm going to use that quote in the story."

"I hope you do."

"May I correct your grammar so the subject and verb agree, or not?"

"Leave it as I said it." Yvonne shuffled the meeting papers and pushed them aside. She leaned over the table. "You're such a hoity-toity thing you're gonna break every bone in your body when you're taken down from your high horse."

"Ladies, please," said one of the men.

When the Board adjourned and the members started to leave, Eleanor remained at the table, scribbling while the details of the meeting were fresh in her mind, including Yvonne's high horse idiom. As she wrote, she waited out the anger electrifying her insides. After all, it wasn't this woman alone who riled her, but a culmination of similar episodes of wrong-thinking locals giving away their wildlands to the highest fucking bidder. She clicked off her Sharpie 0.7 and threw it across the room.

19

ELEANOR STOOD AT THE COUNTER of the convenience store with a Diet Coke, a Milky Way, and a small bag of Cheetos, knowing once she'd eaten the junk food she'd regret it. She already did.

The store owner stood behind the counter and greeted her with a robust "Good day. Can your dog have a treat?"

"Sure." Eleanor looked to her right and read the flyer beside the counter:

Newsom kills babies after they're born.

California was an oasis state for choice, especially if you lived near the coast, but now she lived in conservative pro-life territory, where a person could understand the truth of claims that the state was leaning purple.

She pointed to the flyer. "Do you believe this?"

"Yes," he said earnestly.

She knew nothing she could say would change his mind, so she took her Coke and Milky Way and Cheetos off the counter and carried them back to their spots on the shelves.

"Goodbye," she said. "Thank you for saving me from buyer's remorse."

The owner ignored her.

* * *

Her phone rang.

"This is the State of California Prison System," the recording said. "You are receiving a call from inmate named—" another voice filled in the blank, "—Rex Luciano."

"Will you accept the call? Say 'yes' or press one. If your reply is 'no,' say 'no' or press two."

"Yes," Eleanor said.

A man with a deep radio announcer voice came on. "You called me about the fire."

"You're the man on the Brown's Ferry fire crew who spotted the woman's body?"

"Yeah, that's me. I hear she didn't drown."

"True. Strangled and possibly bludgeoned, then moved to the river."

"That red jacket floating on the surface. Surprised someone didn't spot her first."

"Can you tell me what happened, Rex?"

"I had to take a leak and went down toward the river. I saw that red jacket and shouted for my crew boss. He and a couple other firefighters came down. I pointed her out and the crew boss took over."

"What were your first thoughts?"

"I've seen death. Just wish it weren't a young woman."

"Marisol Rodriguez. She was a student at the community college headed for the university."

"God bless her."

"Was there anything that struck you as odd?"

"One thing. When they pulled her out, turned her on her back, and went through protocols, they pulled something white from her mouth. Looked like flowers."

That would explain the odd look between the Search and Rescue diver and Adelia when she'd asked them if they remembered any details from the ordeal.

"What did you think when you saw the flowers?"

"What sick sonuvabitch shoves flowers in a dead woman's mouth."

"You thought she was murdered at the time, not drowned."

"I did, but I'm a con in prison for killing a man. Murder is the norm. You have any more questions? I'm running out of time here."

"One more. The river is a ways from your crew. Why did you think it was okay to go so far from supervision?"

"Just following orders. My crew boss said, if you got to piss, drain that weasel down by the river."

The line went dead.

That night she had trouble getting to sleep. She tossed and turned, her legs were restless, and when she finally did drift off, she dreamed of one horse chomping the tail of another while standing in a river of leeches that crawled up the horses' legs and attached themselves to their necks.

She didn't hear her alarm and woke up groggy and late for work. When she walked into the newsroom, a note placed on her computer said, Call *Jerry Ward*, with a business card.

"Who put this on my desk?" she asked the threadbare staff of Mac and Billy.

Mac stared numbly from over his reading glasses and Billy shrugged.

"Maybe the sender got through front desk security."

"What security?" She held up the card. "Jerry Ward, Peckham Water Company. This is your beat, Perlman."

"But it was your story, and he's not asking me."

"I don't like him."

"You're a reporter," said Mac. "Be objective."

"An anachronism if ever there was one."

"It was a good story, Wooley," said Mac. "Utility Board meetings are dry, but water issues are the lifeblood of this state and this county."

She called Jerry Ward. He picked up on the first ring.

"This is Eleanor Wooley from the *Tribune*."

"Hello, Eleanor. Just wanted to say that you know how to transform the ordinary into extraordinary."

"Damming the Bear River isn't ordinary."

"I'm talking about that number you did with the Board about leaving the dam off the agenda. We'd probably have a lot more people show up if she hadn't."

"Who's she?"

"Yvonne Ward."

"Are you related?"

"I'd say so. My mother."

Nepotism, but she didn't bring it up. "Why'd you call?"

"Something I want to discuss. Could you come by my office?"

"Can you tell me over the phone?"

"I have a proposition, and I'd rather talk in person," he said. "You have any time this afternoon?"

* * *

The day was already turning out to be a weird one. McKenzie leaned out the window and handed Eleanor a cappuccino.

"I couldn't do what you do. Reporting on dead people, especially a woman who died a violent death. It's so hard to believe one human would do something so awful to another. What other species kills their own kind?"

Eleanor removed the white plastic lid and sipped her cappuccino. "Male lions and chimpanzees. They eat their young to free up the female for sex."

"That's a horrible reason."

"This killer has reasons. We just don't know what they are."

* * *

Jerry sat on the bench outside the project office, dressed informally in a polo shirt and jeans. She glanced at his Frye cowboy boots. He smiled and she detected chagrin, hopefully not attraction. He offered his hand, and she took it. His palm was a wet sponge, as if missing bone and muscle.

A bead of sweat dripped down her back to the middle of her spine.

"My apology," he said. "The building is south facing and doesn't offer any shade."

She wished she hadn't left her cappuccino in the Blazer. She could wipe off her hand without making it obvious.

"What did you want to talk to me about?"

Ward turned toward the office. He opened the glass door and leaned against it as she passed. On the wall facing the plate glass window hung a large topo map of Gold Strike County, the original of the topo map in yesterday's PowerPoint, with a magnified area of the Bear River Dam Project in the bottom right-hand corner.

He pulled out a chair from the table and gestured for her to sit. He sat catty-corner at the head of the table and stuffed papers into a soft leather briefcase.

"I'd like to hire you as the project's public relations director." Ward smiled that sheepish smile again.

Unbelievable. Her attitude at the Water Board meeting and her story should have been enough to make it obvious she disapproved of the project.

"I was expecting you to bribe me not to write about the project."

"I like your writing. It's smart and clear. We could use that." He faked a smile.

"Absolutely not interested." She didn't thank him.

"No surprise, but if you change your mind, the offer stands. We're a fast-growing county and the newcomers aren't all Republicans and illegal aliens. We've got a skilled workforce coming to town that might spread the blue. With that in mind, I thought you might support the project."

"No. And Jerry, if I weren't reporting on your proposed dam, I'd be fighting it."

She stood and he rose quickly and stuck out his hand for a second shake. She kept her hand on her notepad as she opened the door, feeling his eyes on her as she walked into the street to her car, parked out front.

"Eleanor."

She looked up. He had a smirk on his face.

"You could buy a new hybrid if you came to work for us."

She got in the Blazer and turned the key. The engine didn't respond. She tried again.

"Just saying," he shouted.

* * *

She called Easton and told him she'd been offered a job.

"He'd pay me enough that I could buy a new car to spread his fucking lies."

"In that case, baby girl, I'll cook tonight. Steak. Grass-fed and finished."

"What can I bring?"

"Yourself."

20

EASTON WAS STANDING AT THE counter salting two ribeye steaks when Eleanor walked into the kitchen. He wiped his hands on the dishtowel and turned, put his hands on her waist, and pulled her close and kissed her lightly. No smile.

She decided not to ask if something was bothering him. "I'll set the table."

"That'd be great. Steaks in ten minutes."

She kissed his cheek, and he held her tighter and a few seconds longer than their normal embrace.

The table was clear except for his laptop. When she pushed it down the table to make room for their place settings, the screen lit up with a still shot of horses running and what looked like a helicopter.

She placed the knife and fork and water glass on the left side of his plate. She returned to the kitchen and made a simple salad of romaine and tomatoes.

"Do you have avocado?" she asked.

"In the flour bin."

She smiled to herself as she reached into the flour crock and felt for the fruit. She brushed flour from the Haas and halved it, pierced the seed with the blade of the knife and twisted. He'd used real buttermilk for the ranch dressing, which she drizzled over the salad and tossed, sprinkled parmesan on top, salt and pepper. She placed the bowl on the table and smelled onion caramelizing in the oven.

Easton brought out the sizzling steaks on a platter, medium rare, glossy from sizzling fat, topped with the onion in a lake of au jus. Eleanor hadn't eaten all day.

"That is fabulous. I'm starving."

"Let's dig in." He sat down. "What possessed that dude to think you'd go to work for him?"

"He thought he could tempt me by suggesting the dam would turn his red county blue with a new tech demographic." She forked a steak and placed it on her plate.

Easton cut his steak. "That is tempting."

She put her hand over her mouth as she chewed. "He wore this horrible gloating smile and told me if I worked for him I could buy a new hybrid. And then the Blazer didn't start up."

Easton put a hand on her arm. "What's wrong with the car?"

She shook her head. "Beside the point. He ground me like a cigarette butt. Come to the dark side, he was saying, and you won't be working poor. But really, he's afraid of the press and what'll happen once the town gets wind of his scheme."

"Live with me and you'll be poorer and work harder." He had a twinkle in his eye.

"My kind of offer." She forked the avocado slice hard. "And I saw that twinkle, which is a big improvement over your glum look when I came in. What was that about?"

"It's nothing."

"Which is an affirmation it's something."

He shoved his food around his plate. "They got him."

"Got who?"

"The stallion."

It took her a few to connect the dots.

"Goldenrod?"

"Yup."

Goldenrod was the wild stallion who'd escaped a BLM helicopter roundup last summer, leaping a six-foot trap wall, landing on his back, recovering, and running into the protection of juniper forest, escaping captivity. She and Easton had seen this horse up close and had a personal connection.

"Is that him on your laptop?"

"Yeah."

He pushed away his plate and pulled the laptop to the corner of the table, tapped the pad, and brought up the image of the terrorized horse chased through sage brush flats and grasses toward juniper forest on the horizon.

The high desert terrain was familiar. Easton had taken her there on their first real date. And what a date it was. He'd neglected to tell her he intended to free doomed mares from a kill pen because he hadn't been sure that he'd followed through with the plan. Illegal as hell, but she had no qualms when it happened. On the contrary, she was exhilarated.

"Keep watching," he said.

The stallion was running across the sagebrush toward the junipers, a strategy that had worked for him in the past when he outsmarted a helicopter pilot. But this time, three wranglers on horseback tore off in pursuit. The lead wrangler threw his lasso and roped the stallion's neck, pulled the rope taut, yanked the horse around. A second wrangler threw his rope around the stallion's front legs, tripped him. The horse stood, and a third triangulated the horse, who stopped fighting. His light coat was dark from sweat and his mane hung in long winding knots. He was exhausted.

"Shame on them," said Eleanor.

If that beautiful, struggling horse spurred one iota of guilt in those wranglers, it didn't show.

"I've watched this three times and each time it feels worse." He clicked on the next video of the BLM corrals.

"There he is." Eleanor touched the caramel palomino, who stood with his side to the camera, head turned to the videographer. His ears perked forward and twitched, listening to the new sounds, trying to figure out who this person was on the outside of the seven-foot cyclone fence around his freedom.

"Maybe you should bring him here," said Eleanor.

"One stallion doesn't fix the problem. They've got sixty thousand mustangs in holding and plan to round up more over the summer. I don't see a solution."

"That's like saying saving one child from hunger won't solve world hunger. It's saving a life. One life matters. You have a connection with this horse."

Goldenrod's epic escape last summer had flooded social media and moved Easton to release the stallion's mares from a kill pen.

"We could adopt a couple of his mares, too. You have space. If not, the mares you keep sure would appreciate him."

He checked his phone. "I have the number."

"Call them."

"They won't be working this late."

"Leave a message."

He placed the call. No one answered. A woman's pre-recorded voice instructed him to call a cell number, which he did, leaving his name, his ranch's name. Then, "Thanks, I look forward to hearing back from you pronto."

He hung up.

"You're doing this."

"We'll see how it goes."

The "we" felt good. "They need eligible people to give the horses a safe home."

"It's the bureaucracy, Lee. They're in the business of frustrating civilians."

His cell phone rang. The area code was unfamiliar, but his phone identified BLM. He picked up and put the call on speaker. "Easton Jode."

"This is Randy Freeman at BLM. I'm returning your call." Randy was a woman.

"Thanks for getting back to me at dinner time."

"No problem. It's so busy with all the horses coming in, we don't eat dinner."

"I'm calling about the palomino stallion you recently rounded up from the Moraga Plateau. I own a working two-thousand-acre horse and cattle ranch on the other side of the Sierra from you. Do I have to wait for the auction?"

"Typically, yes," she said. "A lot of people are interested in that horse. You might want to come up here to check him out and meet some of the staff. I'm mostly with the horses and a lot are coming in. I do preliminary owner vetting, and you sound like a good home. What do you plan on doing with him?"

"I want a good stud to breed with my mares. I need him intact."

"Then you better hurry. They're gelding every day. I don't know where he is on the schedule, but if he's here, he's on it."

"How do I find out?"

"The vets have gone home. I'll try to get that information and give you a call. If you don't hear from me, it's on you to follow up. Like I say, you might want to come up here and check things out."

"We can be up there in a few days, and thank you, Randy. I appreciate your getting back to me." He hung up.

They stared at each other, absorbing the conversation. His moody cloud had evaporated, and in its place, an urgency.

"You said, *we'll* be up there within a few days."

"Sorry," he clicked. "I figured you'd want to come."

She smiled. "I do, but Mac won't like it, and I am covering a murder."

He put his hands over hers. "I really want you with me."

"I know and I like hearing it. How many days are you thinking?"

He leaned back in his chair, looked at the ceiling. "Four max. Day of travel, day of paperwork. If they let me take the horse, he's never been trailered and would need some recovery time on the road, so another night at a horse motel. Then home."

If she timed it right, they could leave on Friday, return on Monday, and be back at work by Tuesday. That would leave Billy with weekend duty and two days of covering her beat and his, plus breaking news.

"If you can't get off work, I understand." He stood up and gathered their plates and silverware. "I apologize for presuming."

"I'll ask."

* * *

They slept with a sheet covering their naked bodies, damp from the sweat of lovemaking and evening heat. The heat, mixed with the excitement of the horse and the dread of confronting Mac, kept her awake. She probably shouldn't go with Easton, even though she wanted to.

* * *

She decided not to ask.

"I'm taking a few days off to pick up a horse north of here."

Mac glared at her over his reading glasses. "You're kidding, right?"

"Extremely serious. I can work remotely. I can write a feature on wild horse captivity and take some photos."

"We discussed this."

"This is different, Mac. The horse is an icon to advocates, and Easton's going to adopt him."

"He's your boyfriend. It's a conflict of interest."

"Please, Mac. The newsroom is slow right now."

"You call a murder investigation slow?"

"How many times have you quashed my stories because this isn't an investigative paper?"

She took a few angry footsteps across the newsroom and turned. "I found a witness to Marisol's murder, FYI. The witness, an unsheltered woman, saw the killer carry Marisol to the river and throw her in."

"You're telling me this on the cusp of your departure?"

"I didn't tell you because I can't corroborate her story, and she might be crazy. But it was her fly rod at the river."

He thrummed the edge of his desk with his pencil. "Well, go on, goddammit. You got my attention."

"The Sheriff knows all about it and there's nothing to do until another lead breaks. Billy can cover my beat for a few days. He owes me for the Water Board."

Mac pushed back his roller chair. "You can't go."

"Then I quit."

"You quit. What are you going to do, clean cabins?"

"I'd make more money and it'd be a lot less stressful." She walked back to her desk and yanked her charge cord from the plug. Her hands shook.

"You're serious."

Obviously.

He tossed his glasses on his desk. "You win. Here's my offer. Do a personal travel series on wild horse country or whatever angle hooks our readers. I'll get the feed stores and equestrian centers to put in ads."

"Why do I have to go to this length for you to give me some slack?"

"My job."

"Your job is to trust me."

"I trust you. Are we good?"

"No. I'm pissed."

"That's my offer. A travel piece with photos. Let me know by the end of the day."

"This is the end of my day," she said.

21

THE HEAT INSIDE HER CAR was suffocating. The steering wheel too hot to grab. She was high on adrenaline from standing up for herself, but that would collapse into remorse pretty quickly. And now that she was leaving town, her list of errands became urgent. The community college library had sent her two overdue notices. She owed them ten dollars for *Ghost Town*. She'd be charged for its full value if she didn't return the book by tomorrow.

* * *

She parked in the ten-minute zone and rushed into the library, up to the counter to turn in the book and pay the fine. She turned and saw Chad at a long library table, leaning back in a chair, long legs stretched under the table as he pecked at a computer keyboard. He was dressed in his firefighting blues and looked up and smiled.

She walked over to him. "Chad, I'm Eleanor, McKenzie's friend. Fan of the coffee shack drive-thru."

"Oh, yeah." He recognized her now. "How are you?"

"I'm good," she said. "Returning an overdue book."

"People still read books?"

"We do," she said.

He dropped his hands from the keyboard and sat up straight. "I'm studying for a fire-fighting exam. Not so good at calculus."

"You have my empathy."

"Yeah. I understand how fire works and what to do, but the math doesn't stick. Like the difference in velocity between a fire moving uphill and a fire moving downhill, factoring in wind and humidity. I know downhill's slower, wind makes it faster, but I can't memorize the calculations."

"I can help you correct a vague pronoun, but physics, no. My friend could. She was a math teacher and had her students write down the formulas, so the information processes from their eyes to hands to brain."

"Does your friend teach here?"

"She taught high school."

"Taught?"

"She's missing. She's been officially missing for a year."

"Sorry about your friend. Maybe she's in a better place with Jesus."

The Jesus reference threw her, but that was how it was up here in God's country. "Pretty sure she's not with Jesus."

"Why not? Was she a bad person?"

"I thought Jesus loves everyone. She, on the other hand, preferred men with a trade."

"Jesus was a carpenter. What more could she want?"

"She likes her guys clean-shaven."

"You should be careful how you talk about Him."

"I'm sorry if I offended you." Eleanor didn't know Chad was religious, but should've. Seventy percent of Gold Strike residents identified as Christian.

"You didn't offend me." He looked back at the computer.

"Good luck on your test," Eleanor said.

"Thank you. "

She started to walk away, but heard him call her name.

"I'll pray for your friend. What's her name?"

"Rette."

"I hope you find Rette," he said. "Officially alive."

* * *

Easton and Eleanor made plans to have dinner at her house, spend the night, and talk about the trip. She wrote *coffee* in her iPhone notes as she walked into the market. Two young women chatted gaily near the entrance. One of them asked if she could help Eleanor find anything.

Normally, she used handbaskets when she shopped here. The food was healthy and delicious, but expensive, so she only bought the basics: produce, milk, eggs, a loaf of bread, and menstrual products because this was the only place in town you could find organic cotton tampons.

"I need a cart."

"The carts are outside the glass doors." The young woman pointed to the doors. "Can I get one for you?"

"I'm okay." She walked outside as a logging truck roared by with a load of pine heading to the mill. This market used to be a storage building for that same mill, but when clearcutting was banned on federal forest land, the company went out of business and a larger company with privately-owned forest holdings bought the mill.

Eleanor grabbed a cart and returned, the wheels clacking noisily over the uneven wood plank floors. She looked up from dropping red potatoes into a small brown paper bag and saw Adelia of the Forest Service pressing the skin of an avocado.

"Hey," Eleanor said.

Adelia looked up. "The reporter. Wooley, right? Yeah, I'm reading your stories. How are you?"

"Doing my shopping."

Adelia held up the avocado. "Really hard." She returned the fruit and selected a head of garlic.

Eleanor noticed the three white candles in Adelia's cart.

"Where'd you find the candles? I'm making a special dinner tonight."

Adelia pointed to the far aisle. "By the aromatherapy."

Eleanor pushed her cart over to the aromatherapy aisle, picked out a frankincense candle and proceeded to checkout. She pulled out her items, setting them on the counter. The same young woman who'd greeted her when she came in rang her up. She placed the soft box of tampons on the counter.

"I get that same brand," Adelia said, who'd come up behind her.

"Hi," Eleanor said.

"Amazing you can find them up here."

"This town is full of surprises."

Eleanor watched her grocery total mount until it was over one hundred. She tapped her Visa card and lifted a bag to each shoulder.

"Are you going to her service?" asked Adelia.

"Whose service?"

"Marisol Rodriguez."

"I hadn't heard."

"The family invited everyone who was on the scene."

"They didn't contact me."

Adelia lay two gem lettuces on the counter and her canvas tote. A gilded painting with the New York Metropolitan Museum of Modern Art logo decorated the bag.

"You've been to New York?" asked Eleanor.

Adelia looked confused.

"Your bag."

"Oh, this? I bought it online."

"I keep seeing that painting." It was the same painting above her landlady's mantel.

"It's famous. That's why I bought it. The artist is Fra Angelico, a Renaissance guy who considered the Crucifixion of Christ spiritually epic and," Adelia regarded her bag, "he used real gold to honor the spirit realm."

"A canvas of contradictions."

The checker handed Eleanor her receipt. "Thanks." She stuffed the receipt in her grocery bag and looked up. "Adelia," she said. "I have something to ask you."

"Okay." Adelia sounded skeptical.

"I'll wait outside." A blast of hot air swept over Eleanor's face when she opened the market door and stepped into the evening. She listened for sounds of the middle forest. The cicadas had begun to sing, which meant the scorching heat was cooling a bit. The roar of a log truck hauling ass on the two-lane mountain highway down-shifted as the driver raced to weigh his timber before the mill closed.

Adelia's voice startled her.

"So, what's the question?" Adelia's shoulder bore most of the weight of her bulging, artful, canvas grocery bag. Her free arm supported the bottom of the bag, which made it look, accidentally, Eleanor was certain, like she was cradling the image of the Crucifixion.

"When you pulled Marisol out of the river, her mouth and throat contained foreign material, flowers to be exact." Eleanor was counting on Adelia not remembering she'd been silenced at the time. "What do you make of flowers stuffed in a dead woman's mouth?"

"It tells me there's a pervert running free." Adelia covered her mouth in regret, as if she'd just remembered who she was talking to. "Forget I said that."

"That's not possible," Eleanor said. "But I won't report it."

She watched Adelia make a hasty exit to her car, then turn back before rounding the building's corner.

"See you at the memorial," Adelia called.

22

DINNER WAS PERFECT AND SO was their night. They woke at dawn and planned their day over coffee. Easton intended to return to the ranch to prepare for their road trip and give instructions to his ranch hand. Eleanor would attend Marisol's memorial.

She wore a sleeveless cotton print shift and black flats with a cropped black sweater. She parked in the space reserved for the *Tribune* a few blocks down from the church and walked up the sidewalk past the cars lining the street. People spilled from the church onto the steps on a day that had already reached ninety in the shade.

Adelia appeared, dressed in her Forest Service uniform. She spotted Eleanor and squeezed through the crowd, placed a hand on her elbow, and ushered her through the crowd. She'd saved Eleanor a seat in the fourth row. The family of Marisol Rodriguez took up the first two rows of crying infants, teenage siblings, parents, and grandparents. One elderly woman in a wheelchair sat in the aisle. Sheriff Duncan and his wife sat in the third row. She didn't see Deputy Perelli, who'd been at the scene. McKenzie sat beside Chad in the third row. Adelia sat on the outside aisle seat in the same row as Eleanor.

Church protocol was buried inside Eleanor, who'd been raised Catholic. The rituals she'd practiced every Sunday for sixteen years rose to the occasion when the priest began Mass. For one, the hassock was hinged up and she knew enough to pull it down so she could kneel in a bit more comfort.

"Let us pray," said the priest.

She made the sign of the cross with gut-scraping resistance.

When Communion time came, she remained rooted on the hard, wooden pew and moved her knees sideways so folks could pass to the aisle, where Adelia stepped back to make a space in front of her. Eleanor shook her head, mouthing "No, thank you."

She had no intention of walking up to the alter to receive Communion from a church that sheltered pedophiles.

Adelia didn't take no for an answer. She whispered loudly, "If you don't want to take Communion, you can take a blessing. Put your hands across your chest and the priest will anoint you."

Even a blessing felt complacent. She looked at the wall behind Adelia, where a painting of Jesus carrying his cross decorated the space between the stained-glass windows, one of twelve morbid depictions that had always filled her with chilly fear when she was a girl. That was wrong, filling a child with those tortured images. But Adelia kept waving her hands, coaxing her more urgently now that the line was moving and, finally, persuading Eleanor to join the community and stand in line to receive the sacrament.

The larger-than-life marble statue of the Virgin Mary gazed piously downward as she walked by. Mary's white shawl covered her white head and flowed to her white robe, which draped to the floor.

Eleanor stepped up to the priest and reluctantly cupped her hands to receive the Host. She accidentally bumped the priest's forearm. Deep red wine sloshed from the goblet. He held out the cup until the red waves stopped spilling over the rim. The arm of his garment was stained. His assistant blotted his sleeve with a white cloth as the priest placed a host in Eleanor's palm. *Move on*, his expression said. The paper-thin wafer stuck to the roof of her mouth. She again passed the marble statue of Mary, who appeared amused. Eleanor sat in the pew and closed her eyes. She didn't open them until the voice of a woman woke her, introducing Marisol's younger sister. The girl sobbed as she lamented she no longer had a big sister to ask for advice. People lined the aisles to take turns speaking praises and telling sweet anecdotes. Eleanor turned restless. She wanted to get on the road with Easton before it got late. Adelia walked up to the podium.

She raised the microphone to her height. "I was a first responder on the scene of Marisol's recovery from the river," she said. "I assisted our Search and Rescue diver to retrieve her body from the river."

She seemed drained from the experience.

"Her face was peaceful, and I want you to know that." She left the podium, walked down the two short steps and up the aisle, reclaiming her seat on the aisle without a glance at Eleanor.

Sheriff Duncan walked up to the podium next. "When we lose a member of our town we grieve," he said, "even more deeply when the loss is a young woman with their entire life ahead and so much promise. As your Sheriff, I can't undo what's been done. But I give you my word that my deputies and I are working our hardest around the clock to find the person who did this and prevent them from committing anything close to this travesty ever again."

Duncan returned to his seat.

A sudden spray on Eleanor's face startled her. The priest was proceeding up the center aisle, dipping an olive branch into a bowl of water and sprinkling the crowd as he headed toward the church entrance.

She walked out with the slow-moving mourners. Chad and McKenzie were in front of her, holding hands. They exited the wide doorway into the open and proceeded down the steps.

"McKenzie."

When she saw Eleanor, McKenzie's face lit up. "Finally, we see each other outside the drive-thru. You remember Chad?"

He leaned forward and they shook hands. Eleanor registered his firm grip for the second time and noted the gold cross necklace that lay over the collar of his shirt.

"How'd you do on your exam?"

McKenzie looked up at him. She wore a smaller, matching cross.

"I was studying for an exam at the library," he explained to her. "Ms. Wooley was returning a book. Your tip helped, by the way. I passed with the highest score in my class."

McKenzie linked her arm in his. "That's my dude."

Eleanor knew McKenzie was applying to colleges and wondered how they'd manage a long-distance relationship when Chad graduated from his program and had to find a job.

"Are you going to try to find work here in Gold Strike County?" Eleanor asked.

"I'm going to apply for sure," said Chad. "My family lives up north in Humboldt. I'm going to apply there, too."

McKenzie leaned against him. "Whatever he decides, he'll be able to write his own ticket."

"What about you, McKenzie?"

"I got into Stanford."

"Stanford. That's wonderful news. I'm thrilled for you."

"They've offered me scholarships. My parents are really happy, especially Mom. Dad's happy, too. Mom just shows it more."

Chad nudged her side. "She's going to turn into a liberal."

McKenzie rolled her eyes.

"What about you?" Chad asked Eleanor. "Gold Strike County seems limited for a worldly lady like you."

Worldly. She'd taken two-week vacations to Mexico, Paris, and Ireland. That was the extent of her travels.

Eleanor smiled. "I plan to keep on keeping on. Reporting for a tightly-knit community that appreciates the news." She thought about her argument with Mac and wasn't so sure. "Right now, I'm heading north to pick up a stallion."

"Nice." McKenzie leaned forward to give her a hug. "I'm going to the Mountain Music Festival with my friends."

Eleanor held her a few seconds longer. "McKenzie, you need to be careful. Keep your eyes open and don't go anywhere alone, especially after dusk." She glanced at Chad.

"I'll take care of her," he assured her.

23

THE HORSE TRAILER WAS HITCHED to the Dodge Ram, and Granite sat in the back seat, his head out the window, watching Eleanor disappear inside the house.

She found Easton at the kitchen sink, pouring filtered tap water into canisters for the trip. She came up behind him and put her arms around his waist and leaned her head against his back while he fastened the last lid. He turned and lifted her onto the counter. She wrapped her legs around his waist and those pleasant feelings between them grew, until they heard Granite barking.

"To be continued," she said.

Easton pulled her off the counter. He gathered the water bottles, and she went out the door to stand by the front gate, hearing Granite's tail thump for joy as she passed the truck. After Easton drove over the cattle guard and through the gate, she shut and secured it and climbed into the truck.

As they drove away from the ranch, Eleanor described Marisol's service, laying aside her old resentful barbs of the Catholic Church. She wondered aloud how their relationship would be different if they were churchgoers.

"Instead of falling in love on barstools," he said, "I'd spot you sitting in a church pew."

She laughed, sensing their filaments of love wind around each other's and grow strong between them.

Granite fell asleep listening to them talk. By early afternoon, they'd crested the pass and crawled down the Sierras' east side, where they hooked up to Highway 395 and headed north toward Carson City. The Sierra Nevada range shot up like a mohawk. The shale face of Slide Mountain outside Carson City loomed ahead. On their right was Washoe Lake State Park.

She pointed to dots on the horizon. Wild horses. Easton put on his blinker and turned off 395 toward the horses. He drove past a small cattle ranch and pulled into the entrance of the park.

"Would you look at that."

He got out of truck and leashed Granite. Dog and man walked the crushed gravel path toward the horses while Eleanor stayed back to use the restroom and read the park's interpretation sign, which made no mention of the horses or that this spot was known as one of the best places in Nevada to observe wild horses. Or that it was illegal to feed or touch the horses, and a person could be fined if they were caught doing either.

The horses who lived here weren't separated from visitors by anything aside from their own lack of desire to interact. At least that's what Eleanor thought as she caught up with Easton, passing unfortunate red shell casings on the ground beneath a viewing platform, walking through a dry marsh and up a short rise to another walking path.

The horses grazed in the foreground of Washoe Lake, their lips nibbling, seeking new green shoots from Mother Earth. The band was mostly bays, with a buckskin, a few blacks and a paint. A foal stood by its mother. From where they stood, the horses were indistinct on her iPhone camera. She stuffed the phone in her back jeans pocket and simply watched.

The paint mare looked up and ambled toward them. A few others followed, grazing and plodding until they were mere yards from Easton and Eleanor. The paint stretched her neck and took a few whiffs of Granite, who liked horses. He stepped forward and returned the sniff. Easton's hand slipped into Eleanor's and they stood like that, resisting the urge to pet a horse's cheek or run a hand down their neck. A warm sensation filled her chest, nearly breaking her heart with love. She knew it was joy, and the feeling held as they piled back into the truck and kept driving north. They still had a few hours before reaching Susanville, where they'd spend the night before heading to the Litchfield corrals. As they closed in on Reno, the rugged eastern Sierra ridgeline came down and erupted into high rises and casinos. They passed the suburbs of Sparks until the country turned rural again. They decided to take the back road to Susanville and turned off at Pyramid Highway, named for the lake.

Something appeared on the right that they hadn't expected. A big flat ranch property divided into large paddocks crammed with horses. A brown government sign identified the site as the National Wild Horse and Burro Center of Palomino Valley. Eleanor Googled the site. The Palomino Valley Wild Horse Adoption Center, the land they were now passing, was the largest wild horse and burro facility in the country. Nevada has more wild horses than any state, and this is where most rounded-up horses were hauled, where they're freeze branded, gelded, vetted, processed, and shipped to other locations in the west for adoption and auctions.

They passed a weathered billboard on their right welcoming them to the Paiute Reservation. The shift to a sparser high desert was quick. The land exuded isolation. Occasional weathered homes sprinkled the base of the range.

They turned down at the marina sign and pulled into a parking lot crammed with RVs fronting Pyramid Lake, a huge oblong desert lake stunning in its remoteness. The rolling dun landscape on the opposite side of the lake was completely nude. Conical tufas rose out of the water like calcified gnome hats, raising the question, *What lay beneath?* On the shore, giant rocks formed ancient sentinels. Fishing boats dotted the lake. A jet ski jumped the lake's waves.

The long building to their right housed the marina, the police, and the ranger stations in one.

"I'm going inside to ask how long to Susanville." She left Easton to walk and water the dog.

A Paiute Reservation police officer stood behind the counter. "Can I help you?"

"Yes," said Eleanor. "We're driving up to Susanville and taking the backroad. I'm wondering what the conditions are like out there?"

"There's no pavement and no road signs, so if you don't know the area, you shouldn't go."

"Cell service?"

She shook her head. "No."

Granite was lapping water from the stainless-steel bowl Easton had filled. She relayed the officer's recommendation.

"I've grown up on back roads," he said. "Hell, I live on a backroad. In fact, we met on the eve of a back road adventure."

She nodded but quickly remembered her last solo experience on a Nevada backroad that had become dire straits in the name of her search for Rette. The landscape was brutal, and she'd become convinced the wilderness was deciding whether to kill her or let her live.

They drove with Pyramid Lake on their right. The lake marked the end of the Truckee River. The early Paiute who lived here killed more white invaders than anywhere else in the far West. The soil was layered with bones. Easton stopped the truck at the dirt road. "End of civilization and beginning of the Wild West."

"Cool."

"I'm spooked."

"This doesn't sound like off-road Easton."

A hot gust shook the truck.

"Uh-huh," he said

A herd of tumbleweeds somersaulted across the barren land, bumping along on prickly feet in front of the truck from small fry to papa and traveling on.

"That's kind of amazing."

"Sometimes when I'm on the road and there's no other cars, I think to myself maybe I shouldn't be here, either."

"I'm guessing this is one of those times?" She stared at the cut of his face and his Adam's apple moving up and down as he spoke. Eleanor knew this man. He was no coward. He took risks, like setting free those doomed mustangs. When he said he was afraid, her heart filled with love for his vulnerability.

"We could look at it this way," she said. "No one else is seeing what we're seeing right now in this time and space."

He looked straight ahead and gripped the steering wheel. "I say we turn around." He rolled up the windows.

"Okay then, we should definitely turn around."

24

ELEANOR HADN'T THOUGHT OF MARISOL Rodriguez since leaving the wild horse facility. But once Easton's foreboding seeped into her, the fearsome events surrounding Marisol ran through her mind as they drove north along the northern terminus of the Sierra Nevada. Right now, it seemed like they were passing a lot of geological endings and the beginning of something strange.

She rolled down the window. The air was a mixture of freshly cut hay and sage. The high desert sky was brilliant blue. The air so dry you could snap your fingers and start a fire. Ahead the flat, dun-colored geothermal dry lake, named Honey Lake, was a glaring metaphor for the turmoil beneath tranquility; in peace-loving Gold Strike's underworld, a killer was preparing their next move. Eleanor pulled the scrunchie out of her hair and shook her head.

"What is it?" asked Easton.

"My mind. An awful thought."

"I'm listening."

She turned to him. He looked so earnest, she almost cried.

"I don't want to give it power by saying it out loud."

"Maybe the thought will fly away if you speak it."

She looked out the window as they passed a small hand-painted sign on the shoulder of the road that said ICE CREAM AHEAD.

"I could use an ice cream," she said.

"Ice cream sounds good," he said.

They pulled in front of a small shop roughly twenty yards off the highway. A spindly palm tree grew out front of this sweet oasis. A sign hung on the doorknob: *Please shut the door when you come inside.* The thermometer on the wall read one hundred and four degrees.

Granite lapped from the water bowl the owners had placed outside for dogs. Posted beside the thermometer was a small, printed sign with the profile of a handgun. *Registered sidearms are allowed inside.* The sign gave Eleanor pause.

The screen door squealed as they filed inside. The pink interior walls and the black and white checked floor gave the parlor a crisp, old-fashioned look. The small white board behind the ice cream counter listed eight flavors and several toppings, including homemade toasted marshmallow and caramel. The clerk spotted Granite. She smiled, looking too nice to be someone who'd post a sign welcoming guns.

"He can come inside," she said. "It's way too hot out there, especially for dogs."

Granite flopped on the cool linoleum. Eleanor ordered a one-scoop vanilla ice cream in a cup, with marshmallow and caramel toppings. Easton ordered a double-scoop mint chocolate chip and strawberry cream on a giant sugar cone. They sat outside, savoring the flavors and watching the cars whizz by. She watched Easton manage the drips as the heat melted the ice cream faster than he could lick. She laughed and he looked up, his tongue on the cone.

They'd been together nearly a year. She still liked everything about him. Except his son, who only came around the ranch when she wasn't there. That was Easton's rule, which made it easier for all three of them, especially Eleanor. She couldn't erase from her mind his history of violence toward women and the revulsion she felt toward him.

"Where are you?" Easton tilted his head looking at her while sucking melted ice cream from the tip of his cone.

She stared at him. "I'm thinking the way you eat ice cream cones has strong sexual connotations." She ran the wooden spoon around the sides of the cup and collected the remaining caramel, surprised at herself—a dodger of innuendo—feeling comfortable enough with Easton to invent her own.

"You know the wilderness guide who deserted me on the river last summer?"

"Why are you bringing him up now?

"Sugar high, and I've been meaning to tell you."

"You juxtaposed that dude to an oral sex tease."

"I've been meaning to tell you. I ran into him at the Rancheria."

"He shouldn't be a guide if he can't keep his clients safe."

"No argument here."

"What's he doing in Gold Strike?"

"Investigating Bull Livestock Company contracted by the Gold Strike rodeo, the same outfit that was so eager to put down that poor horse."

"I haven't read anything about a livestock company scandal."

"That's because we're a paper of news and record, and even if I did blow Leonard's cover and propose a story, Mac would remind me the *Tribune's* not an investigative paper and turn it down. If Leonard finds fault and officially documents it, we'll have something solid to write up."

He ate the cone from the bottom up and she couldn't tell if he was savoring the flavor or dwelling on Leonard.

"How'd he end up at the Rancheria?"

"Renee, the hydrologist for the Forest Service. They're a thing."

The small white paper napkin made a crinkly noise when he wiped his lips.

"What are you thinking?" she asked.

"Glad he has a girlfriend."

"You're jealous."

"I don't like a guy who abandons my woman to the lions." He pointed at her empty ice cream cup. "Want another?"

She slid her hands across the table. He put his free hand in hers. "It's human to be jealous, but it's a waste of energy when your woman is crazy in love with you. I'm going inside to use the ladies' room."

Eleanor went up to the counter and ask the owner if she could use the bathroom. The lady handed her a key attached to an orange nerf gun. "May I ask you something?"

"Sure."

"Why do you have a sign saying licensed sidearms are allowed inside?"

"That sign's been up there since before we bought the place, and we kept it. You're the first person to ask. Why?"

"I get paid to ask questions," she said.

"Are you some kind of census taker?"

"I'm a reporter."

"There's bad people out there, intending to do harm and we want as many good, Christian folks as possible to arm themselves against evil."

"Aren't you worried the sign will scare off customers?"

She pulled back her shoulders and stuck out her chest, as if the question were absurd.

"The opposite. They'll feel safe. We want them to know our ice cream parlor is a haven where they can enjoy life but don't have to let down their guard."

"Honestly, I felt less safe when I saw your sign. I don't like to think about guns when I'm about to enter an ice cream paradise."

"Well, then, you live your life in a different world than us, and I'll pray that evil doesn't pop your bubble."

Eleanor decided she'd pee on the side of the road and returned the nerf doll to the woman. She headed out the door.

"What'd you say you do for a living?" asked the woman.

"I'm a reporter."

"Like a newspaper reporter?" she said with disdain.

"Yes, a newspaper reporter."

"What do you report on?"

"Murder."

25

THEY FOUND A FUNKY MOTEL that was dated but clean and allowed dogs. Their room was big enough to host a family. Two queens were made up in the main section of the room by the door with two twin beds in an alcove. Eleanor claimed the first shower. But the hot water faucet was either on the wrong side or her brain was fried. The latter. She adjusted the knobs to the desired temperature and stood under the thin stream for a long time and thought about Marisol Rodriguez. The women of Gold Strike would never feel safe again hiking alone or taking a solo road trip. Even she, someone who vowed she'd never buy a gun, fantasized about buying one. That way when she encountered a bad man while hiking with Granite and the man's smile turned into a devil-grin, she'd pretend to lean over to vomit and pull out her derringer from her front pack and shoot him in the chest, shoot again, then a third time in his head. Her body convulsed.

"Holy shit." She turned off the water. She reached outside the shower curtain and felt for the towel she'd left on the toilet seat. Instead, her hand touched human flesh, and she screamed.

"Lee," said Easton. "It's just me." He handed her the smallest bath towel she'd ever seen. She could barely wrap it around her chest and tuck it in. She went into the room and flopped down on the bed. She listened to the shower, then, no sound. A few minutes later, Easton, holding the small bath towel around his waist, flopped down beside her.

"How was it?" she asked.

"The water's hot and plenty of it. What do you want to chat about?"

"Marisol."

He turned on his side, facing her.

"Why would someone move a person they'd murdered?"

He thought a while. "They didn't want the authorities to find the body in the same place they murdered her because of evidence."

"What if it wasn't about the killing but about the burial?"

"Not following."

"What if they wanted to make sure the body was found?"

"That would be weird."

"Not really," she said. "Remember Cary Stayner? He sent a map of Lake Don Pedro to the FBI so they'd find Juli Sund's corpse. Whoever killed Marisol could've started a fire to draw people to the river so they'd find her."

He stared up at the ceiling a few seconds. "You think the killer set the fire to attract authorities to the body?"

"Maybe."

He rose from the bed, scratched his scalp with both hands as if rubbing away the conversation. "I'm going to shave." He came back seconds later. "My thought. Water purifies. The killer dumped the body in the water to purify the act and set fire so the body would be found and properly buried for closure."

"Makes gruesome sense." She rolled onto her side and fell asleep hating the roar of the air conditioner and woke up trying to figure out where she was. It was daylight, but dim. Dawn or dusk. And she was on the wrong side of the bed.

"Lee?" Easton put a gentle arm over her.

"It's time to pick up Goldenrod." He handed her a paper cup of hot coffee poured from his thermos. She drank the coffee and got up. After opening the door of their motel room, she inhaled the cedar and sage descended from the volcanic mountain slopes and mixed with the virgin clay risen with Honey Lake's subterranean fluids. She was hungry.

The restaurant didn't open until seven, so Easton made motel coffee with the automatic drip machine. They sipped the coffee, grimaced, and giggled over the room's unused beds—all four of them.

"We'll have to remember this place for the future," said Easton.

"What are you talking about?"

"You never know."

"Know what?" She took a sip of coffee and shivered from its bitterness.

"We might want kids someday."

She imagined children scampering and chattering, their voices a soft rain of hope.

* * *

When she stepped out of the truck, the morning air smelled of horses. She glanced around the corrals. Their truck and trailer were the first to arrive in the parking lot.

Easton's hand brushed hers as they walked down the aisle along the six-foot cyclone hog wiring fencing. Each containment area had a number. They stopped at pen number six, where the stallions and bachelors were placed together according to the date they'd been rounded up.

The stallions would undergo gelding and a final vet check. Easton had given strict instructions that he wanted Goldenrod intact. They didn't see the stallion in any of the pens and walked down the next aisle checking out the paddock of mares. What most surprised Eleanor was the beauty and health of these horses. Why would the BLM remove wild horses who clearly thrived in the wilderness? A habitat that, by federal law, was put aside to protect them.

A small cremello mare caught Eleanor's eye. Tragically, the BLM tended to euthanize these rare beauties, citing eye problems due to their blue eyes and light pigmentation.

A high-pitched squeal rose from the corral.

"That's a mare crying for her baby," Easton said.

"How sad." Eleanor clung to the fencing and put her head against the hog wire to discern which mare was in distress. The foals were in the next pen over, chewing hay from bins in the center of the enclosure.

"Why separate them?"

"There's a reason," he said. "Not a good one. They want to sell the weanlings. C'mon. There's not much you can do at this point."

They came to a gate with a sign that said, Restricted Area. Beyond the gate were a couple of small paddocks and a long metal warehouse building.

"This is where they do the vet checks, vaccinate, geld the stallions, and treat the mares with fertility drugs." Easton tipped back his ball cap. "You okay?"

"I'm fine."

They walked down the aisle to the last pen, all bays in one large corral. Bays were the last horses adopted. They were more likely than the rest to be auctioned off to kill buyers and end up hauled out of the country for slaughter. Or transported to off-range holding facilities. Or a rancher's land where they competed with cattle for food and access to water at exorbitant costs to the taxpayers.

A stricken look came over Easton's face, his forehead skewed with worry.

"What's wrong?"

"He's not here."

"Goldenrod?"

"I don't see him in in any of the corrals."

Eleanor scanned the stallions and couldn't spot him. "Let's go ask at the office."

A middle-aged woman sat at the desk, looking up, a little surprised, when the two of them walked in.

"I'm looking for a particular horse. Goldenrod."

"Name?"

"Easton Jode. I had my name on that stallion."

The woman checked her computer. "I see you here, Easton." She studied the screen. "He's in recovery."

"Recovery from what?" He was pissed.

"Gelded this morning."

"Gelded. I specifically requested he not be gelded. I need a strong stud for my mares. I was clear."

"Sorry, sir. I don't see that on your request."

"You gotta be kidding me."

Eleanor knew enough about Easton to worry that he was outside the limits of his mild-mannered temperament.

"May I see your screen?" he said.

"I'm sorry sir. I can't do that. I'll make a call." She picked up the phone and punched some numbers. "Travis, this is Bonnie at the corrals. I have an adopter in here who claims he's scheduled to pick up a stallion we gelded this morning. He says he required the stallion be left intact. You have a record of that? Doesn't show up in my file. I'll wait."

The office was quiet. Bonnie said thank you and hung up.

"You're correct. You did state you wanted the stallion intact."

"What's the matter with you people? Where is he now?"

"I told you, sir, he's in post-op, probably still recovering from anesthesia."

"Where *exactly* is the horse now?"

"Sir, you have to settle down or I'm calling security."

Eleanor stepped forward. "Please tell him where Goldenrod is so he can be assured the horse got through the surgery safely."

"His location is off limits to the public."

Easton turned to Eleanor, his tanned neck rage-red. "I'm going out to the truck to calm down before someone gets hurt." He left the room, muttering, "Fucking bureaucracy."

Eleanor remained in the room. "He had his heart set on that horse."

"He's still a good horse. You can look around, maybe select one that's already had its vaccines and needs a good home."

"Are they all gelded?"

"Not all. I'd say ninety percent."

"Ninety percent of the rounded-up stallions are gelded? Why so many?"

"People don't adopt stallions, ma'am. We can always put them back on the range and if they're gelded they won't be a problem."

"The problem isn't the horses," Eleanor said.

"Ma'am?"

"The problem is how you manage them."

26

ELEANOR HEADED TO THE TRUCK to find Easton. Several rigs had parked in the BLM lot since they'd arrived. That was the first thing she noticed. The second was the empty cab. Easton wasn't in the truck. Which meant he was looking for the horse in the only place they hadn't looked.

She walked briskly past the scattering of folks who stood outside various pens on both sides of the yard, gazing at the horses: mares, foals, stallions.

She stopped short at the gate with the sign posted Restricted Area and turned back. If Easton were in there, it was his business, and she'd just have to wait.

She stopped beside a little girl who stared at the horses in awe and gazed up at Eleanor.

"See that light one," the girl said. "I love her."

"She's a beauty," Eleanor said to the girl. "I noticed her earlier."

"I wish I could bring her home," she said. "My dad mostly takes the bays."

"Do you have a name for her?"

She took a deep breath. "Shimmer."

"Because she's so shimmery." Eleanor smiled down at the girl. She was young—eight or nine, and tiny.

The girl smiled back. "Do you have a favorite horse?"

"We do. His name's Goldenrod."

"Do you have a ranch?"

"My boyfriend does. A big ranch. We're here to take Goldenrod back to live on it. My name's Eleanor."

"I know who you are. You saved the horses."

"Oh yeah? That's a nice thing to say."

"My dad was going to sell those horses for meat, but you freed them. You ride a paint. She's pretty, like you."

Not possible. This little girl couldn't know what she and Easton had done that day a year ago.

"I was in the cinder block shed," she said. "My mom lets me sleep in there to keep the horses company." The girl looked up at Eleanor, her young eyes fully serious. "I won't tell." She held up her little finger.

Eleanor linked her pinkie finger with the girl's. "Thank you."

"You should adopt Shimmer."

"I'll see what I can do. No promises."

"You won't get in trouble because you weren't on the security camera," she whispered. "You were on the other side of the shed. But the man you were with was on the camera. Daddy is so mad. He's going to get even."

"His words?"

"Without the cuss words which will send me to hell and the devil will eat me for breakfast."

"Who told you that?'

Someone shouted and the girl turned.

"He did," she said.

"Would you like my business card so we can stay in touch? It has my cell number on it if you want to call me." Eleanor handed the girl the card and she stuck it in her sweatshirt pocket and ran toward the man Eleanor assumed was her father. He looked familiar, a wiry man with a high voice. He seemed to recognize her as well, as he caught the girl's wrist and pulled her with him. When he got close, she saw the gun under his denim jacket. It was too warm for jackets, never too warm to carry.

He jabbed his first finger in the air. "You're the nosy bitch reporter."

"Yep, a crime reporter, in fact, investigating the BLM's incentive program that attracts criminal kill buyers. I got a lead there'd be a few of you here today. Mind if I take your photo?"

She looked straight into the man's eyes and watched them narrow. He turned his head to the side and spit tobacco. The little girl stared at the ground, looking like she would burrow a hole in the dirt if she could.

Eleanor spoke before he could cough up more nastiness. "Would you care to comment on the horses?" she asked. "For the record."

"What kind of comment?"

"Why are you here?"

"I don't care to comment for no goddamn newspaper."

The little girl tugged on the man's arm. "Daddy, tell her we're adopting the bays." She looked up at Eleanor.

"What a wonderful thing to do." Eleanor looked at the man. "The bays go last, I hear, often to buyers who haul them to slaughter."

The man seethed.

"Would it be okay if I quote your daughter, sir?"

"I'm her stepfather. And no way in hell can you quote her, and if you do, I'll sue your ass or die trying."

"Buy yourself a coffin, then." She held up her iPhone.

He pulled back his vest revealing the butt of his pistol. "Better not take no goddamn picture."

"What's going on here?" Easton took her arm and pulled her behind him.

Recognition lit the man's face. "You stole my mustangs. I got you on video, you sonuvabitch. You think I'm leaving my livestock out there without a security camera? I'm taking your license plate and you're gonna hear from me one way or th'other."

"That's fine," said Easton. "I've had your number for a long time now."

He sneered. "If the girl weren't standin' here, I'd use this." He opened his vest for the second time. "You git in the truck, Sissy. Now, or I'll smack you."

The girl looked up at Eleanor. "That's short for Narcissa." She ran to the truck and turned to look. Eleanor gave her a short wave as she struggled to pull open the Silverado's passenger door.

"How many horses are you hauling to slaughter today, man?" asked Easton.

"None of your goddamn fuckin' business you phony ass cowboy still sucking on his mama's tit and hasn't worked a day in his life." The guy was reaching a pitch and leaning forward onto the toe of his cowboy boot. "And you're lucky this nosy bitch reporter wasn't on that tape, or I'd ream her tight ass in court right along with yours."

Easton lunged, flattening the guy in the dirt, Easton on top, gripping his collar with one fist and slugging the dude's face with the other. One. Two.

"Easton," Eleanor shouted, as two men ran up the aisle toward them. It took both to pull off Easton, who worked to catch his breath, head bent over his knees.

"This asshole threatened my lady with his side arm and foul mouth."

"Nothing to be sorry about, man. We know this guy. He's bad news."

The bad news man rolled onto his side and spit blood into the dirt. He felt for a loose tooth. Spit again. He got up groaning and snake-eyed Easton.

"You'll regret this." He slapped dirt off his jeans as he walked to his truck, where the little girl was looking out the rear windshield. His truck shot a cloud of exhaust, and he drove out of the yard, his clattering horse trailer empty.

"I have his license," Easton said.

"I'm worried about the girl." Eleanor said a quiet prayer the man didn't take it out on her.

She put her arm around Easton's waist and rubbed his chest as they walked toward the truck.

She waited until they cleared the corrals to ask where he'd been.

"They haven't gelded him," he said. "They've shipped him out to Palomino Valley, that holding facility we passed in Nevada."

* * *

Two hours later they arrived at Palomino. The outdoor corrals were crowded with horses from the recent series of roundups. Goldenrod's pen was supposedly inside the building.

It took an hour for the administrator to find Easton's paperwork. At first, the man in charge told him he'd have to go through the same process as everyone else—put in a bid and wait for the auction date. Easton reminded him he was taking a stallion off their hands, and they'd already fucked up. The man must have liked him. After he made a few calls, he sent Easton and Eleanor to the big metal warehouse of pens and paddocks. They roamed the aisles and checked the numbers.

The palomino stood tall, his mane in dreadlocks, and his full tail falling to an inch above the ground.

"He's gorgeous."

"That he is," said Easton.

The horse lowered his head and drank water from a bucket, an eye on them. When his thirst was quaffed, he walked to the opposite side of the paddock, head held high figuring out what these two-leggeds were up to.

"What are you thinking?" Eleanor asked.

"I'm thinking he's bold. I'm a little worried about the way he holds his neck so high. He'll rear if he gets too unhappy about things. Just be aware."

They went back to the truck and Eleanor stood outside as Easton backed the trailer to an inside chute, opened his trailer door, and backed in some more.

A wrangler came up to him. "Looks like you're taking home Goldenrod," she said. "He's a lucky horse."

"I hope so," Easton told her. "Bureaucracy's damn quick when someone's pulling strings."

"Bureaucracy's hardheaded and new ideas just can't find a way into its calcified brain," the wrangler said. "So, who's pulling strings?"

Easton shrugged. "Beats me."

The wrangler stood by and another cowboy at the end opened Goldenrod's paddock gate. The stallion ripped down the aisle, hooves pounding. He pulled up to a stop short of the trailer and reared. Another wrangler leaned over the rail and slapped the horse's rump with a flag.

"Hold off, Cody," shouted the woman. "Let him decide." She climbed the rails and back down into the chute and stood there a distance from the horse, who turned toward the trailer.

"You put hay in the manger?" she asked.

"I did," said Easton.

Goldenrod turned again and took a quick step into the aisle, looking to bolt. She sidestepped and he turned back and faced the trailer again. When he turned toward her, she took a small step forward and spread an arm until he turned back to the trailer. It went on like this for a long time, the people waiting patiently while the horse sniffed and pawed the trailer. One questioning hoof stepped up, and the rest followed. Easton swung the door shut.

They drove out of the compound slowly, not talking, barely breathing, listening for sounds of distress. Goldenrod was calm, and Eleanor thought of Narcissa looking out the back of the cab window at a world where adults made a mess of things.

27

THEY PULLED INTO THE TRUCKEE gas station. Easton filled both tanks and checked the stallion while she went inside and bought two Cokes and Häagen-Dazs ice cream bars. It was a long haul to Gold Strike, and they planned to stop halfway at a horse motel to give Goldenrod a break.

Easton got back in the truck. "Horse is good."

"Great." Eleanor brought up the online edition of the *Tribune.* "Oh shit."

He shot her a look. "What?"

"A woman drowned in the river today." The breaking news story hadn't named her. "And they're reporting fire further up the gorge."

"Better call Mac," said Easton.

She put the call on speaker.

"Mac, I just read about the woman who drowned."

"I tried to call you," he said. "She went over the falls."

"Which falls?"

"Gooseberry Falls, above the pools."

"Someone must have seen her."

"There's a witness. Not giving out their name."

"That's awful. Do they have an ID?

"They can't retrieve the body. Conditions are too dangerous for the divers. Pools too deep, too cold, and too turbulent. Add fire."

Her stomach dropped.

"When are you getting back?"

She turned to Easton.

"We'll drive straight through," he said.

"A few hours. We're out of Truckee, on our way." Her voicemail notifications pinged, three in a row, all from the same unknown caller. She read the messages.

"This is Tracy Wilson, McKenzie Wilson's mom. Call me, please."

The second voicemail: "I haven't been able to reach McKenzie. She hasn't been home for two nights. Please call."

And finally: "I read the story about the woman who went over the falls, and they don't identify her. They haven't even found her body. Please call me."

Eleanor called the Sheriff and left a voice message. "This is Eleanor. I'm out of town and heard about the woman going over the falls at Gooseberry Lake. A worried parent is calling me. Do you have any information I can pass on to her? I'm on the road but reception is okay."

Eleanor called Tracy Wilson. The call went to voicemail.

"Mrs. Wilson, this is Eleanor Wooley from the *Tribune* letting you know I have a call into the Sheriff and when I hear anything—"

Wilson picked up, breathless. "I'm here. This is Tracy."

"I've been out of town or would've called sooner."

The mom spoke rapidly.

"Slow down, Tracy. Have you heard from McKenzie?"

"No," the mother said. "Do you know who the dead girl is?"

"They haven't recovered the body and no identification, but I'll let you know as soon as I get word. Have you reported McKenzie missing?"

"I have not."

"I'd call the Sheriff's Office and file a missing person report." Eleanor remembered the advice Sheriff Duncan gave her when Rette had vanished. "File a missing person report, and when she shows up, good end of story. Where did you last see her?"

"Home, but no, McKenzie would be humiliated. I'd never hear the end of it."

"I'm on the road right now and Easton Jode is driving. You know him."

"Easton. Please say 'hi' to Easton."

"Give me some of her friends' phone numbers and I'll make calls."

"Hold on."

A long minute went by, and Eleanor thought if she were the mom, she'd panic, too. McKenzie was probably at the music festival.

"I'm back. Here are some phone numbers."

Eleanor's gut tightened at the thought of McKenzie as the victim.

"Tracy, try to remember an eighteen-year-old woman is severing the umbilical cord regardless of how close you are, and I know you two are close. I don't know if that helps."

"Nothing'll help until I hear her voice."

"She's probably hanging with her friends."

Her effort to comfort the mother didn't assuage her own anxiety. McKenzie was smart and responsible. She wasn't the kind of kid who wouldn't let her family know where she was.

They hung up with a promise to keep in touch until one of them heard from McKenzie. Eleanor placed her hands over her face and swore quietly. Easton's hand gently rubbed her shoulder. He turned off at the In-N-Out Burger on the right side of the highway and drove up to the speaker.

"One large French fry and two medium Cokes."

As she brought the cold, sweet liquid to her lips, her hand shook. Easton looked over at her. "Doesn't she have a boyfriend?"

Chad. "Joined at the hip." She set the Coke in the holder between the seats and shoved French fries into her mouth, flooding her senses with salt and fat, tapping Chad's number.

"Chad here."

"Chad." Eleanor and Easton exchanged a look, and she put the phone on speaker. "It's Eleanor Wooley."

"How can I help you?"

"Thanks for picking up, Chad. I'm looking for McKenzie."

"McKenzie. Why're you looking for McKenzie?"

"Her mom's worried because she hasn't heard from her and another young woman has drowned."

"I read that. It's tragic. Can I pass on a message if I see her?"

Something was off in Chad's reaction. "Do you know where she is?"

The rustling sound of a phone changing hands came through the phone.

"I'm here."

"McKenzie."

"Yes, Eleanor. This is McKenzie. Is my family okay?"

Eleanor slumped back in her seat. Easton pulled over to the side of the road.

"Thank God you're safe. Your mom called me because she's very worried about you."

"Why? What happened? I told her."

"An unidentified young woman became another victim, and your mom hasn't been able to reach you."

"Why are *you* calling and not her?"

"She tried calling you, numerous times."

"This is so embarrassing."

"You weren't picking up."

"My cell phone doesn't get reception up here."

"I told her I'd call a few of your friends and get back to her."

"Does anyone else know my mom is stalking me?"

"She was panicked. A woman is being reported drown up at Gooseberry Falls, the second in two weeks, and another fire's broken out." Now Eleanor was impatient. "What would you like me to tell your mom?"

"I'm sorry."

She sounded earnest.

"I left a note on the fridge that I was going to a music festival with my friends, and we'd be gone all weekend."

"Are you at the music festival?"

"I'm here now next county over and we're camping."

"You with friends?"

"I'm with Chad, and my girlfriends are somewhere around here. I can't believe my mom."

"McKenzie, any mom who doesn't know her daughter's whereabouts is going to freak out."

"Did you say the woman's dead?"

"Missing and presumed dead. Someone witnessed her go over the falls and they're trying to recover her body."

"Do you know who she is?"

"Not yet, another reason your mom panicked. I would, too. She thought I might know the woman's name, which I don't. She didn't want to file a missing person report with the Sheriff, even though I suggested she do that because she didn't want to embarrass you."

"You suggested she file a missing person report?"

"I did, and I'd press her to do so if I hadn't found you."

She sighed. "I'll call her."

"How are you going to call her if your phone doesn't have reception?"

"I'll use Chad's."

"Want me to tell her I spoke with you?"

"You don't have to. I'll call. Promise."

"Do it now. Pass the phone back to Chad. I have a question for him."

"What can I do for you?" Chad asked.

"Do you have any information on the fire?"

"Sounds like it's being held."

"It's far from under control and the smoke alone is hindering Search and Rescue. I'm returning to town from up north, and any piece of information no matter how small could help me get a better idea of what's going on."

He didn't answer right away. "I can tell you what I've been thinking."

"I'm listening."

"Whether on purpose or accidental, can't say, but person-caused. If it were one fire, case closed. Two fires under similar circumstances there's probably more coming down the pike unless the arsonist is caught."

"What do you mean 'similar circumstances'?"

"Both fires unseasonal. May's early. Not lightning-caused. Female victims nearby."

"Related?"

"Coincidental. So, yes, I think the fires are related and the women are related. It's one thing to kill someone and hide the evidence by starting a fire, but the bodies are outside the fire."

"This second one hasn't been found."

"They will recover it eventually and forensics will figure it out because they always do. I'm junior in this field, but my bet is whatever sicko set the fires was drawing attention to the scene. Probably a guy because women don't normally kill other women, and I haven't heard of any female arsonists."

Easton looked at her and shrugged. He'd said the same.

"Make sure you hand your phone to McKenzie so she can call her mom."

"Yes, ma'am."

"I mean now."

"Yes'm. Mitzi, here, call your mom."

28

A CHARRED SNAG HAD THROWN out new sparks and reignited the fire overnight. Low-flying planes dropped clouds of bright red flame retardant, and helicopters dipped bucket after bucket into the lake, gathering water to drop over the blaze.

The Hotshots hiked in with chainsaws and hand tools to take down trees and chaparral, creating breaks to stop the spread of the blaze. And the Forest Service helitack crew with their heavy gear rappelled on ropes from choppers into difficult terrain to build firelines.

When Eleanor arrived Monday morning, the smoke was dense and Gooseberry Lake parking lot was full of first responder trucks. Two Sheriff patrol cars had parked on either side of a shiny new dark blue water tender rig. She recognized it as the same truck that had worked the Browns Ferry fire. A stocky middle-aged man with a trimmed beard sat on the water tender's back fender talking to Deputy Perelli. Eleanor snapped photos of the business sign on the driver's door panel and approached the two men.

She skipped acknowledging Perelli and held out her hand to the driver. "Eleanor Wooley from the *Tribune*."

He offered his hand. "Jeffrey Turnbull."

She kept her attention on Turnbull because she knew Perelli would be uncooperative and try to bias the water tender operator, as well.

"That's a nice truck," she said. "How much does the tank hold?"

Turnbull glanced at Perelli, but his pride of ownership outweighed Perelli's eyeball roll.

"My rig is holding four thousand gallons of water and could pump three hundred gallons a minute," he said. "When I run out, it only takes thirty minutes to refill the tank. Unfortunately, both sides of the fire road are curtained with flames so it's inaccessible for my rig, but they're cutting new road, so I'm on standby."

Eleanor turned to Perelli. "Any updates on the victim?"

"Updates from when?" asked Perelli.

"I was told the pools are too dangerous for Search and Rescue to dive in the area the victim was seen falling. Do you know what SAR is doing at this point?"

"Searching for a body," Perelli said.

Smartass. She inhaled. "As they should be. Have they found the body?"

"Why don't you go up there and find out?" he said.

"That's the plan." *Jerk.*

A yellow gurney had been set up, in wait mode, on the tarmac. An older man in a faded T-shirt with the word "FIRE" paced the lot with a radio. Down at the loading ramp, another wave of search and rescuers stood on the lake's main dock. They stepped single file onto the fire boat. The siren was quiet, but the rotating emergency lights blared, preparing to cross the smokey lake.

She asked the man in the FIRE T-shirt, "How is everything?"

He looked grim. "There's a lot happening up there," which she translated as not going well.

Eleanor called Mac and told him another team was taking off from the dock, heading toward the falls. "I'm going with them."

"You don't have to do that," Mac said. "That canyon is steep, hot, and smoky, and there's a fire nearby."

"Exactly why I'm going."

"You prepared?"

"I brought my CamelBak and sunscreen."

"Find out the name of the witness who saw the victim go over the falls. Watch out for rattlers. Don't go stepping on rocks with overhangs. Got it? And wear a KN-95 for God's sake."

She'd kept a KN-95 in her backpack since the last wildfire. "I'll wear a mask, and I'll be with folks who know how to handle snakebites. Anything else?"

"Keep your eyes open and stay away from the river's edge. Repeat. Stay away from the water's edge. My guess, the body's lodged deep in one of the lower pools and a lot of those pools aren't even accessible on foot. Don't get any stupid ideas. Stay with the crew. Get quotes and take pics. The story angle will be about rescue attempts, unless they find her."

She looked up at the faint sound of a helicopter traveling from the east but couldn't see it through the smoke. The sound grew deafening as it flew toward the canyon, and she discerned its silhouette as it flew overhead. A dangerous route, threading the smoke-filled slot between the canyon's two massive granite walls. She assumed the chopper had been sent to retrieve the body, which meant they'd possibly spotted the victim. But minutes later the chopper returned, a length of cable dangling from the end with nothing attached.

The man in the FIRE T-shirt talked on the phone. He glanced at Eleanor, and she heard him say, "Conditions are too dangerous for the divers to retrieve the body."

After he hung up, she approached him and asked, "Is there a PG&E station above the falls where they can shut off the flow?"

He looked at her in mild surprise and posed the same question into his radio. "Has anyone contacted PG&E to cut off the outflow at the high country dam?"

A crackly voice came over the radio. He kept her gaze and listened.

"Roger." He placed the radio in his back pocket. "No dams up there, but it was worth a try."

"I need to get up to the canyon to cover the rescue for the *Tribune*."

"You can go with the boat. They're about to take off. You got water and a hat?"

"I have water, sunscreen, and a mask."

He removed his cap with the Gooseberry Fire District emblem and handed it to her. Gratefully, she placed the sweat-stained cap on her head.

He got on his radio. "Newspaper lady needs a ride up canyon. On her way to you now."

The all-men team of rescuers wore red shirts and black harnesses. One of them held out a hand to help her step into the boat. They shoved off and proceeded full throttle across the lake, leaving a wake on the glassy surface, the windless air heavy with smoke. Eleanor fastened her mask.

When the boat pulled up to the eastern dock at the river mouth, the crew disembarked. Each was dressed down to short-sleeved T-shirts, carrying easily fifty pounds of gear. She looked down at their feet as they stepped off the boat in front of her. She heard them tromp ahead of her and followed the feet of the last in line as he jumped off the boat in front of her. When he moved too far ahead, a slight panic rose in her throat, and she glued her eyes on his shadow as if she were following white stripes while driving at night on Gold Strike's curving back roads.

She crawled through the low limbs of a stunted cedar that grew out of a fissure in the granite wall. She climbed the next boulder using crevices as handholds. She worked to keep up, her legs burning, her chest sore from the smoke. They were at forty minutes in when the rustic trail turned to blasted rock. She made out cairns that affirmed they were on course to the pools. She glanced down from the trail and at the river, barely discernible in the smoke. The spray of the river misted her face. She thought of the priest and the holy water and his olive branch at Marisol's service.

Soon, the sound of the cascades was deafening as the stampeding snow melt plummeted to the life-sucking whirlpool below. The top of the falls was even louder. Eleanor could barely see clearly to the river's far side. SAR picked their way down the cliff to the river. Two divers in full wetsuits and scuba gear entered the water, roped to teammates on shore. Eleanor didn't have time to photograph. In seconds, the whirlpool sucked the divers into its vortex and pulled them under. Immediately, the ropes went taut. There was panicked shouting as the crew pulled hard on the ropes, their faces strained with exertion until the divers surfaced and were dragged to the base of the rock, where they climbed the vertical ledge to the crew. This was mountain rescue.

She remembered the diver at Marisol's retrieval, blue lips and chills. How Adelia helped him put away his gear because his hands were too numb from cold to work properly. That water was a fraction of this water's frigidity, born from the mountain's frozen womb.

As the crew helped the divers out of the river and removed their tanks, something hot pricked Eleanor's arm. White ash trimmed with hot orange flame. She flicked it off, but the ash had left its brand.

Another helicopter was flowing up the canyon with the bucket of water suspended by a cable sloshing water over its sides. The heli flew so low she made out details of its red and white underbelly and watched until it disappeared up mountain. And there was Adelia Shepherd standing on the ledge above her. She leaned against a pine, bent over, hands on knees, breathing heavily. Her face was streaked black. Her pants looked wet. Eleanor stepped back, out of her line of vision. A firefighter was conversing with two rescuers. His voice was urgent.

"You can't be standing here," he said to them, "checking your manual to analyze the situation. By the time you figure it out, the fire will have grown ten thousand acres and cost us a bundle more. Don't figure. Get up there and fight the goddamn fire."

The young men hustled away.

He removed his helmet and wiped his brow with a red handkerchief, aware of Eleanor. "Either I'm too old for this or they're too young."

"I'm sorry," she said. "I'm a reporter."

"Of course you are."

"Why are your firefighters down here with SAR?"

"My point exactly. I'm here because they need me to report information of the rescue to the fire crew. Those two are the fire crew and they're analyzing the situation when they should be fighting it."

"What's *your* analysis?"

"I'd say forty percent contained. We've called in the prison crew to keep an eye on overnight flare ups. And these snags, they're punks, and as soon as the sun hits they can flame up and send out sparks."

"Are you ruling out natural causes?"

"There's been no lightning and it's still moist up here."

"So possible arson?"

"Not ruling out anything. We don't know. But my crew's working round the clock to fight this one, and we'll continue until it's contained and the forest and critters are safe."

"What about the victim who went over the falls? Who's the witness?"

"Don't know who the witness is, but the water's too dangerous and too deep for the divers." He glanced at his watch. "You should get the next ride back to the dock. We're wrapping this up and the last boat out is gonna be crowded with gear." He pointed to a group of SAR guys in yellow vests. "You want to go with them."

She followed them down mountain to the inlet and boarded the fire boat, surprised to find Adelia sitting alone on the stern, arms across her chest, eyes closed, legs stretched out in front of her. Eleanor let her be.

29

A LATE AFTERNOON WIND WHIPPED the lake to chop. The wind would feed the fire. One of the men nodded to Eleanor. She moved up to the seat across from him.

"Thank you for your work today," she said.

He nodded, pressed his lips, and tipped his hat.

"How are you feeling?"

"Been better."

"I'm sorry."

"We failed our mission. We're fatigued and disheartened."

"Do you know for certain there's a victim?"

He shrugged. "There was a witness."

"A reliable witness?"

"Above my pay grade." He mumbled, so she leaned in and asked him to repeat. "The witness is one of us." He tilted his head toward Adelia. "Ask her."

They reached the docks. The crew disembarked and headed to the lodge and refreshments. Adelia stayed put, her eyes shut, her body a slant board. Eleanor followed the crew, taking a few photos of their sweaty slumped backs. *Disheartened* was an apropos adjective.

The community room inside the old lodge was cool. Electric fans blew at top speed. A large orange water cooler sat on each end of the table. The men lined up for water and grabbed energy snacks—Cliff Bars, etc. She grabbed two, stuffed one in her vest pocket, unwrapped the bar, and bit off chunks, ravenous, her head filled with the sound of chewing as she stared at the parking lot full of emergency vehicles, including the water tender, apparently still on standby. When she turned, Adelia walked by and stood in front of the snack table between two of the men, staring so blankly Eleanor suspected her work on the search effort had depleted her. Adelia picked up one of the energy bars and read the label. Eleanor walked up to her.

"Adelia, how are you?" she asked.

She turned a blank stare on Eleanor and tossed the bar back on the table. "Egg whites. I'm vegan."

Eleanor kept it light. "No guilt when you drive by the cows."

"Or the turkey sheds."

"What's your take on what happened up there?" Eleanor asked.

"My take?" Adelia said. "My take is I hate men right now. Sorry to be a downer, but I started my fucking period. I get enough shit from the guys without bleeding all over the place."

"I understand," said Eleanor. "You know who I can talk to for an update?"

She scanned the room. "The public information officer is around here somewhere." She got on her radio. The crackle of radio waves filled their space.

"Reporter from the local newspaper needs to talk to our PIO."

A male voice replied. "He's on the fire coordinating teams. He can't talk right now."

She looked at Eleanor and shrugged. "Which means this is bad and getting worse."

"Can you tell me why it's bad and getting worse?"

Adelia coughed. "Well, to start with we lost another civilian in the high water. Don't quote me on that because it's not confirmed. If we keep on like we're doing with the diving, we're going to lose one of our crew. There's no one on our team or SAR who is expert enough to handle this high water, which means we can't retrieve the victim's body. And then there's the fire."

"About the fire," said Eleanor. "Apparently, the wind came up by the time our boat returned to the docks. Can you explain how this might affect the blaze?"

She inhaled deeply. "Badly," she said, and looked around with a restlessness that told Eleanor if she had any more questions she'd better hurry up and ask.

"Are you going back up to the site?"

"Of course. We were getting it under control until the afternoon wind came up from the west and didn't die down during the night. Usually, it dies down by evening. Last night, it didn't and that changed everything fast. Flames jumped our fire break, absolutely torched the pines which are near dead from beetles anyway, exploded the crowns, and sent a fireball across the canyon. I saw it fly overhead. A giant comet soaring across the sky as if someone had thrown it. Never seen anything like that. It happens, but I'd never seen it before now. Kind of awesome to be honest."

"Can you predict how you're going to contain the fire?"

She shoved her arm back into the sleeve of her fire jacket and trudged toward the front door. "I leave that up to my captain."

"One more question," said Eleanor.

Adelia stopped "Ask away."

"Is there a witness who saw the victim go over the falls?"

"There is."

"Was it you, by chance?"

"Why are you asking me that?"

"One of the SAR crew said to ask you."

"Bastards. Back to my original comment. You'd hope they'd enter the twenty-first century and stop harassing women in a traditionally male-dominated workplace, especially in a government job. Then again, look who's president. To your question, the Sheriff won't release that information until they find the body. The press ... well," she scoffed, "you know how you are."

"So, you didn't witness the fall?"

"What I saw was snow melt traveling at twenty-two thousand plus cubic feet per second because the Sierras received one hundred and fifty percent of its normal snowpack. When that water nears the crest the flow rate accelerates and the velocity increases as it crashes down the face and the force of water and sediment pummel the river bottom so hard it erodes the rock and creates a whirlpool with the power to suck a victim down and pin them thirty feet below. The current drags the body until it wedges under a rock, creating dangerous conditions for divers and making rescue impossible."

Adelia watched Eleanor's reaction.

"What then? Wait for receding waters?"

"That's one option."

"The poor family."

"Yup. I have to get going or I'll be giving the guys ammunition."

"Wouldn't want that."

The corners of her mouth turned up. "Call me if you need anything," Adelia said. "Or if you don't, call me anyway."

"Thank you. And be safe."

"I appreciate that."

* * *

Deputy Perelli stood in the parking lot beside his partner with the K9. He looked down at her and took a deep breath. "Wondering when you'd show up again."

Eleanor acknowledged him with a nod. "I got back from the canyon about a half-hour ago."

"See anything?"

... asks the deputy who rolls his eyes when she raises a question. "It was extremely smoky and hard to see, but the divers are having a hard time in that water. They were pulled out as soon as they went in. Are you treating this as a crime scene?"

"Can't comment," he said.

"Someone called in the incident and said a witness saw the victim go over. Can you give me the name of the witness?"

His mouth turned down. "Same answer."

"What about the fires. Any idea who's setting them?"

"Who was it in that movie who said, 'Follow the money'?"

Deep Throat. Perelli's way of saying, "Suck my dick."

The K9 deputy looked down at his boots.

* * *

Eleanor sat on the toilet, crying, as her bladder emptied. This was the longest she'd sat still all afternoon. The cubicle smelled female and not in a fragrant way. The tampon and Kotex receptacle on the cubicle wall was so full the top didn't close. She recognized the paper wrapper, her and Adelia's choice of organic cotton feminine hygiene. Her period was due. This had to explain her meltdown. And Perelli's incorrigible meanness. She wanted to lay her head on her mother's lap and feel the soft brush of her hand. But her mom was dead. Eleanor had been in her mid-twenties, married, working full-time as a journalist for a large newspaper when her mom died of breast cancer. Eleanor's lids filled and her eyes stung. She cried, and soon she was sobbing. The person in the next cubicle asked if she needed help.

"PMS," she said. "Thanks. I'm missing my mom."

* * *

The helicopter was audible and then it became visible. This time the cable hanging from the belly was weighted with a crib that appeared to contain a body. The chopper hovered and lowered the cable. Paramedics circled the crib like protective doves circling a crow-pecked brethren. It was too late to bring back the life inside that crib. At this point, it was protocol. She saw the ritual in the EMTs and firefighters in blues, the deputies in green, and the onlookers, mostly campers who refused to be driven out by smoke, craning toward the energy emanating from death, unknowingly absorbing spirit as the body ceased to exist. Eleanor looked at the scene with detachment. She scanned the crowd of humans drawn to a tangible death they could almost understand. And she watched for some small expression or gesture that felt off.

30

SHE WAS LIGHTHEADED AS SHE wound down mountain, dehydrated despite drinking her water and carsick from the curves. She removed her hat, hoping that would relieve the first sign of headache. Easton was calling.

She pulled the Blazer over to the side of road.

"Easton," she said. "Hold on. I'm going to throw up." She opened the door, and heaved, hearing him faintly shout her name.

"I'm here." She wiped her mouth with the tail of her shirt and tamped the groan. "I'm here."

"What's happening?"

Sweat drenched her body, and she remained lightheaded. She closed her eyes. "I threw up. I'm better now." She put her palm to her forehead. Cool, whatever that meant.

"It sounds like hyperthermia," he said. "Why don't you drop in at Urgent Care soon as you get down mountain. They'd have electrolytes to hydrate you."

"Ugh."

"Look, you just returned from a long road trip, headed back to the high altitude, and spent the day under the sun, breathing smoke, reporting on another dead woman."

"They found her."

"They did?"

"The body was thirty feet down wedged under a rock. One of the divers got hypothermia and they almost lost him."

She began to cry, again.

* * *

Eleanor turned into Urgent Care. The nurse swabbed her nose for Covid, took her blood pressure, temperature, and oxygen level. She handed her a small plastic cup and asked for a urine sample. She peed into the cup and placed the cup inside the small square cubicle. Then, she returned to the room she'd been assigned and texted Easton.

"Keep me posted," he texted back, with a heart emoji.

She tapped her NYT app and played the Spelling Bee game. The beehive of letters made her nauseated.

A doctor in his white coat entered the room. She looked at his name tag, Dr. Casey. He was handsome and smiled reassuringly. He put out his hand and she took it. Warm and dry.

"How are you feeling?" he asked.

"Not great," Eleanor said.

"You don't have Covid." He smiled.

"That's good."

"You're pregnant." He pulled up a stool on rollers and sat down in front of her, looking too big for the small seat.

A sudden warmth filled her chest clear to her throat, and her head was so full of joy she could sprout flowers.

He nodded, reading her face. "Congratulations," he said, and rolled up close. "Mind lying back?"

She lay back on the table's white paper and felt the doctor press her stomach, watching his eyes for the slightest tell as he touched his stethoscope to various spots on her torso.

"Do you take vitamins?" he asked, head bent over her stomach.

"No."

"Start taking them, a simple prenatal vitamin with folic acid."

"I'm not married."

He was unfazed. "Women don't need to be married to have babies." He offered his arm for her to sit up. "You'll make a wonderful mother."

"How can you tell?"

"I know who you are. I recognize your name from your byline. Your compassion for the people you write about comes through. Are you using birth control?"

"A diaphragm. Most of the time. I took fertility drugs a few years ago."

She could tell by the serious shift of expression and the slight tilt toward her this was serious information.

"The drugs won't hurt the baby. But I'm a little confused why you took them."

"My ex-husband convinced me I was infertile."

"There are tests for that," said the doctor.

"He's very convincing."

"But you didn't conceive?"

"Nope, and every time I got my period I felt like I'd lost another child."

He put a hand on her forearm. "Women endure tremendous grief when the fertility drugs don't work. I'm just curious about this ex."

"He had a vasectomy and didn't tell me."

"I see. You said you're not married?"

"He's my ex. His girlfriend told me."

"Your ex, not the father of this baby?"

"Right. I've been divorced for five years." She shook her head softly, chasing the shame.

He slumped comfortably with his arms between his knees. "You're very healthy. You're going to want to come in once a month at first and more as the pregnancy goes along. We'll order routine prenatal labs and advanced maternal age labs. But no need right away."

"Okay." But it didn't feel okay. It was a scary reality check that she was approaching a dramatic physical and life-altering change. "I'd like to FaceTime my boyfriend."

"I'll give you some privacy."

"He's the father."

The doctor turned at the door. "I'm happy for you. Five minutes and I'll be back."

* * *

"We're pregnant," she told Easton, smiling.

His brief and notable silence was followed by a loud whoop that Eleanor was certain could be heard through the walls of the room and down the clinic's hallways.

"You stay right there," Easton said. "I'll pick you up."

"Easton," Eleanor said. "I have a car."

"We can convoy."

"Sweet man, it'll take you too long to get here."

"What then?"

She laughed. "Meet me somewhere?"

"How about the Steakhouse. We can celebrate."

She felt queasy at the mention of steak. "Maybe potato chips and ginger ale?"

The doctor walked in. "How's he taking the news?"

She held up the phone so the doctor could see him. "Over the top."

"Is that your doctor?" Easton asked. "I'd like to talk to him."

She held out the phone. "His name is Easton."

"Hello, Easton. I'm Dr. Casey. His eyes looked intently into the FaceTime screen. "Congratulations."

"Thank you."

"Eleanor's healthy and she's two months pregnant based on her last menstrual period."

"What do we do for now?"

"So far it sounds like you've done everything right. She's feeling some morning sickness so you could make her a light soup and herbal tea."

"When's her next appointment?"

"In a month unless she wants to come in earlier."

"Can I come with her?"

The doctor smiled. "That's up to Eleanor." He handed the phone back to her.

She grinned. "Hi."

"I'll pick up a couple of things at the market. Potato chips, ginger ale, chicken noodle soup, and meet you at your place. How's that?"

"Sounds like I have the stomach flu."

"We can curl up on your couch and watch TV."

"I don't have TV."

"We'll stream."

"I'm sleepy."

"Maybe you shouldn't drive."

"I'll go straight to my place."

"Where's Granite?"

"Shoot. In the screened porch. I need to let him out."

It seemed an era ago that Easton had decked a bad man and saved a horse. Across that span of time—roughly twenty-four hours—she'd rescued a wild horse, tracked down McKenzie and assuaged her mother Tracy's worst fears; she'd covered a second wildfire and second death. And now there was a future she could touch.

* * *

They sat on Eleanor's futon with her laptop between them and ate potato chips. They fell asleep in her bed, spooning, Granite taking up the entire bottom of the bed, so she had to pull up her knees. Throughout the night, as they turned and stretched their tired limbs, they slid like wands of kelp against each other's skin. Intermittently, she used her feet to shove Granite off the bed.

They woke up happy and convoyed into town to the little café that made fresh croissants and brewed organic coffee. Eleanor ordered toast and a mocha with extra milk. He ordered biscuits and gravy and black coffee. They did the math, and he sketched a calendar of the months on his napkin, marking December as the baby's approximate due date. She reached for the napkin, folded it into quarters, and placed it in the fold of her wallet meant for cash.

31

ELEANOR'S BLAZER IDLED NOISILY AT the four-way stoplight, the only stoplight in Gold Strike. She was content, but something was missing. The woman she regularly saw every morning jogging up Main Street wasn't there. A cluster of teenage girls headed toward the bakery to grab breakfast before school looked exceptionally sloppy in their black sweatpants and oversized sweatshirts. It was as if a palpable fear had created an unspoken curfew and curled out like the devil's tongue into the town's nooks and crannies. And this oppression persisted throughout the day until evening when teenagers disappeared from their nighttime hangouts, and the mall was deserted before the nine p.m. closing time. Friendly chitchat became a rarity in daily commerce because people's trust in each other had dissolved. Nothing felt safe. Dark alleys hid perverts. A friendly face was a façade.

Eleanor climbed the stairs to the upstairs newsroom with a palm on her flat belly and an unfamiliar sense of joy. She walked into the newsroom, headed to her desk.

"It's early for you to be smiling," Mac said.

"I got laid," she lied.

"That explains it."

"Must have been good," said Billy. "You're grinning."

She caught her grin in the reflection of the picture window in front of her desk and suddenly felt like throwing up.

She placed her routine call to Sally at the Sheriff's Office.

"Hi Sally, it's Eleanor. Do you have any updates on the drowned woman they pulled from the falls."

"We have an ID."

Eleanor started typing.

"Cleo Gunderson, a twenty-five-year-old woman from Gold Strike County. We've notified her next of kin."

"Cause of death?"

"Undetermined until the coroner's report comes out." She paused. "There's something else."

"I'm listening."

"Plant matter was found in the victim's throat."

"What kind of 'plant matter'?"

"Haven't identified it."

"My guess? Dogwood, just like Marisol. Thanks, Sally."

The image of someone pressing plants down a woman's throat infuriated Eleanor. She shoved her chair back and slammed down her laptop, swearing.

Mac and Billy turned, wide-eyed by her outburst.

"They keep shoving plants down their throats." She pulled open her desk drawer and pulled out her backpack. She stood and kicked the drawer shut and slung her pack over her shoulder. She felt sick to her stomach and heaved into her palms as she ran to the bathroom.

Eleanor was covered with sweat and her legs felt heavy. She cleaned up the mess, and when she returned to her desk, the expression on Mac's face said she looked ghastly.

"What's wrong?" he asked.

"They just ID'd the woman upriver. Cleo Gunderson, twenty-five. They found plant debris in her throat." She dry-heaved.

He rested his chin on his hand and studied her. She knew what he was thinking.

"I can handle this," she said.

"Doesn't look like it."

"I have morning sickness."

"You're pregnant?" He leaned back with his arms behind his head. "That's something. Who's the father?"

"That's inappropriate, Mac," Billy said. "Congratulations, Eleanor. That's cool."

"Thanks, Billy. Keep me on the story and I'll tell you who the father is."

"Also inappropriate," said Billy. "You're bargaining with your unborn child."

"No secret," said Mac. "This is a small town. A good guy. Good choice for a dad. Going to raise yourselves a genuine Gold Strike County cowpuncher."

"Thanks, Mac. That's nice to hear."

"But I'm taking you off the Gunderson story," he said. "You're temporarily on general assignment, and I want you to take a few days off to get some rest, and this Saturday at noon I want you to cover the Black Powder gunfight," an annual reenactment based on local history.

She resented Mac's orders, but a few days off didn't sound bad. Eleanor could clean house and organize. Peruse maternity clothes online and spend more nights at the ranch without worrying about getting up early. She could hang out with her horse, and then there was Goldenrod. She could observe his first days on the ranch.

* * *

Easton had put Goldenrod in the far pasture next to the mares. That way the horses could check each other out at a safe distance from each other. Whichever mare exhibited curiosity and calmness could be the first to go near him. One at a time, hopefully, they'd form a new family structure.

Goldenrod loped back and forth along the fence line, neighing to the horses, shaking his mane. No question he liked them, but the only mare who showed interest in him was the white boss mare, Blanca, who'd tried to bite Eleanor a couple of times when she rode through their field. Blanca went up to the barbed wire fence and extended her neck.

Goldenrod nibbled her mane. For the first time, the mare was oblivious to Eleanor as she opened the gate while Easton drove Blanca through. It didn't take much. The mare walked up to Goldenrod and sniffed. They took off loping, her tail flagged with spirit. Easton and Eleanor turned back, and by the end of the week two more mares—a black and white paint and a roan—were let in the stallion's field.

* * *

Saturday arrived too quickly. Eleanor guessed the guy in the ten-gallon hat with scraggly brown hair and a droopy handlebar mustache, dressed in all black, was the villain. The man in the tan felt hat with the trimmed goatee, long salt-and-pepper ponytail, and fringed suede jacket had to be the chosen one.

Onlookers filled the sidewalk in the alley beside the newspaper building. Heads poked out of the Stolen Horses Saloon door with beers in hand. Eleanor checked the time. Ten minutes till noon.

She took photos of both gunslingers and zoomed in on their pistols with the polished wooden handles. She took random shots of the crowd. One couple looked like they'd just come off ranch work. A strapping guy with worn flat boots and a gray felt cowboy hat stood next to a smaller woman, dressed in worn jeans, Western shirt, hair in braids. Both wore small knives on the back of their belts. They looked like a pair of freshly plucked heirloom apples that begged a little dusting off.

Eleanor took a profile shot of the man, who turned toward her as if a lifetime of working with horses had trained him not to startle.

"I'm Eleanor Wooley from the *Gold Strike Tribune*. On assignment to report on the gunfight. May I take your picture?"

"You might've asked me before you took it." He wore the same serious, down-to-earth look as the man in the hay truck who told her to slow down.

"I apologize."

He was a foot taller than his woman and a good hundred pounds of muscle heavier. Eleanor showed her the photo she'd taken of his stoic profile with the bad guy rustler in the background.

"That's nice," she said. "But he's right, you should've asked."

"I'm sorry. Really."

The man put his arm around the woman. "Can you take a single of Crystal?"

Eleanor held up her camera and zoomed in. "When I say 'three,' smile." The young woman relaxed and Eleanor kept shooting. "Now for the two of you."

They moved even closer together, his arm draped around her shoulder, their smiles a tad bit north of neutral. She took their names and number and gave them her card with a promise she'd text them the photos.

She scanned the crowd. The hermit stood on the sidewalk, staring at her. He wore the same railroad overalls and a long sleeved, very off-white henley, stained at the neckline. Steel-toed logger boots. His shaved head looked sunburned and his long, pointed beard was longer than she remembered.

"I know you," she said.

He looked at her like she was the oddball.

"I was hiking near the fire trail above the old Boy Scout camp and saw your cabin and your dog. You came outside."

"I did, did I?"

"He's a pitbull you keep chained to an oak."

"If I don't, he chases deer. He'll run them into the reservoir, and they'll drown from a heart attack."

"That's awful."

"Yup."

"Have you lived there long?"

"'Bout twenty year. Ever since my wife left me. I prefer poverty to working for the man, and she wasn't keen on my philosophy."

"That could be hard on a partner," Eleanor said.

He stared at her. "You know you're in danger."

She stiffened, taken aback by his bluntness and no less by the content of his pronouncement. "What kind of danger?"

"The dangerous kind."

"Don't kid about this. You walk up to a near stranger and tell her she's in danger, you damn well better elaborate."

"I can't see the specifics."

"Is it life-threatening?"

"That's the only kind of danger I know, ma'am."

"There's emotional danger, psychic danger, physical danger—" She glanced at the gunfighters. They were eyeballing each other, their arms hanging loose at their sides, waiting for the first move.

She readied her camera.

The man in black crossed his arm to his gun.

The other pulled out a pistol with his draw hand.

Cr-aaak, cr-aaak. Smoke mushroomed from the guns. The man in black staggered and fell to the ground yards from Eleanor's feet. The air smelled chemical and her eyes burned. The good guy twirled his pistol and shoved it back in his holster. He walked through the cloud of gun smoke toward his dead opponent as if the heavens were parting, and she took the photo. The crowd hooted. If only it were this easy, Eleanor thought, to discern good from bad.

32

ELEANOR SUSPECTED THAT JESSIE SENSED the baby energy radiating from her womb. The horse acted abnormally edgy and restless and kept moving ahead of her. Maybe Jessie, being a mare in her prime, smelled Goldenrod. Whatever the reason, a two-thousand-pound equid had the upper hand—which was dangerous, no matter how sweet a horse. Jessie could freak and ram into Eleanor with the power of a wagon train. Maybe that's what the hermit saw.

Easton suggested she twirl the end of the lead rope in front as they walked to the round pen if she got in front of Eleanor again. The rope would create an invisible wall. She tried it out. When the rope accidentally hit Jessie's face as she moved ahead, Jessie startled but stayed back at Eleanor's shoulder.

Eleanor tied Jessie to the rail and picked up a curry comb. She held the comb out to Jessie and let her sniff.

"Good girl."

Eleanor closed her eyes and ran her hand down the swale of Jessie's back and over her flank. The mare licked her lips and dropped her head, surrendering, Eleanor swooning from their bond.

Which was why, that evening, Eleanor understood what Lawrence Standin felt when he stood at the podium in front of the Gold Strike County Supervisors and asked them on behalf of his people to turn down the Bear River Dam Project and respect his people's sacred site.

* * *

Renee and Lawrence Standin sat in the second row of the Supervisors' chambers. The dam project manager sat in the front row behind a long desk. Eleanor took the catty-corner seat reserved for the press. Tindale, Everett McKinney, Harvey Johnson, and Stephanie Lindstrom, each representing a different area in the county, sat on an elevated platform behind a long oak desk, each with their own name plate and mic.

Roscoe Frecceri called the meeting into session with a pound of his wooden gavel. He asked the assembly to stand for the Pledge of Allegiance, and everyone did, turning slightly to the corner of the room where the flag hung at an angle from the wall. They held their right hands over their hearts and recited the Pledge, except Eleanor, who'd just lost an earring, her favorite, a turquoise stone set in silver. She bent down, following the skittering noise across the oak floor. *With liberty and justice for all*, she said as she reinserted the earring into the tiny hole on her earlobe.

Roscoe glared at her before calling the prison warden up to the podium to receive an accommodation. The warden walked to the podium with the prison fire crew supervisor, who'd been on the last two wildfires. The supervisor was an attractive man who looked to be in his forties. The warden turned the mic over to him. His name was Cody Singleton, and he said a few obligatory words to the Board and gave earnest praise to his crew of inmates. Eleanor made a note to ask Singleton about the inmate who'd discovered Marisol's body.

Next on the agenda was the Bear River Dam project. Jerry Ward straightened his tie as he walked to the podium to present a PowerPoint, which produced the opposite effect Ward intended. The photos of the river and meadow in the high country were hands-down gorgeous. The drawings of the proposed dam were oppressive. Citizens who had lived here when the original project was turned down booed, and Roscoe had to pound his gavel.

At the public comments portion of the meeting, Standin strode up to the podium in canvas workpants, brown suspenders, and a red Henley long-sleeved shirt under a sheepskin vest that couldn't hide the hunch of his shoulders from decades of bending over his work. His long white hair was pulled back into a thin ponytail.

"My name is Lawrence Standin. I'm a woodcarver by trade. I know two of you gentlemen up there. Roscoe, you bought one of my bears, and Jim Tindale, you bought the pair for your entryway."

"The grandkids love those bears," said Tindale. "They named him Smokey and her Smokin' and put my wife's apron around her waist and my posse vest over his chest."

"I'll bet neither one you had break-ins or strange people coming to your doorstep since then," said Lawrence.

Roscoe leaned into his mic. "With a little help from my Colt .45. It's good to see you here today, Lawrence."

"I'm here to speak for the record. My people have lived here since before recorded time and the river this man intends to change with a dam will destroy what is sacred to us."

Everett McKinney spoke into his mic. "Do you have any documentation of the sacredness of this site, Mr. Standin?"

The room fell silent, waiting for a response. Lawrence closed his eyes thickening the hush. "We don't build statues or erect monuments to our sacred places," he said. "We don't broadcast, either, or people will ransack what remains of our old people. The place is not identified in legal documents because you ran us out and snuffed our voices nearly two centuries ago."

"Then you can't expect us to regard your claim of this being a sacred site as credible," said McKinney.

"You should be careful disturbing a sacred place," said Lawrence. "There are consequences."

"Like what?"

"You could wake up a curse."

McKinney scoffed and looked aside at his fellow supervisors.

Renee walked up to the podium and stood beside her grandfather.

"I'm Renee Standin, a hydrologist for the US Forest Service."

"Only one person at a time at the podium," said McKinney.

"I'm helping my grandfather to his seat," said Renee, "after my turn to speak."

"He got up there on his own, he can sit back down on his own."

"Oh, for God's sake, Everett," said supervisor Lindstrom. "Go ahead, Renee."

"My grandfather, Lawrence Standin, has told me the stories of this place."

Lawrence closed his eyes, and Renee held his arm to steady him.

"He won't tell these stories to the outside world because that's how *we* do things. Ironically, this prevents us from documenting the sacredness of a place for the benefit of saving it. But I invite you to accompany my grandfather and me to the site to help you understand its importance."

Lawrence opened his eyes. McKinney shook his head in disgust.

Lindstrom leaned toward her microphone. "I, for one, am honored to accept your invitation. I move the Board schedule a day within the next two weeks to visit the proposed dam site on the Little Bear River with the Standins."

Harvey Johnson, the supervisor who represented the upscale mountain lake district where Bay Area folks kept their second homes, seconded the motion.

"I object." McKinney's face pruned up.

"Care to explain your objections, Everett?" asked Roscoe.

"A field trip is a waste of our time and the county taxpayers' money, and it won't prove anything."

"Point taken." Roscoe called for a vote. "All in favor?"

Lindstrom and Johnson put up a hand. "Aye," in unison.

A man from the audience shouted, "What the hell are you waiting for, Tindale? Raise your goddamn hand."

"Order in the room." Roscoe pounded his gavel. "No outbursts from the audience." He snake-eyed the offender.

Jim Tindale raised his hand. "Aye. And not because someone opened their fat mouth and badgered me. Lawrence deserves consideration."

"For the record, three ayes in favor of the motion. Opposed?"

Everett McKinney raised his hand. "No."

* * *

The outcome surprised Eleanor. She'd been reporting on this county long enough to understand the elected city officials rarely hesitated to give away huge parcels of land to the highest bidder, even when the town turned out to object to the latest ranchland-turned-shopping-mall or a hilltop-turned-subdivision. Most of the supervisors still called development progress. But tonight, the vote was different.

"That went well," said Eleanor.

"Compared to what?" said Renee.

"The last four years I've been reporting on the supervisors. I'm coming on your field trip."

"Not as a reporter."

"Fair enough." Eleanor scanned the room for the warden and Singleton, the prison crew supervisor. She'd report on his award for tomorrow's paper, but she also wanted to interview him about the inmate who'd spotted Marisol's body. Apparently, Singleton had already left the chambers.

"I want to ask you something," Renee said, an imploring expression on her face.

"Yes, ma'am." Eleanor smiled.

Out of the blue, she asked how Eleanor had met Leonard, which told Eleanor she was a threat to Renee.

"I met him in a smoke shop."

"You smoke?"

"Nope, not anymore, but driving by Wells, Nevada, my craving for a cigarette got the upper hand. I went into the smoke shop to post a missing person flyer and ask the clerk if she'd seen a particular man I believed had abducted my best friend. Leonard had spotted this man driving north with a trailer of horses. I ran into him a second time in a small town in Northeastern Nevada where he was a wilderness guide. I hired him to help me find my missing friend."

"Did you—sleep with him?" She looked at Eleanor hopefully.

"No way."

"'No way' means what?"

"He guided me into the center of this wilderness and vanished."

"Vanished?"

"I woke up and he was gone. I spent days fending for myself and ended up thinking how rich it was I'd gone out there to save my friend and I was the one fated to die. Sort of like your comment about sacred sites."

"That's a story I'd like to hear someday."

"More like a nightmare."

"You're here. Probably stronger from the challenge."

"Don't even." Eleanor inhaled and ran her hands through her hair to pull the loose strands from her face. "Wanting to know if I slept with Leonard says a lot more about your lack of trust than my relationship. A healthy relationship bolsters trust, and you wouldn't have to ask." She ignored the recent memory of Easton asking about Leonard on their trip.

Renee's eyes glassed over. Her vision moved from Eleanor's face to a vague place in the distance. "I was such a goner the second I saw him. He seized my heart."

"Ouch."

They laughed the laugh of women whose better judgment has been shrink-wrapped.

Renee inhaled. "I was scheduled to give a guest lecture at Stanford about water issues on tribal land. I stuck around for the Mother's Day powwow because it's one of the best pow wows in this part of the country. Leonard was standing in front of a vendor stall speaking to the flute maker. He glanced at me and did a double take."

"Struck by your lightning," Eleanor said.

"Struck by something. He picked up one of the vendor's flutes and played. I told him his playing was beautiful, and he said, 'So are you.' I put out my hand and introduced myself, and he put his hand in mine and held it to his chest. Kind of uncomfortable, you know, until I looked up at him and he says, 'I'm honored to meet you, Renee. We have so much work to do.'"

"Not exactly a romantic come on."

"It was if you're a workaholic."

Lawrence, who'd been talking it up with Roscoe, came up to them.

"End of story," said Renee.

"What story?" asked Lawrence.

"Secret, Grandpa."

"Thank you for what you said and the invitation," said Eleanor. "But the trip is a long ride."

"Once I get up, I ride like a virile young man."

Renee rolled her eyes. They said their goodbyes and walked to the exit.

Eleanor remained in the chambers and noticed the topo map on the opposite wall. In the center of the Grizzly Wilderness, the proposed dam site had been starred. A bit downriver from the project was the small virgin lake Easton called his sacred fishing hole. Follow the river west, down mountain, to the pack station. Just below the station, the river split into north and south forks. The north fork flowed through a notably steeper rock canyon and emptied in Gooseberry Lake reservoir. She touched the falls above the lake, where Cleo's body was found at the bottom of a thirty-foot-deep pool, pinned beneath a rock. The south fork became the Little Bear, where Marisol was found at the inlet to Brown's Ferry reservoir. The three spots on the river—the dam site, the falls, and Brown's Ferry formed an equilateral triangle.

"What do you think?" Jerry Ward stood there beside her staring at the map.

"Are you going?" she asked.

"I'm the project manager proposing to develop the site. It'll be an adventure. Not often we get to hear authentic stories from real Indians."

Racist idiot.

"And once that old man's had his chance and failed to drum up spiritual hocus pocus, the supervisors will be on my side."

33

As Eleanor drove down Main Street, passing the rows of Gold Rush-era facades on both sides of the road, she asked Siri to call the prison. She punched 5 for operator and asked to be connected to the prison fire crew supervisor, Cody Singleton. She was connected to his voicemail.

"Mr. Singleton, this is Eleanor Wooley, reporter for the *Gold Strike Tribune*. I was at the supervisors' meeting and would like to follow up briefly on the success of your program for a story in tomorrow's paper. Please call me back."

She left her personal cell number and refrained from telling him about her interest in the inmate who'd spotted Marisol's body, fearing he wouldn't return her call.

Her phone rang. Her screen showed a call from the prison.

"Cody Singleton here, returning a call from Eleanor Wooley."

"This is Eleanor. Thanks for returning my call so promptly."

"What can I do for you?"

"I watched you receive your commendation this afternoon, and it's well-deserved. I'd like your insight on why the inmate fire crew program is successful."

"The inmates. If they demonstrate unquestionable integrity while serving time and pass the physical tests, they get a shot at being on the crew. They've done great work with those two fires."

"Some of their success must be tied to your supervision. What about you helps them?"

"I appreciate your question, but it's the program. I'm a coach at heart. Everyone needs constant positive reinforcement and guidance. I'd say, also, I have my own God, and I believe in Jesus Christ as my savior."

Eleanor cringed. "I see. Can I ask what your crew's doing now up at the Gooseberry Fire, Mr. Singleton?"

"Call me Cody. We're mopping up the parts that have been extinguished. When the ground is hot, fire travels underground and will exhibit all kinds of strange behaviors, like popping up out of the ground twenty yards from a flame."

"How much longer do you think before the fire's under control?"

"Don't know, but it's being held, and I'd guess at least another twenty-four hours and we'll have some significant containment."

"Downriver from the fire, the Sheriff's Office identified the victim, Cleo Gunderson—"

"I heard that."

"—a young woman in her twenties who's an EMT and decided to go backpacking for the weekend."

"Alone, not so smart."

"I don't know if she was alone, but someone witnessed her fall."

"That witness wasn't with her, from what I hear."

"Really? Can you tell me about that?"

"Someone was working up top clearing brush and saw the body moving downriver before it hit the falls."

"Do you know who?"

"Nope. They're keeping that under wraps so the media doesn't go crazy with it."

She decided to come at the interview from another angle before he got personal. "People in town are freaking out. I had a mother call me because she hadn't heard from daughter in a couple of days and the body hadn't been identified. High school girls are wearing baggy sweatpants in the heat. What's going on?"

"Not sure I'm following you, ma'am."

"Do you have children, Cody?"

"Yes, I do, ma'am. A boy, six, and a girl, three."

"As a father, does Gold Strike feel any less safe than it did before two young women turned up dead?"

"My wife would say definitely less safe, and if my wife doesn't feel safe in our own home when I'm not there, I'm not a happy camper."

"I understand, and thanks for that. Do you think the Gooseberry Fire is arson?"

"In my opinion? Safe bet."

"Think it was the same person behind the Brown's Ferry fire?"

"Maybe, but no one's officially saying so."

"Do you see any connection between Marisol Rodriguez and Cleo Gunderson?"

"My wife does. Hands down. I try to have more common sense. People hike these mountains every summer thinking it's Disneyland."

"Marisol and Cleo lived here. Cleo was an EMT."

"I was an EMT. They're trained for emergency protocol on the scene and in the ambulance. They're not trained not to do stupid things in the wilderness."

"Sounds like a grudge."

"No grudge. Truth. They think they know as much as a fireman or a paramedic, and they don't."

"Do you think Cleo's death was an accident?"

"There's no evidence otherwise, yet, and I don't spread rumors, especially, no offense, ma'am, to reporters."

"Understood."

"You have any more questions?"

"Do you think there's a serial killer out there?"

"My wife does."

"How about you? I'm asking because you work on the ground and might have heard something."

"Off the record?" he asked.

"Off the record."

"There's always a serial killer out there. They're like time bombs. The ingredients have to mix before they combust."

"What ingredients?"

"Abusive childhood, extreme religiosity, addiction, mean mother, sick mother, boarding schools, bad genes—sometimes a kid is born with a neurological architecture headed for violence or a kid becomes damaged goods. The wounds fester, then *boom*. Is that why you called?"

"No, I wanted to get your reaction to the county's commendation for your work with the fire crew."

"I'm honored. To be recognized for my work is the highest compliment."

"Speaking of remarkable work, what about the inmate who spotted Marisol in the river? Has he been acknowledged?"

"Good catch on his part. But no, we like to keep low profiles in the prison. It's safer for the inmates."

"Why'd you give him permission to go to the bathroom so far away from the crew?"

He didn't respond right away, and she apologized for being blunt.

"Yeah, well, whatever the reason, it worked out considering he found the woman."

"It just seems strange you let him go so far away from supervision."

"I see where you're going. This program is based on trust. If I can't trust the inmate, he's not on the crew. That it?"

"May I call you if something comes up?"

"Anytime."

* * *

She was trying to parallel park outside the café when a white-haired gentleman dressed in a casual business suit walked outside with a cup of coffee. He fumbled with his brown paper napkins. A young man dressed in a T-shirt and jeans, sporting a red MAGA hat, pulled back the cafe's glass door and walked inside. Could either of them kill a woman or be scheming to murder the next? Three hundred and sixty spokes in a circle and countless degrees between. A person could grow their pain from the hub in countless random directions or come into the world bent.

Her Blazer was too big and she lacked patience. Eleanor pulled out and headed to the drive-thru coffee shack.

She drove up to the service window. "I'll have a cappuccino with whole milk."

McKenzie, sounding glum, repeated the order back to her and asked if she wanted anything else.

"This is Eleanor, and yes, would you throw in a chocolate muffin?"

"Eleanor," McKenzie said brightly. "I didn't recognize your voice."

"You sounded different, too."

"I'm pulling two shifts for extra money. Tired, I guess. What're you up to?'

"Covered the supervisors meeting to discuss the Bear River Dam project and called the prison for an update from the fire crew supervisor."

"What'd he say?"

"Basically, he doesn't want to spread gossip to a reporter." She smiled. "I have something to ask you."

"Ask away."

"I'll wait until I'm at your window."

The car in front of her idled. A man's arm poked out the window and reached for a frappe with a caramel-colored swirl down the insides of the tall plastic cup, topped with whipped cream. He drove off and Eleanor pulled up, watching the man pause at the exit onto the main road. He made a dash at the next break in traffic and crossed, swerving into the far lane that would take him back to town. The next stream of cars with recreation equipment on top came down from the mountains headed toward the Central Valley and Bay Area. A full four-horse trailer passed on its way back to the lowlands.

Eleanor startled at McKenzie's voice.

"Here you go." The girl held out the muffin and cappuccino.

Eleanor placed the white paper cup carefully in the cupholder on the dash.

"You were going to ask me something," said McKenzie.

"The supervisors are planning a field trip to the proposed dam site," Eleanor told her. "An elder from the Rancheria is going to help them understand why the site is sacred and shouldn't be disturbed."

"Interesting."

"We'll get up there on horseback."

"Even better."

"I'd like you to join us. Our group could use your equine expertise, and I want you to meet Lawrence Standin."

"I'd have to check my work schedule." She smiled. "But I'd love to."

* * *

The group needed a campfire permit. Eleanor called Renee and told her she had to check something with the Forest Service anyway and would go in personally to take out the permit.

Kate, the Forest Service volunteer, stood from her desk and walked to the counter. "What brings you back, Eleanor?"

"I need to take out a permit for a campfire at the Bear River. We're taking the supervisors up there to look at the dam site." Eleanor told her about the Standins' invitation.

"That project's a travesty. The feds should designate that meadow a wilderness, and they should've done it twenty years ago."

Kate pulled up the site on her computer and Eleanor filled it out.

"Done." Eleanor finished typing in the information. "Did you know the Sheriff identified the woman found at the falls?"

"Yes. Tragic."

"She'd planned to hike that day and told people where she was going. I'm hoping she took out a permit. Could you check for me?"

Kate scrolled through the permits.

"We've got two people for that weekend. No Cleo Gunderson." She paused and peered more closely at her screen. "Their permit numbers aren't sequential, though, which is odd. You want to come around and look at this?"

Eleanor walked around the counter and stood beside Kate. She noted two permits skipped the number between. Kate clicked a permit link and pressed "delete file." A screen came up with the notification ACCESS DENIED.

"Doesn't mean a file can't be deleted," Kate said. "It only means I can't delete it. I'd need a code which I'm not privy to."

"You're saying someone could have deleted Cleo Gunderson's wilderness permit and that's why the numbers aren't sequential?"

"Very possible. The permit could have been cancelled or had errors. But there's always a record."

* * *

Eleanor went back to the newsroom thinking of the missing permit as she wrote up her notes from the supervisor's meeting and her interview with Cody. Her cell phone rang with a Forest Service number.

"Wooley," she said.

"I thought of something."

"Is this Kate?"

"Yes. The victims may have taken out a fire permit online rather than a camping permit. I checked it out. Get this. Marisol Rodriguez and Cleo Gunderson both took out campfire permits."

Which meant someone knew where these two women were headed shortly before they lost their lives.

* * *

Eleanor rode out with Easton in the truck to the field where the wild horses lived to throw out timothy hay from the truck bed. The horses trotted beside them, their tails high. He stepped on the gas, bringing them up to a lope, and slowed to a stop.

"You're saying if you follow the rules for how to find solitude in the great outdoors, someone will know where you are. That's rich."

"It could be a lead."

He gazed out the windshield at the rolling horizon. "Lee, I hope, well, Jeez—"

"Say it."

"We're having a baby." He reached over to the bucket seat and put a hand on her knee. "Following a lead to a killer doesn't sound safe. You want some action, get in back and toss some hay."

She opened the passenger door and swung around into the truck bed. She tossed two flakes and heard Easton shout, "Hold on." He drove slowly and she tossed another flake. Two mares stopped and the rest followed. She tossed another. They came up to the gate where the stallion and mares grazed. She climbed down and opened the gate, standing aside while Easton drove through. She closed the gate and climbed back in. The stallion raised his head as they drove close. She tossed the rest of the hay and swung back inside the truck cab and watched. The boss mare walked toward the truck and the other followed her. Goldenrod remained where he was, watching.

They drove the long way out. She turned and kneeled and pressed her chest against the back of the seat as the horses got smaller and the land rose and hid all but Goldenrod, who stood on the rise, facing the wind and their retreating vehicle, chest erect, head high, long, knotted mane blowing.

She showered and Easton made dinner. When she got out, a hot cup of chamomile sat on the bedside table. She climbed under the covers and sipped the tea until she was so warm she threw back all but the top sheet.

"Granite." She patted the bed. He hopped up and curled at the foot. She photographed him and checked the shot. So many photos of Granite on the bed. She scrolled the photos of the rescue operation. A helicopter lowering the crib, carrying the body of Cleo Gunderson (a front-page photo), the helicopter heading across the lake toward the inlet before it was enveloped in smoke, a cumulus fire cloud billowing in the background. The crew on the fire boat, a close-up of Adelia leaning against the tree. Her blackened face was bewildered and her eyes wide as discs. She didn't remember taking the photo.

The water tender's blue truck. She'd zoomed in on the sign: *Hell's Dipper.*

She Googled his Facebook page. Yep. That was him. Jeffrey Turnbull. He'd posted pictures of his family, his attractive wife, healthy kids, all looking like they were having a fun time enjoying a wholesome backyard barbecue. She felt like a voyeur and an outsider. She should at least be married to count as part of this community. She let the thought swim by. His bio said he worked for the Bureau of Reclamation and hauled water in emergencies and special jobs. His reviews were fours and fives. He belonged to the Trinity of Christ Church. She scrolled down to his religious posts. A sexy contemporary Mary Magdalene with a low-cut gown coming out of Christ's tomb with a seductive smile on her lips and the line, "I revived the fuck out of Him." Eleanor shrugged it off. The picture of a white supremacy Othala rune gave her pause.

She tossed the phone to the foot of the bed and pulled the sheet over her head. Granite pounced and dug his paws to pull back the sheet.

"Ow. Ow. Stop."

He scratched a nest and lay on her feet.

"What's going on in here?" Easton held a tray. "I brought us dinner in bed. Scoot over."

"I was checking out my photos and Googled the water tender guy." She told him about the metamorphosis from backyard barbecue to white supremacy.

"That's how they are," said Easton. "They say they're Christian out one side of their mouth but don't tolerate anyone different. My way or the highway."

"His family looks so nice," she said. "And he fights fire."

"I know those guys. Where are they when someone's lost or hurt? Fire Service, Cal Fire, HP, Sheriff, SAR, ready and able. Water tender? Sitting on his bumper."

"He was, in fact, sitting on his back bumper."

"Don't get me wrong. Need water, he's got it. But he can't manage the firefighter challenge. Probably couldn't pass the physical."

"I'm surprised at you, Easton." She reached for her phone and scrolled down to an earlier post. Turnbull's thick torso was naked except for a black leather vest. His arms the diameter of melons were crossed, and a Dixie flag draped across his shoulders.

"That's him."

"Rest my case. Man scaring the shit out of anyone who looks twice."

34

THE NEXT MORNING, EASTON CARRIED two folding chairs into Jessie and Fred's paddock, and she carried a thermos of coffee and two mugs. He set up the chairs facing the sunrise. She poured fresh hot coffee from the thermos for their first cup.

Fred lumbered over, neck low. He sniffed Easton's hat, bit and tossed it. Easton caught the hat in mid-air, and she laughed. Then Fred laid down and rolled on his back for a dirt bath. At her first caffeine lift, Eleanor decided this was a good time to discuss where she would live as the pregnancy went along.

"Easton," she said, "I think I want to keep my place up mountain."

He took a sip of coffee and pushed Fred away from his face with his other arm.

"We're going to have this talk right now?"

"Dolores asked if she should put the cottage on Zillow. I've lived there four years."

"And?"

"I might want to keep it."

"You need your space."

"I think so."

"Look around. There's so much space out here."

"It's your space."

"It can be our space. You could make your own space."

Eleanor thought of her ex. She'd spent so many years living a lie, going to work, coming home, making dinner, having wine-drenched conversations about the fertility drugs he convinced her to take, her sense of failure and grief every time her period arrived. All his predictable jabs, his reminders that if she wanted kids they'd better get to bed and maybe, just maybe—and the entire time, he'd had a vasectomy and chose not to tell her. When she'd left him, she couldn't even decide what to buy at the grocery store. She'd only ever bought his favorite cold cereal, his favorite apricot jam, tortilla chips (she liked original Cheetos), and Pepsi. With him gone, she'd gaze for minutes at a time at the shelves lined with processed foods until she skipped the center aisles altogether and shopped only the outer shelves, filling her cart with fruit and vegetables, eggs, milk tofu, hummus, and fresh, locally baked bread that was still warm from the oven. She'd return to her one-bedroom apartment and sit cross-legged in front of the full-length mirror, eating figs, never so alone. *Who are you*? she'd asked her reflection. Four years later, she'd figured it out. She wanted to keep that person and learn more about her.

"Where are you?" His voice brought her back.

"It's not you, Easton."

"That's what they all say."

"I don't trust myself."

"I trust you." He took her hand and kissed it.

They watched Fred get up and shake off the dust until his feet nearly came off the ground. He stood in front of them, ears twitching. Jessie plodded over to the three of them and stood above Eleanor, lipping her hair affectionately. She rubbed Jessie's cheek.

"Good girl." Easton picked up the thick metal thermos on the dirt between them. The same thermos he had with him that morning he drove her to the Leapfrog operation to search for Rette. They'd met in the Bear Clover bar the night before. The next morning, she had been surprised to find him in the barn, loading his horse Chester into his trailer. She had realized they were headed to the same place, deep in the Sierra Nevada river canyon to search for Rette. He'd given her and

Jessie a lift. They'd ridden horseback for miles up that canyon and found no sign of Rette. She had asked him that day what he did when he was discouraged. Move forward, he'd said.

Now Easton held the thermos and she brought her cup to it, watching the clear brown liquid laced with steam fill her cup and the pleasant scent filled her head. She leaned forward and sipped, and they sat awhile taking in the morning until Easton broke the silence.

"I'm worried."

"About what?" Eleanor was nonplussed by his sudden admission.

"I don't think you should go on the Standins' field trip."

"In my condition, you mean?"

"We've ridden up there on horseback and it's pretty steep in some places, and that dam site is even further up some rough river canyon." He added that it wasn't because she wasn't fit and able—she was, no doubt—but his protective instincts were on high alert.

"Aw," she said. "I understand how you feel, but we're in this together." She listed all the things pregnant women did these days, which didn't appear to assuage his fear one bit.

"Yeah, but I heard about one young woman went on a pack trip seven months pregnant and went into labor way up there with no cell service and if it weren't for the fact that one of the riders was a nurse, she and the baby wouldn't've made it. And another one, a PE teacher at the high school was taking an everyday hike around Gooseberry Lake and miscarried and by the time search and rescue got to her, she'd bled out."

Eleanor listened at the same time Jessie was rubbing her rear end on the fence rail. She'd just seen some progress on growing back the mare's chewed tail, so she got out of the chair to move the horse away from the fence.

"It feels like I'm talking to the backside of southern-bound geese," said Easton. "So I'll tell you what."

She turned.

"I'll go with you on this field trip and oversee the horses."

She smiled. "You're coming? I was counting on that." She ran her palm along the hardening wall of her womb, which was becoming a frequent gesture. "And for the record, you have every right to worry."

They headed back to the house, got a few things, and went their separate ways: she back to town and the newspaper, Easton in the opposite direction to the outskirts of Merced, where he planned to flatten forty acres of undeveloped prairie for a future turkey farm.

*   *   *

The evening was warm, and the summer heat mixed with the smell of the hay barn as she approached Jessie's paddock. Easton hadn't returned from Merced, it was still plenty light, and she decided to saddle up Jessie for a ride.

She went into the tack room and picked up a grooming box, fetched Jessie, and tied her to the outside rail. She curried then brushed off the ground-in dust until Jessie's coat glistened. Eleanor scratched the spot below the mare's hip that made her head crane forward and plucked a cobweb from Jessie's upper eyelash. Standing at her left flank, Eleanor rubbed product on the top layer of the tail that Chester had nibbled to six inches below the dock. The hair had grown back some. She gathered the long tail and brushed out the cords until the entwined hairs were separated. Now for the feet. Eleanor ran a hand down Jessie's front leg, prompting the mare to lift her front hoof. Eleanor picked the dirt and manure. A pebble was lodged in the frog. She pushed the pick under the ridge and dislodged a sharp-edged nugget of white quartz. She held up the stone and turned it. A metallic yellow vein ran through. She shoved the stone into her back pocket to show Easton and finished her horse's feet.

Flies clustered on Jessie's back. Eleanor sprayed them with citronella and squirted the repellent into her hand, cautiously smoothing the strong-smelling liquid over Jessie's face and around her eyes.

"Hey," a man's voice shouted.

Eleanor shrieked and dropped the bottle. Jessie lurched sideways.

Bart Hargrove stood with a smirk on his face. "Didn't mean to scare you. Easton wants me to fix some fence up where the mustangs are. Mind if I go in the house and fill my canteen?"

She and Easton had agreed Bart could not be at the ranch when Eleanor was there. And his full-of-bullshit expression made her want to slap his stupid face.

"There's no way Easton would tell you to fix fence while I'm here. That's the rule, Bart, and you know it."

"Thought you'd be at work. The splice in the barbed wire broke 'cause they used the wrong patch grade and this coming winter it's gonna rust, unless they put some forty-weight oil on it and some anti-freeze. But the anti-freeze is a problem, too, because it's sweet and the horses are going to lick it, especially the foals. So I need to go out there and figure a way to keep that wire together without poisoning that stud you put out there."

His lying eyes infuriated her as he spewed his crap. If bad thoughts could kill, Bart would be pushing up daisies. But this was Easton's kid.

"I'll walk up there with you." Eleanor shoved the hoof pick in her back pocket and petted Jessie goodbye, letting her dwell at the tie rail. Eleanor walked briskly to the house, staying a couple of yards in front of Bart. She poured herself a glass of water, moved over, and drank it as Bart filled his canteen, an old-fashioned round metal container covered in gray and red wool plaid.

"I need to ask you not to be at the ranch while I'm here."

"I don't know when that would be, ma'am."

"When I'm not working at the paper. You need to call first before coming out."

"When do you work at the newspaper?"

"I arrive at seven and leave around dinner time."

He crossed his arms over his stocky chest. "So, I'll get here earlier next time."

"Next time, call first."

He looked at the floor and shuffled a boot, nodding. That was the extent of his apology.

"How's that story going on those dead women?"

She studied his face and decided his question was in earnest.

"Because whoever's doing this," he added, "is scaring the shit out of my girlfriend. She won't even drive by herself."

"Everyone's on edge until we catch the guy."

He scoffed. "Why do you think it's a guy?"

"Figure of speech, mostly. Eighty-five percent of serial killers are male, and eighty-two percent are white."

"No *guy is* going to do what this killer's doing."

"Why do you say that?"

"Or what this killer's not doing, 'scuse me. The coroner said no rape or signs of sex abuse. It was in your article. A *guy* who's going to all that trouble would rape his victim."

"And coming from you, I'd say your claim is worthless." She was insinuating his participation in a gang rape of an underage woman.

"I've changed. Six months clean and sober. That should count to you, of all people."

She wondered how he knew she was in recovery.

"I know," he said, "because of that necklace you're wearing."

She fingered the dime-sized gold triangle encased in a delicate circle, the symbol of Alcoholics Anonymous.

"People can change, Bart, that's true," she said. "The damage done to others likely won't. Have you made an amends?"

"I will. When it's right." He screwed down the top of his wool-padded canteen. "A few of us have banded together to protect our girls."

"You need to be careful not to jump to conclusions and start harassing innocent people."

"The Sheriff isn't doing shit, so we got a responsibility to protect our women."

"I know for a fact the Sheriff is working very hard on this case. And the FBI might come in on this. Don't go out there with your buddies like a pack of vigilantes and create more violence and fear."

He scoffed. "I gotta go." He opened the front door and turned, looking like a hulking shadow.

"I want to know something," he said.

"What is it?"

"Am I having a sister or brother?"

He knew. She wasn't having this conversation. She called Easton's number and let it ring. It went to voicemail.

"Easton, Bart is here in the house. He says you told him it was all right to come out to the ranch and fix fence. Come home."

"You're calling this place 'home'?"

She held out her phone, recording Bart's words.

He jabbed the air with his finger, "You're not only a bitch. You're a fucking gold digger."

"And now you're going to have to explain yourself to your father."

Bart moved his hand to his hat and tipped it. As if his guilty conscience interfered with his coordination, he bumped into the door frame before charging outside and slamming the door shut. She twisted the dead bolt and leaned against the door until she heard the roar of his pickup. She watched out the window as he tore out of the yard and zigzagged onto the rock road, and when the dust settled she hurried to the ranch gate and swung it closed.

As she walked Jessie from the tie rail to her paddock, Bart's face blared in her mind. The way he measured her gullibility as he lied, and that infuriating smirk reminded her of something she couldn't put her finger on.

35

WHEN ELEANOR HADN'T HEARD FROM Easton, she drove into town for an eight p.m. AA meeting, entering the room as a woman read from the *Big Book of Alcoholics Anonymous*:

"Our thought life will be placed on a much higher plane of consciousness when our thinking is cleared of wrong motives."

Right now, her consciousness was drowned in anger and resentment toward Bart and worry that something had happened to Easton on his way home.

Leonard walked in. He circled the perimeter of the room, looking for a seat while trying to be invisible, which was impossible for a tall, broad shouldered Native man with a long black braid, wearing jeans and a black T-shirt with a photograph of four Native warriors and the words:

Homeland Security
Fighting Terrorism since 1492

He took an empty seat in the back of the room and put his to-go paper cup of coffee on the floor between his feet. He spotted Eleanor and nodded. She gave him a short wave and a pressed smile.

As people took turns sharing, she spaced out, looping back to her exchange with Bart. She was unwilling to share about him, and she wasn't ready to share the news of her pregnancy. They'd figure that out soon enough.

It was early, anyway.

As she gazed around the room, she noticed Charlotte sitting in a corner. Her makeup was freshly applied, her nails long and polished. The last time they'd talked, she'd been pretty chipper, slinging burgers at the grill. Tonight, she looked glum.

Leonard's voice broke through her musing.

"For me," he said, "I got to love myself to give it away. When I was drinking and using, people weren't happy to see me walk into their stores. They'd see me on the sidewalk and cross to the other side of the road to avoid me. I thought they were the problem until I realized I was the problem. These days I go into the Flying J for my RC Cola, and I'm met with a smile and a 'Hey, Leonard, how's it going?' I try not to stand in the way of the Great Spirit's miracles for me. I surrender every morning before I set foot on the floor, and every time a mean thought enters my mind, I ask forgiveness and gratitude. Thoughts create emotions and emotions create actions, so I got to keep my head straight and stay connected or I'll end up dead or hurting someone."

That was compelling.

When the meeting closed and everyone stood in a circle, Leonard crossed the room and took her hand during the closing prayer.

When the prayer ended and they dropped hands, she asked, "Can I talk to you a minute?"

"Sure," Leonard said.

"I'm pregnant."

"Hmm."

"Hmm what?"

"I thought something was different about you. Thought maybe you and Easton were going through something."

"We are going through something. We're having a baby and we're really happy about it."

"You don't look happy."

"He has a twenty-year-old son who scares me."

An angry expression scuttled across Leonard's face.

"When I go to the ranch to take care of the horses, Easton's not always there. This evening, his son shows up out of the blue without calling while I'm grooming Jessie." She heard a tremor in her voice and her words caught in her throat. "He startled me so badly I screamed." She smoothed her hand instinctively over her nearly decipherable mound.

"Did you tell your old man?"

"He's not returning my calls. And I'm worried about that. Easton told Bart not to be on the property when I'm there. Bart knew I was there. My Blazer's parked out front of the house. But he came right up to me and lied, saying Easton sent him out there to check fences."

His eyebrows knit. "What's Easton say?"

"I left a voicemail which included his son's angry voice calling me a bitch and a gold digger. And then I came here." She took a breath. "Easton's trying hard to provide some guidance for his son."

"His son needs guidance?"

"Understatement. He committed a violent crime against an under-age woman, and I can't forgive him."

"You know what we say in these rooms about forgiveness."

"Forgiveness heals the one forgiving."

"That, too. Forgiveness isn't fast food."

"I don't understand."

"Forgiveness takes effort. We got to search for it, Nell, and then shine that light on darkness so the stench retreats without poisoning the present any more than it already has."

"I don't have it in me."

"You forgive the kid, and he becomes a better person."

"I forgive the kid, and he worms his way into my relationship with Easton."

"Anger's not good for the baby." He gave her a hug. "Gotta go. Renee made us dinner. I'm here for a while longer. Don't be a stranger."

It was dark outside and tank-top warm, and the cicadas hummed in the wildland beyond the parking lot. Eleanor wasn't one for sticking around after a meeting and talking, but the sight of Charlotte sitting alone at the patio table smoking a cigarette got to her.

"Hey, Charlotte," said Eleanor.

"Hi." Charlotte's walls were like gelatin. They melted at the first sign someone cared. Eleanor sat down. "You look sad."

"You'd be sad, too, if you had to put up with the shit I put up with."

"Want to talk about it?"

"Not really." She stubbed out the cigarette. "My boyfriend is a jerk." She pushed the ashtray across the table. "I can't handle it."

"Sounds rough."

"He's ragging on me I should stop taking birth control pills. I didn't tell him I was pregnant and I'm not going to. So, yeah, I'm sad. I'm not ready for a kid and if I were, it sure as fuck wouldn't be his."

"That's serious. I'm sorry."

"Yeah. I need some financial leverage. I'm going to buy the laundromat. It's for sale and I know the owner, and he'll help me get a small business loan. I'm going to make it nice. I already have a name for it." She raised her arms and blocked the air with her hands. "The ... Laundry ... Room. We'll have a fluff and fold and sell home-baked snacks. No vending machine that never works."

"I can see that. You'd be a stellar businesswoman."

"So how come you don't come in on Tuesdays anymore?"

"Boyfriend has a laundry room."

"Well, I miss you."

"Thank you, Charlotte."

"You shouldn't let a boyfriend take away your independence or your meetings. You haven't been going to as many as you used to since the boyfriend."

"Noted."

"It sneaks up, you know. Cunning, baffling, and powerful."

"Yeah." Eleanor thought of her anger at the beginning of the meeting. "I have a question. Do you know Bart Hargrove?"

"Doesn't ring a bell. How old?"

"Twenty. He's one of us?"

"I'm not into blowing people's anonymity." Charlotte raised her eyebrows in admonishment.

"Right. Sorry."

"See what happens when you stay away? Anyway, twenty's too young for me to pay attention."

"What about an older woman, not one of us, but she might do her laundry at your place."

"What's she look like?"

"Like she's had a hard life, lives outdoors. She takes care of coyote pups in the river canyon outside of town."

"It don't register."

"She has a habit of flicking her false teeth in and out."

Charlotte nodded. "I do know her. She comes in and washes her sleeping bag about once a month. Why?"

"Probably shouldn't say."

"Oh, come on. You can't do that."

"She was at the river and witnessed the killer dispose of Marisol Rodriguez's body."

"Are you shitting me?"

"Nope."

"It was a man, right?"

"She couldn't tell. Big coat and hood. I need to find her."

Charlotte pulled out a fresh cigarette from the pack of Spirits. "I could text you the next time she comes in. It's been a while, so she's about due. My number's on the phone list." She flicked her purple Bic.

The first whiff of tobacco about did Eleanor in. "I don't have a phone list."

"How do you expect to stay sober if you don't call people?"

"You're right."

"I'll go inside and get you a list." She started to stand.

"Just give me your number. I have to go."

"Whew, pushy." Charlotte recited her number. Eleanor tapped it into her contacts and called, let it ring once, and hung up.

"Now you have mine, too."

"Keep your ass in that chair while I go get you a friggin' phone list."

* * *

Eleanor headed up mountain to spend the night in her cottage, everything looping. Charlotte's surprising wisdom. Her knowledge of the coyote woman. Leonard's advice and Bart's lies. *That smirk.* It reminded her of Adelia the day in the lodge when she was speed-talking about the falls to avoid answering the question: Were you the witness?

* * *

Easton was furious. "I pulled over as soon as I heard your message."

"Where've you been?"

"The Merced job. I stayed outside until I couldn't see two feet in front of me, grading that property for turkey sheds. No cell service out there."

"I was worried."

"I'm sorry, Lee. Bart's done. I'll let him know as soon as we hang up. He knew the rules and blew it."

"What if your decision makes him angrier and he comes back?"

"He won't come back."

36

THE NEXT MORNING, ELEANOR NEEDED to borrow a cup of milk for her oatmeal. Dolores opened her front door and pushed out the screen before Eleanor had entered her patio.

"Come in, dear," she said. "You haven't been at your cottage for days."

It had been days. She'd lost track.

"So glad you're here." Dolores ushered Eleanor inside. "I want your opinion on something." She led Eleanor over to the fireplace and pointed at the gilt-framed print of the Crucifixion.

"I want to move this to the dining room so it's not the first thing my guests see when they walk into my home."

Dolores never had guests.

"Plus," she lifted the print off its nail and walked it across the living room to the dining nook, "the gold frame and the painting's gold leaf match my Annie Glass. You should know about Annie Glass."

Eleanor did know about Annie Glass. The internationally praised dinnerware was made in Santa Cruz County. Its most famous line featured a thick gold leaf trim on the perimeter of each plate. Dolores had arranged six dinner plates with matching salad plates, white cloth napkins, and real silverware. She was right: the print's gold leaf did pop the Annie Glass gold trim, but even gold couldn't mask the grotesquerie of humans crucifying another human.

"Honestly, Dolores, you don't want the image of a bloody, tortured man overlooking your guests while they eat. Maybe *The Last Supper*, but not this. I lose my appetite looking it." She held out her Pyrex measuring cup. "May I borrow a cup of milk?"

"Of course." Dolores set the print on the table, took the measuring cup, and headed for the kitchen.

Eleanor remained in the dining room, studying the painting, and her gaze rested on the three grief-stricken women at the base of the cross. She recognized the Virgin Mary and Mary Magdalene. "Who's the other woman?" she called to Dolores.

"What other woman?" she shouted back.

"In the painting. There's the Virgin and Magdalene. Who's the third?"

Dolores walked in with the measuring cup full of milk. "Mary of Clopas. Three Marys."

Eleanor took the cup.

"And see that cross?" said Dolores. "That's from the dogwood tree. That tree's never been the same."

A vague dread wound its way up Eleanor's spine.

"They found plant matter in the latest victim's throat, same as Marisol."

"My arm hairs just stood at attention."

"Is that biblical?"

"Apocryphal, but true. It used to be a milling tree, but after the Crucifixion the tree would never again grow to support an evil purpose. Just look at our dogwood out back. Spindly, weak as vines in some spots."

Eleanor had already learned that from the internet. "Can I take a photo of the painting?"

"As long you don't post it on social media. I don't want that photograph to be an attractor for bad energy."

"If you're worried about bad energy, why keep it in your house?"

"In my home it keeps me safe. Out there where some ne'er-do-well is trolling the internet, the image could trigger something."

"That's weird, Dolores."

"What's weird is something you said earlier. The girl's name: Marisol Rodriguez. Marisol is the Spanish name given the Virgin Mary. Maria de Soledad."

Eleanor felt lightheaded.

"And then there's Cleo. Another version of Mary of Clopas is Mary of Cleopas, depending on who you're talking to." Dolores glanced down at Eleanor's stomach. "You're pale, dear. I'll get you a glass of orange juice. Orange juice fixes most things."

Eleanor drank the juice, realizing how thirsty she was. "Thanks. I need to get back to my house and lie down before work."

"Yes, you need to eat that oatmeal."

She went outside and the vanilla scent of pines hit her senses. She heard the click of Dolores's screen door, followed by the front door lock. She started across the lawn with her cup of milk. Granite barked inside her cottage. The crunch of gravel behind her got louder.

Easton pulled into the mobile park, window down. "I thought I'd take you out to breakfast."

She walked up to the truck and leaned against his door. "I'm so glad to see you."

He kissed her cheek. "You look pale."

"So I hear, and yes on breakfast, but Granite needs a walk."

"I'll walk him, and you get ready for work, then we'll catch breakfast at that place with the outdoor patio. We can bring the dog, and I'll take him back to the ranch for company."

* * *

Easton ordered eggs over medium, biscuits, and gravy. Eleanor stuck to her original plan: oatmeal and fruit.

"Did you tell Dolores you're pregnant?"

"I didn't have to. Those X-ray eyes of hers saw right through me."
She sniffed the coffee. It didn't appeal to her. "This strange idea came
to me." She reached for the cream and lightened the coffee to beige.

"Strange, like a new brand of marmalade?"

She broke open two packets of raw sugar and sprinkled the contents
into her coffee. "Not like marmalade."

Easton stared. "You're putting sugar in your coffee."

"I could be eating pickles and ice cream."

"God save us."

"Speaking of which, are you familiar with the painting of Christ's
Crucifixion?"

"Everyone is."

"Would you humor me and Google the Crucifixion? Tell me what
you see."

"I'm eating." He pulled out his phone anyway.

"Tell me what you see."

"One-hundred-ninety-three dollars on Wayfair."

"Do you see the women at the base of the cross?"

"Yeah."

"Can you name them?"

"His mother the Virgin Mary, his girlfriend Mary Magdalene,
and—"

"That's my point."

"Who's the other one?"

"The third Mary. Mary of Clopas."

"Where you going with this?"

"Marisol stands for Maria de la Soledad, the Spanish name given
to the Virgin Mary."

"I'm getting a bad feeling."

"Mary of Clopas is also identified as Mary of Cleopas." She spelled it.

"I just got chills."

"That's only two of three Marys."

He leaned back into the bench seat. "You know, Lee, I don't think you should be involved in stuff that gives me chills."

"We talked about this."

"We did, so let me put it this way. It scares me to think of what you're up to. Maybe you should talk to someone, a priest or something. Someone who knows about these things. The church has a new priest, and my friends say he's young and smart. Maybe you want to talk to him about what I'm perceiving is your new hunch."

"A theory," she said. "I met that priest at Marisol's service and he's not that young."

* * *

Out front of the stone rectory was a rose garden in full sunlight. Among the rose bushes was the priest in his black robe and white collar. He was bent over holding red-handled pruning shears and lopping the tops off spent blooms. She inhaled the floral perfume.

"Good morning," the priest said, straightening.

"Morning, I'm Eleanor Wooley from the *Gold Strike Tribune*."

"Nice to meet you, Eleanor." He placed his pruning shears inside the basket of trimmings. "I'm Father Braxton. How can I help you?"

"I'm following up on the death of the two women who were each pulled from the river."

"I read the stories," he said. "You do good work. Difficult work, I imagine. One of the victims attended this church. God rest her soul."

"Marisol. I attended her service. You sprinkled me with holy water."

He smiled in a way that made her feel blessed.

"I'd like to run something by you, Father, if I could."

He waited for her to go on.

"I was studying a print of the Crucifixion this morning."

"Which one? A lot of famous paintings of the Crucifixion. My favorite is Fra Angelico's with the gilt background."

"That's the one."

"The Met has it. You should check it out. It's worth the price of airfare. More beautiful than any photograph.

"Is the gold significant?"

"Fra Angelico's intention with the gold? Yes. The gold transforms Christ's death into a spiritual occurrence that extends to the supernatural and sanctifies death. I can attest that when you stand before the original painting you are transported to another dimension."

"That's sort of what I'm curious about. The three Marys in the painting. How powerful is that threesome in theology?"

"Very." He glanced around the garden as if someone might be watching them. "Shall we go inside and talk?"

"It's so pretty out here with the roses. And a perfect temperature before the heat climbs. Could we sit on one of the benches?"

"Like minds."

He sat on one, leaving the bench facing the roses for Eleanor.

"What do you mean 'sanctifies death'?"

He nodded. "In this case sanctify would mean purifying death by ritual, consecrating an action or event. Like a church wedding makes holy a union of two souls."

"I'm pregnant but the father and I aren't married."

"If we're human, we're born with Original Sin," said Father Braxton. "Try this on: A union sanctified by the sacrament of holy matrimony makes everything leading to that marriage holy in the eyes of God."

"That's beautiful," she said. "I'll think about it, but what I'm going to ask is not beautiful, and I hope it's not sacrilegious."

He leaned back against the bench, hands clasped on his lap. "All ears."

"It's about the three Marys. The first victim the Sheriff pulled from the river was named Marisol."

"Yes, a lovely name which means Maria de la Soledad, a Spanish name given to the Blessed Mary."

"Right. The second victim's name is Cleo Gunderson, as in Mary of Cleopas."

A mild tic grabbed the priest's cheek. "Mary of Clopas or Cleopas. The Virgin's sister-in-law, according to some scholars. God rest the girl's soul."

"That's two of three Marys. My gruesome thought is whoever killed Marisol and Cleo is going to kill a third Mary."

Father Braxton slid his hands inside his sleeves and lowered his head. Eleanor thought he might be praying. She waited.

"Not sacrilegious. Gruesome. Here's what I can say. The symbology of the Three Marys has been a subject of religious scholarship and contention for centuries. Separate from Trinitarians, which is a whole other avenue of contention. In Christian theology, two Marys create duality and tension, but the third defuses the tension and brings the energy to neutral. Another way of considering your question is that to neutralize the power of our three sacred Marys would signify destruction of the feminine and a genesis in the mind of some sects for a new order, synonymous with restoring the patriarchy to its original power."

"Could someone interpret this as a rationale for killing women?"

"If a person needs a rationale for killing, they can conjure up anything. Your theory infers the killer suffers religious psychosis. In such cases, the perpetrator may not rest until they fulfill what they deeply believe is their spiritual calling, regardless of whether it's a false calling."

She rubbed the goosebumps on her arms. "What about Mary Magdalene?"

"Magdalene wasn't the destitute prostitute portrayed washing Christ's feet," said Father Braxton. "She was born into a very influential family. Jesus helped her find her path and she repaid him with loyalty and substantive financial support. Her status was equal to the Apostles. After all, she witnessed Christ's Resurrection and retold her story throughout the Mediterranean. She died a martyr and a saint. Today she's an icon for the power women once held in the church. Women today are making good strides reclaiming their power in the hierarchy."

"Who are the extremists trying to undermine the feminine?"

"I'm not sure who, specifically, but there's always been a sick fringe who rely on the patriarchy to subjugate women."

She felt validated as she thanked the priest and rose to leave.

He surprised her by asking, "You're the one who spilled wine on my sleeve?"

"I am. I'm still embarrassed."

"On the contrary. In Italian culture accidentally spilling wine is a good omen. *In vino veritas.* Our meeting was meant to be, and on your quest, you'll find the truth, and truth will prevail." He held both of her hands in his. "May the Lord Jesus Christ be with you, keep you safe, and guide your path." He kissed her cheek and crossed himself.

On her way to her Blazer, Eleanor let go for the time being of decades-long resentment against the Catholic Church and narrowed her hatred to one misguided executioner.

37

ADELIA SHEPHERD DIDN'T HAVE A Facebook or Instagram account. She wasn't on LinkedIn or the other platforms. When Eleanor Googled her name, a dozen links came up, but none of them her, and she began to wonder why. She brought up Truth Finder and entered *Adelia Shepherd*.

It took five minutes for the app to list relatives in boxes, none with the same last name. Another five minutes for the aliases screen to come up. Lucia Rocha.

Eleanor Googled the alias, and her screen instantly filled with links to newspaper headlines of a husband who drowned his wife in a bathtub.

"Holy shit." The wife-killer was serving a life sentence in San Quentin. A child was involved. A little girl, Lucia. She was five when the murder occurred. According to the Stockton newspaper, she had witnessed the murder.

Eleanor called the newspaper and asked for the reporter. She was told the woman who'd written the story had retired a year ago, and the paper was not at liberty to give out her number. Another Google search brought up the reporter's number.

"Yes, I remember the story," the retired reporter said. "One of those you can't forget. It had taken awhile to gather enough evidence to convict the husband. Eventually, the court allowed the daughter to testify, and because the reality of going back to live with her father horrified her, she told the court what she'd seen and that put him away."

The girl ended up in foster care. She'd been baptized Catholic, and her birth parents had been active in the church, so she was sent to a Catholic orphanage in Arizona that also served as a boarding school for local Navajo kids whose families lived on the reservation.

"The girl is a grown woman who's changed her name to Adelia Shepherd," said Eleanor. "She's gainfully employed by the Forest Service and living in Gold Strike County where two young women have been murdered, each discovery of the body accompanied by a nearby wildfire."

"That's odd because she is attracted to fire," said the ex-reporter. "When she was a kid, she got caught for lighting grass fires. Small ones. She'd build grass houses and burn them down. She managed to stomp out the fires with one exception. That fire got out of hand. It's documented in a Child Protective Services report."

"I used to make grass fires when I was a kid, but I didn't become an arsonist."

"You didn't have a father who killed your mother in your presence."

"This is true."

"Where exactly is this orphanage?"

"In Arizona outside of Tuba City. I visited her a few years after the murder. She'd spent time in juvenile hall after beating up her teacher."

"She beat up a nun?"

"She claimed she was being bullied, and the nun was complicit in the bullying. Another student hid pot in her backpack and ratted her out. The nun humiliated our girl in front of the class. I can understand why she'd change her name and move on."

"She changed her name. Not so sure she's moved on."

* * *

Adelia lived on a dirt road in the middle of the forest in one of those subdivisions built up from a patch of privately-owned land surrounded by public land. The wood-framed houses were cheaply constructed and buffered from each other by native pine and manzanita.

The neighborhood had that woodsy mountain look where the potholed roads added rusticity, and folks didn't worry about landscaping because the forest took care of it. Yet, a sense of neglect overshadowed the neighborhood, seen in weathered siding and broken window shades.

Eleanor drove up to Adelia's. The garage door was closed, and the driveway was empty. The only way past the six-foot wooden fence that surrounded three sides of the house was a tall gate on the right with a square yellow sign that said "No Trespassing" in black lettering.

Eleanor parked around the corner on the shoulder of a vacant lot. She got out, and with Granite at her heels, walked back to Adelia's. She approached the front door and pressed the yellowed round plastic doorbell, assuming Adelia was at work and wouldn't return until after four in the afternoon.

She glanced down the street at the neighboring houses. If the absence of cars was any indication, no one was home across the street or on either side of Adelia's. The only sign of life was a squirrel dropping cones from the Jeffrey pine beside Adelia's house.

Eleanor petted Granite as if she were merely a lady with her cute dog visiting a friend. She paused on the front porch before feeling confident enough to walk to the six-foot side gate. A glance through the garage's side window confirmed no one was home, and she pulled the string to unlatch the gate and slipped inside with Granite. The yard consisted of dead lawn and blown out dandelion, the round white seed heads spent. An uneven brick patio sported one chaise lounge. The chaise was unused, judging from the layer of pine needles covering its brightly flowered cushion.

Floor-to-ceiling blinds on the sliding glass door blocked the view into what she assumed was the living room. A large ceramic pot by the door held a dead geranium. Further along the patio was a smaller window with open curtains, the sill too high for Eleanor to see in. She pulled the pot along the patio, scraping the bricks, until it was under the window. She stepped up onto the pot, mindful of the poor geranium, and peered inside to a room with twin beds, one unmade. Between the beds a print of a bear sow and cub was hung to look like an actual window. An Art Deco lamp sat on the bedside table and what looked like a Gideon's Bible. The doors of the closet were partially open, revealing Forest Service shirts on hangers and a jumble of boots and running shoes on the floor. Two boxes were stacked above on the closet shelf, one labeled "Rum" and the other "Libby's pineapple juice." Drab-colored clothes lay in heaps at the foot of the beds.

Eleanor stepped off the garden pot and walked around the side of the house where a pop-out bay window revealed Adelia's kitchen table and four matching chairs. The table was bare except for three white candles placed in a triangle, two of them with blackened wicks, the other unused. A light green Southwestern-style cross hung on the wall above a small telephone desk. Catty-corner to the cross was a grid map of the forest that hung on the wall. She made out two red circles drawn around the locations where the two dead women had been pulled from the river. Above each circle was the acronym "RIP."

"I need to go inside." Saying it aloud bolstered her courage.

She started to drag the pot back in place when she spotted a small brass key within the ring of dirt that had accumulated around the pot.

The key fit easily into the sliding door. Eleanor stepped over the aluminum track and ordered Granite to stay outside. He sat on his haunches and whined as she walked through the living room to the kitchen and studied the map. Adelia had numbered the circles #1 and #2, aligned with the locations where Marisol's and Cleo's bodies had been found. Eleanor glanced at the old-fashioned telephone desk and her eye caught a greeting card with the striking image of a brown-skinned Mary Magdalene dressed in a red cloak, holding a white egg. Magdalene's gold halo possessed the same vibrant effect as the gold in the Crucifixion painting that hung in Dolores's living room. She plucked the card carefully from its picture stand and read the backside. This image had been commissioned by Grace Cathedral in San Francisco. The card emphasized Magdalene's power during the time of Christ and asserted, "she bears witness to the important role women once held in the Church," symbolizing the modern resurgence of the feminine. The card read, "As women reclaim their ancient rights in the church, Mary Magdalene challenges all Christians to re-examine their cultural prejudices about gender and leadership."

Eleanor returned the card to its stand and headed to the bedroom, mulling over Adelia's connection to this powerful version of a biblical woman most people regard as a submissive prostitute. And why set the card in such a visible spot?

She pulled down the rum box first, and set it on the unmade twin bed, opened the flaps and peered at stacks of old files. Nothing struck her. She pulled the Libby's pineapple box down, opened it, and found an assortment of trinkets and memorabilia. The relics were of a religious variety: a white china dinner bell from a California mission, a statue of the Virgin Mary, a collection of laminated cards with images of saints. A small photo album.

Eleanor picked up the album and opened it to a photo of a baby she assumed was Adelia. She flipped the plastic page. Adelia as a toddler. A mother in blue jeans and a flannel shirt crouched down, holding her arms out to receive the wobbly child. *Flip.* A photo of mother and child embracing, their cheeks pressed together. She returned the album to the box and saw a front-page newspaper lining the bottom.

Sacramento Husband Found Guilty of Drowning Wife.

The back of her neck itched as a hair or two rose. Granite barked. She felt a chill.

"What are you doing here?" said a voice.

Eleanor whirled around.

"What the hell are *you* doing in my house?" Adelia stood in the doorway. She looked huskier than Eleanor remembered.

"I brought you a box of produce," Eleanor said. "Carrots and little gem lettuces."

"The kitchen's out there." She pointed. "Which is totally beside the point. Why the fuck are you in my bedroom?"

Granite trotted in and barked.

"The back door was open," Eleanor said. "I was looking for you."

"Tell your fucking dog to stop barking." She took a puffed-up step toward Eleanor, looking like she might take a swing.

"Granite, no barking." She reached down and grabbed his collar.

"So where are the veggies?"

"I left them in the car." She pulled the still barking dog past Adelia and out of the bedroom.

"You're lying." Adelia followed, inches from Eleanor's hunched back as she tugged Granite over the sliding door track into the yard.

She stepped in front of Eleanor. "You know, I was beginning to like you, but you can't break into someone's home like this. It's fucking illegal. Why are you here? And don't tell me you think so highly of me you're bringing carrots and lettuce to my doorstep. I'm not an idiot."

"I'm sorry." Eleanor glanced down at her feet. "I know what happened to you."

"What do you mean, 'what happened to me'?"

"I know about the trauma you experienced as a child. I know you witnessed your father kill your mother when you were five. I know you testified at his trial, and I know your birth name is Lucia Rocha."

Adelia's neck reddened, and she pointed a straight arm at the fence. "Get the fuck out."

"And I saw your candles and that map of the forest. I had to ask myself—" She couldn't finish.

"Ask what?"

"You circled the sites where the two dead women were found. I had to ask myself *why?*"

"Not your goddamn business."

"I'm covering their murders. It is my business. And your house is very strange."

"What's strange?"

"Your religious regalia."

"You got into my boxes? Get out, now. I'm calling the Sheriff."

"I doubt that." Eleanor backed toward the gate, pulling Granite by his collar.

"I'm not going to forget this."

Eleanor reached up to close the gate, holding on to Granite's ruff. Her steps quickened as she headed to her Blazer and piled in, Granite first, grateful she hadn't locked the car. The engine started right up as if it knew they were in trouble. She sped off and the sensation of someone chasing her diminished with each mile she put between Adelia and herself as she headed down mountain to town.

38

"SIRI, CALL EASTON."

He picked up. "Hey there."

"Can you talk?"

"You bet. You okay?"

"I'm okay."

"What's going on?"

"I just got back from Adelia Shepherd's house, the fire technician for the Forest Service."

"Do I know her?"

"Maybe. She's worked both the Brown's Ferry and the Gooseberry Falls fires. Adelia Shepherd is her alias. Her birth name is Lucia Rocha."

"Okay."

"She was a child when she witnessed her father murder her mother. There are front-page stories in every newspaper in the state."

"That's bad. Where are you going with this?"

"During the Gooseberry Falls incident, I rode the fire boat back to the staging area with the Search and Rescue crew. Adelia was on the boat. One of the SAR team inferred she witnessed the woman's fall. I asked her and she skirted the question."

"What does this have to do with going to her house?"

"I found the key and went inside."

"You broke into her house?"

"Says the guy who released someone else's mustangs. I went merely to get a sense of where she lived and see if anything came up. She had a map of the forest with the body recovery sites circled."

"That doesn't sound unreasonable for a first responder who worked both incidents."

"Yeah, well, she walked in on me."

"Is she reporting you to the Sheriff?"

"I don't think so. But I might report her."

"What you're saying is compelling, Lee, no doubt about that, especially her background, but I don't think it's enough hard evidence to present to the Sheriff."

"She was busted as a kid for a grass fire that got away."

"That's weird. But here's the thing. You're the one who did something illegal. You tell the Sheriff and you're admitting you broke into someone's home. A private investigator would get their license revoked for that."

"What should I do?"

"You *could* ask the Sheriff if he has a person of interest and follow up saying something like 'It's rumored among SAR volunteers that Adelia Shepherd was the witness to the woman's fall,' and you did some research and found out Adelia, whose real name is— "

"—Lucia Rocha."

"—whose real name is Lucia Rocha, has a traumatic background and a record of starting fires."

"Sounds good."

"Where are you now?"

"Home. I just pulled in and I'm going to take Granite for a walk and fix a bite to eat."

"Will I see you tonight?"

"I'm going to stay here and turn in early."

"Are you okay?"

"Definitely processing, but I'm fine."

"Can't say as I am."

"Don't worry. I'll call you when I'm in bed."

* * *

She walked with Granite down the path behind her cottage, pausing at the dogwoods. Something was off with the tree nearest her. The limbs within her reach were bare. There were no white six-petal blossoms sprouting from branch tips or fallen on the ground. She glanced at the surrounding dogwoods. Their branches were laden with blossoms, even the vining dogwood that wound around the fir, competing for light in the treetops. She stared at this partially barren tree, mulling over what might have happened.

As she hiked the fire trail across the mountainside, she picked up her pace and let Granite run ahead as she mused over the tree, thinking of scenarios. The tree could have had bugs attractive to bear. Or Dolores may have picked them. She'd thought of doing the same except they were so fragile they'd brown within hours of plucking.

She stopped at the clearing with the view of the far-off horizon where neon shades of persimmon and eggplant colored the western sky as the sun set in the crotch of the river canyon. She said a prayer, nothing fancy, just a request to lighten up on work for the well-being of Easton and their baby. She started walking, feeling lighter.

Someone approached from the opposite direction. They walked with purpose. Granite loped as if he knew the person, a man. He wore dark blue clothing and patted the top of Granite's head before continuing toward her.

"Chad," she said and held up a hand.

He grinned and said a friendly, "Hey Eleanor."

"What are you doing here?"

"I'm surveying for the Forest Service."

The Forest Service?

"I'm assessing fuel buildup to see if the slash qualifies for a controlled burn," he said, picking up on her skepticism.

"This entire mountainside is a tinderbox," she said. "That's for sure."

Both sides of the trail were a tangle of fallen dead branches and limbs that had accumulated from two years of extreme winter storms. The forest understory had become a dry, gray web of fuel.

"I thought the forest service oversaw controlled burns."

"They're low on staff and working with Cal Fire," he said, "and Cal Fire works with the college program and internships. That would be me."

He stepped off the trail and picked up a rock. Granite growled. She called him and he came to her and sat at her side on his haunches, alert but quiet.

"Sorry about that," she said. "The rock threatened him."

He removed a knife from the back of his belt and flipped open the blade. "You really should think of moving. It's not safe here."

She watched him score the rock with his blade.

"You sound like my boyfriend."

"Smart guy. You could literally be toast."

A rustling closed in, and an animal charged through the grove of cedar saplings from the down mountain side of the trail. The dog stopped in the path, baring its fangs at Chad, who held the rock in mid-air and stared at the vicious creature.

"Peck," bellowed a man's voice. The hermit who lived alone in the abandoned Boy Scout camp walked through the clearing his dog had blazed.

He held his dog by its stud collar. "Who's this?"

"This is Chad," Eleanor said.

"I'm asking him."

"I'm Chad. Surveying for potential controlled burns."

"You're gonna burn the place down?" the hermit said.

The pit snarled.

"Call off your hound."

"He's not a hound. You need to run the hell outta here before I sic 'em on your sorry ass."

"What's with you, man?"

"I know what goes on. Now get outta here before I count two. One."

Chad glanced at Eleanor and pointed his finger at the hermit. "You're going to be sorry about this."

He retreated hastily in the direction he'd come. She felt both embarrassed for Chad and oddly relieved. She stroked her stomach to quell the anxiety and murmured soft words of comfort to the baby before turning to the hermit. He'd disappeared. On the ground, footprints of the men, dogs, her own remained in the soft dirt. The rock Chad scored was on the ground. She picked it up. The size of a bocci ball. Scratched on the face were three blaze marks. Whatever that meant, it gave her chills.

She glanced up. The tops of conifers swayed in a high afternoon breeze coming down from the mountains. She headed to the cottage and went around locking her doors.

"Please pick up," she grumbled into her cell phone and slung her backpack over her shoulder.

"Lee, how was your walk?"

"I'm not staying here tonight."

39

ELEANOR HADN'T BROUGHT ANYTHING BUT her backpack, laptop, and dog. She was so shook up she'd blasted out of there without a toothbrush or a change of clothes. Easton was waiting at the cattle-guard. She stopped the Blazer, and he got in and rode with her the short distance to the house. They went inside and she started for the stairs, but he pulled her back.

"Whoa," he said, and held her tight. She felt safe.

In the bathroom, Eleanor saw the brand-new toothbrush and tooth-paste. He'd left a pair of his flannel bottoms, a white V-neck T-shirt, and a clean towel on the counter, along with a tube of Burt's Bees lip balm and a new bottle of Lubriderm lotion. His kindness made her cry. Or maybe it was hormones. She wiped the last tear with the trim of the bedsheet.

"I've been thinking about our conversation in the arena," said Easton, an arm around her shoulder.

"Which part?"

"The part where you said you didn't trust yourself."

"And you said you trusted me. That was sweet." She looked up at him, smiling.

"I've been thinking about what you said, and I'm wondering if fear of losing yourself is worth depriving yourself of happiness?"

She inhaled deeply and glanced out Easton's bedroom window to the crown of the walnut tree. "It's a fair question."

"Would you ponder it?"

"Yep."

"And let me know what you come up with?"

She grinned.

* * *

"You're late." Mac peered over his reading glasses as she walked to her desk.

"And you're observant." She picked up the acorn from the window-sill in front of her desk. "And this is Truth."

"You okay?"

"Actually, I'm blessed, but my personal life is getting very strange, and I should probably tell you about it."

He laid his glasses on his desk and stood. "Let's talk in the conference room. Get a cup of coffee and I'll meet you there."

In the break room, pouring rank coffee, Eleanor organized how to tell Mac the odd events and which to tell first. She began with Father Braxton for credibility before she told him about yesterday's encounter with Chad and the Hermit.

"And I should probably tell you I broke into a woman's house, and she busted me."

"You probably had a reason."

"She may have a psychological reason for killing women and placing them in a river and purifying the scene with wildfire in order to process her own mother's murder by her father."

"You've been busy. What do I do when your good friend Perelli comes in to arrest you for breaking and entering? Tell him you're not here?"

"That's nice of you, Mac. I don't think she'll press charges. She's hiding something."

"That it?"

"For now."

They went back to their desks, and she heard Mac call downstairs to the front desk. "If anyone comes in asking to talk to Eleanor, tell them she's out on assignment and let me know immediately."

Thank you, Eleanor mouthed.

She opened the email from Renee Standin with "Field Trip" in the subject line. She and Lawrence had scheduled the trip to the dam site for this weekend, the only weekend the supervisors could agree on. Eleanor needed to talk to Easton before she confirmed.

"Short notice," he said. "I have a meeting this Saturday with a cattle broker from Lubbock, Texas, but I'll see what I can do."

"Why a meeting when the cows are up mountain?"

"He wants to check out the ranch. See how I run things. S'okay. I'll make sure the trailer's good for hauling the horses. Might need a new tire. Should upgrade my first aid kit and make sure my radio works."

"I'm a little worried about Lawrence Standin. He's a little old and hasn't been riding. If you can think of anything that'll make him comfortable, let me know."

"Maybe some fleece for the saddle. I'll see what I can do."

"I want some fleece for my saddle." Her sit bones had been worn raw on her ride through the Moraga Plateau last summer. It had taken two weeks for the sores to heal.

"I'll fleece your saddle any time and any place."

She realized she was smiling. Her cell rang. Charlotte was calling. "Hi, Charlotte."

"She's here, the lady you're looking for. She usually stays through the wash and dry cycle, but no guarantee."

"I'll be there as soon as I can."

*　*　*

Eleanor gathered the dog blanket she kept in the Blazer for Granite and carried it into the laundromat. The woman sat in one of the unmovable orange plastic bucket chairs reading a paperback. Charlotte stood at the office Dutch door writing in a notebook. Eleanor said hi and put a five-dollar bill in the change machine. The coins tumbled out.

"Which machine do you recommend for a dirty, heavy dog blanket?" she asked Charlotte.

"Use the big one in the middle." It was the coyote woman. "It'll end up cleaner than if you use a small one." She rested her gaze on Eleanor. "You're the one who gave me the ride."

"Ah, yes." Eleanor faked surprise. "How are your coyote pups?"

"They're not mine, but getting bigger and stronger every day. Costs a lot of money if you happen to have any extra on you."

"Certainly a good cause." Eleanor reached into her backpack and dug out her wallet. She pulled out her ATM Visa, inserted it into the machine, accepted the extra fee, and punched $20.

The machine processed her request and spit out the bill. She held it out to the woman.

"I need to talk to you."

"Not about washers, I figure. Dogs like the smell of their dirty blankets. I wouldn't waste my money changing the scent with laundry detergent. I figure you're not in here for that. Who told you I'd be here?"

Charlotte ducked into her office.

"I thought so."

"I found your fishing line in a tree." She pulled out a sandwich baggie and held it up. "I got your fly."

"Be nice if I had a pole to go with it."

"The Sheriff's Office has the rod as evidence. I told the Sheriff your story and we checked it out. He believes you."

"You told him? That's bad. Now I have the law and the criminal hunting me down. You shouldn't've done that."

"We need to catch this person before they kill again. Is there anything else you remember about that day? What time it was? Sounds? Some detail about the killer, the way they moved, their hands?"

"Gloves. The color of rawhide." She got up, opened the washing machine door, and pulled out several unzipped sleeping bags, placed them into a metal cart, and wheeled the cart to a big dryer. "You wouldn't happen to want to give those quarters you don't need to use on that dog blanket? I need them."

Eleanor fed her the sleeping bags, and the woman stuffed them into the dryer.

"One thing's eating at me," the woman said.

Eleanor wiped her hands and inserted her quarters. She turned on the machine and waited.

"Eleanor," Charlotte called from behind her half door. She held out a container of disinfecting hand wipes. Charlotte pulled a wipe from the container.

"Ask the nice lady if she wants one."

Eleanor took the container to the woman. "Would you like one?"

"Are you kidding? Those things are toxic with chemicals."

"Right."

"I'll tell what's buggin' me," she said.

Eleanor put the container on the folding table and said nothing. One word from her could change the woman's mind.

"You know how the sun sets and casts a glow on the mountainside?" She flicked her dentures. "The mountain has to be in the exact right place, and you have to catch the light at the perfect time or it disappears. That's why I picked that spot to fish. The fish like the color as much as me and they're easy catching. Around six the sun lowers and its light shines on this granite wall with quartz crystals. The rock turns rosy and for one second those crystals flash."

The woman waited for Eleanor's reaction. "It sounds beautiful."

"Right before the killer threw that poor girl's body into the river, I saw something. I thought it was the quartz, but the flash was in the wrong spot. I tried to make myself think it was just different today and must've put it out of my mind. But it keeps coming back. Something flashed, like glasses or a keyring, maybe a cellphone. A flash, like a glass bottle or tin can. I thought maybe that's how the mountain caught fire. Now I know better. That flash came from the killer."

* * *

That night, Easton explained the technical name for this optical phenomenon was "alpenglow," and if Eleanor wanted to experience it, there was a place on the property where they could see it just before sunrise.

"It's a long ride and I never went out there with the objective of watching it. More like, I'm here working the cows and, wow, isn't that beautiful?"

"Would you take me there?"

"Sure. It's past sunrise so we'll have to make it another day."

"Let's plan it after the field trip," she said. "Right now, I have to call McKenzie and give her the logistics."

"You going to ask her about Chad?"

"We'll see how it goes."

* * *

The two women sat in a booth by the picture window at the front of the cafe. The building's owner had intentionally peeled off layers of plaster and paint down to original brick added an historic aesthetic to the cafe's interior.

Eleanor ordered a decaf cappuccino and McKenzie, a hot chocolate. She sipped the whipped cream, and Eleanor poured raw sugar on top of her foam, trying to think of how to open the conversation.

McKenzie started. "I'm so excited about the field trip." Despite her smile, she looked tired. A small dark patch lay under each eye.

Eleanor listed items she should bring: sunscreen, water, candy bars. McKenzie wrote everything in her cell phone notes even though she probably knew better than Eleanor how to pack for a daylong trail ride with a string of adults whose equestrian skills were an unknown.

"My mom wants to know if there's going to be cell service."

"Probably not. There wasn't any when I was up there. We can figure out a plan, so your mom feels comfortable. Easton has a high-powered radio."

"Who all's coming?"

Eleanor recited the names of the attending supervisors, Ward and the Standins.

"And Easton, of course. You're going to like Lawrence."

"It sounds really special."

They held their mugs and stared at their hot drinks.

"Have you told Chad you're going?" asked Eleanor.

"Briefly. We're both working long hours. He seemed upset the first time I told him. I think it hurt his feelings I was excited about doing something without him." She took another sip of her drink.

"I saw him yesterday," said Eleanor.

"You saw Chad?"

"He was conducting survey work for the Forest Service."

"I thought he was taking exams."

Eleanor looked out the front window to the sidewalk. The sun had traveled behind the hill enough to cast elongated shadows of the buildings across the street, the largest being her blocky newspaper building. She felt the shadows in her bones and braced herself for the vespertine fear that lurked this time of day.

She told McKenzie the story about running into Chad.

McKenzie took another sip of her drink and put the mug on the table between them. The dark, puffy crescents punctuated her big eyes. "He scored a rock?"

"He said he was marking the spot."

Her brow creased. "That's strange."

"How long have you known him?" Eleanor asked.

"Our one-year anniversary is in September." She looked up and gave Eleanor a wan smile. "We met at a college political rally. He was a security guard, and I was speaking for my environmental class defending heritage oaks the campus planned to remove to build a new road."

"Does he share your opinion?"

"No, but he respects it. Or he wouldn't be risking his life to save trees."

"That's why he wants to be a firefighter? He loves the forest?"

"And its critters." She jutted her straight jaw forward. "I'm guessing. I never asked."

"I'm a reporter. I don't write stories because I like to write. I report to find truth."

"You're saying he's not a firefighter to protect the forest?"

"I'm saying you'd think a reporter loved to write, but I'm motivated by something more primal. A love of justice. I want to be a hero and save the world."

"And Chad is motivated by, what, a love of fire?"

Eleanor shrugged. "Maybe he wants to be a hero. What do you know about him?"

"His mom lives up north near Humboldt. She's confined to a wheelchair. He goes up there to check on her when school and work permit. I want to meet her, but he isn't keen on the idea. I think he's afraid of what I'll think of her."

"Does he have siblings?"

"He's an only kid of a single mom."

"Do you think he's capable of hurting women?"

McKenzie gasped. "No way." She turned her head, and Eleanor followed her gaze and saw their reflection in the plate glass window. McKenzie looked angry.

"I'm sorry. I've been covering this story and find I don't trust anyone, and everyone is a suspect."

"You just poisoned my relationship." McKenzie rose, slipped on her backpack, and stood up to leave. "I can't even talk to him about this meeting, which means I can't be honest with him which creates a wall and kills a relationship."

"Then you should tell him."

"Eleanor Wooley, the reporter for the newspaper, suspects you're a serial killer. He was with me at the music festival, Eleanor. How could you forget that? You called looking for me."

"Was he with you the entire time?"

"I went early with my girlfriends," she said. "He joined me after they got the fire twenty-five percent under control. Why are you doing this?"

Eleanor placed her hand on McKenzie's forearm. "You okay?"

McKenzie pulled away. "*No*, I'm not okay. *You* are freaking me out."

"I'm sorry. Two women were murdered, and their killer is out there."

"I was going over to his place after our meeting to tell him more about the field trip. Now I can't because he'll know I'm upset and won't let up until I tell him what's bugging me."

"Maybe just go home tonight. I'll follow you, if you don't mind."

"I do mind."

"I need to reassure your mom you'll be in good hands with Easton and me. Why don't you call her and tell her we're coming?"

"You call her."

She decided not to call and followed McKenzie, who lived out in the ranchlands south of Easton's ranch.

* * *

Tracy looked relieved to see them. Even more so when Eleanor told her Easton would be on the trip.

McKenzie left the living room, and Tracy spoke in a low voice until an older gentleman came into the room. "What are you ladies whispering about? What'd you do, hide the whiskey?"

Tracy laughed. "This is Farley Wilson, McKenzie's grandpa."

"Howdy, ma'am," Farley said. "Happy to make your acquaintance."

"She's a reporter for the *Tribune*."

"Uh oh," he put his hat back on. "What'd I do now?" He was an older man, with a round, weathered face and a bit of a paunch. His plaid short-sleeved Western shirt pulled at the snap buttons. He must wear his white straw cowboy hat and boots from the time he gets out of bed until he slips back between the sheets, Eleanor thought.

"My daughter-in-law here was pretty darn worried about our Kenzie until you found her up at that music festival. You any closer to finding that dirt bag so us old folks can get a good night's sleep?"

"No, sorry to say, sir. The sheriff hasn't had any leads as far as I know, which doesn't mean they don't have leads and persons of interest. It means they're not telling the press."

"Can't blame 'em for that now, can we? And call me Farley. Some people call me Far Off when I get out there with my philosophizing."

"I'm just glad she'll be getting some space from Chad," Tracy said. "He's too old for her. And controlling."

Farley considered his daughter-in-law's comment. "You know, Tracy, if that boyfriend weren't too old and controlling, he'd be too immature and wimpy. He seems like a fine boy training to be a firefighter. He just might stick around when our girl gets out of high school."

"When McKenzie graduates high school," said Tracy, "she's going to college."

"There's plenty she can learn around here," said Farley.

"You just don't want her to leave home." Tracy put a hand on his crossed arms.

"That said, I'm glad she's coming along on the field trip," said Eleanor. "We need her expertise."

"Sounds like some field trip," said Farley. "I hear Lawrence Standin's gonna give those politicians some local history."

"Maybe she'll get some perspective on her relationship," said Tracy. "She's too young to be so serious."

"Her mom just don't quit," said Farley.

Mom and Grandpa walked Eleanor to the foyer, leaving behind their different approaches to raising a girl in the twenty-first century.

They stood in the doorway as one, blocking the light from the hallway, united in their love for McKenzie, which was so palpable Eleanor felt a surge bordering on tears. She backed up her Blazer and quickly drove away, wishing she could put a damper on the worry, which wasn't possible while a killer roamed free.

* * *

The next morning, the tenant in Rette's place reminded Eleanor that he was moving out and wanted his deposit returned. Eleanor promptly put the house on Zillow and within five minutes her phone started to ping.

She drove out to Rette's and gunned the Blazer up the driveway. The house seemed to be falling apart as never before. Eleanor hadn't noticed the sagging trim beneath the south-facing window. She could nail that back up easy enough. The peeling brown paint exposing silvered wood siding was more problematic. She nearly tripped on a loose board on the back porch. The yard was littered with mounds of poop from the outgoing tenant's dogs.

Inside, the tenant had left bags of garbage on the floor and random trash was scattered about as if he'd left in a hurry or were coming back to finish cleaning up. Eleanor doubted the latter.

The tenant had left screws in the pine walls where he'd hung things. The kitchen door handles and light switches were covered with grime. Eleanor plucked a dusty heater vent from the floor and found its underside duct-taped shut on the bottom, probably to save on the heating bill. A year's worth of sticky dust clung to the blinds and windowsills and microwave.

* * *

During her lunch hour, Eleanor went to the hardware store. The clerk wore a red company vest and was sweating bullets. It was hot outside, over one hundred. Inside, the air conditioning was on in addition to several fans. The clerk's dripping head reminded her to pick up an AC unit for her own cottage, which would be hot enough inside to make beef jerky. He was friendly and talked a blue streak about AC options.

"Where do you live?" he asked.

"Up mountain a way. Halfway between here and Gooseberry Lake."

"I don't go up there anymore," he said. "The lake, I mean."

"You mean since the drowning?"

"Too many people." He waved his arms. "They're rude slobs throwing their garbage and cigarette butts wherever they want. I go a couple of times a year, but only in the winter when the summer people are back where they fucking belong."

He wasn't finished railing on summer people when Eleanor selected the smaller AC, because installing it herself would be more manageable. He looked for the price tag while explaining his theory that the more people on earth, the crazier they were, and to escape the hell of the city, they came up here and ruined things for the locals. He was a young man, not bad looking if his anger hadn't made him appear mentally challenged.

"They're arrogant and they can go fuck themselves."

He carried the AC unit to her car, commenting on the Blazer. "Cool wheels. If you can't install the AC yourself, give me a call and I'll come up after work and install it myself."

"Thanks," she said. "That's considerate of you." She had no intention of calling and asking a questionably sane man to install AC in a cottage where she lived alone with her dog. If he knew her thoughts, he'd think her arrogant, too. And she was an outsider by Gold Strike standards, who could just go fuck herself.

Another ping. A woman wanted to see the house today and had all cash. Eleanor had a half hour before she should return to her desk. She texted the woman back, saying she could meet her in twenty minutes and gave her the address. She headed back down mountain to Rette's.

The prospective tenant gave her an envelope. Eleanor looked inside at the cash.

"Three thousand," she said. "First and last months' rent, plus a security deposit."

"I can't legally collect last month's rent," Eleanor said. "And you do need to fill out an online application. Zillow charges twenty-five dollars."

"No problem." The woman was two inches shorter than Eleanor and stout around the middle, as if she drank too much beer. She wore a flowered cotton shift that came to her knees. Skinny legs, flip-flops. Her brown hair was cut in a bob with highlights framing an ordinary face.

"I'll fill out the form while I'm here," she said.

Eleanor pointed to the brown leather couch that had a tear in the cushion she hadn't seen before. She didn't want to rush the woman. "I'm going outside to clean up a few things while you're doing that. Come and get me when you're finished."

Eleanor retrieved a hammer from the tack shed and nailed the exterior trim back in place. With two whacks, she hammered down the loose porch board. The peeling paint would have to wait. Painters were expensive and she couldn't afford to pay one, and she didn't have time to do it herself. For the second time that day, she understood more deeply why Rette had been so keen on men who were handy at fixing things.

The woman came outside and told Eleanor she'd finished. Eleanor checked the name on the application. Grace Bilbo. Odd name. These days people reinvented themselves, including people who fled from their past lives for a new start in the Sierra Nevada. She couldn't forget, she was one among them.

Grace came outside and scanned the three-acre backyard of mostly pasture and fencing with her hands on her hips. "Do you have horses?"

"I do," said Eleanor. "Two horses. Not here right now. How about you?"

"No." The woman said. "But I love horses. Maybe I'll get one."

"Do you ride?"

"No, but I've always wanted to."

"One of my horses belongs to the woman who owns this place. Sometimes I bring the horses here if it's okay with the tenants."

The woman pondered the suggestion without a trace of enthusiasm. Eleanor assumed her love of horses was conceptual.

"Can I show you the rest of the house?"

"No need," Grace said. "I breezed through while you were outside. I'll take it."

40

LAWRENCE STANDIN OPENED THE PASSENGER side of McKenzie's truck and climbed in. Jerry Ward showed up in polished cowboy boots and hat. He sat in the backseat. Easton hauled five horses in his trailer. Leonard, who insisted on coming, rode with Renee, Easton, and Eleanor. The double cab was thick with uncomfortable energies. Eleanor let go of manipulating the conversation and filling the silence to ease what she perceived as tension between Easton and Leonard, who'd never met each other face-to-face. Leonard knew Easton as the new boyfriend when she hired him to guide her search into the Jarbidge Wilderness and knew Easton now as the father of her coming child. Easton knew Leonard as the guide who abandoned his woman in dangerous wilderness and showed up out of the blue to test his patience.

She tried to let the conversation alone, but the silence was coiled tight as barbed wire.

"Renee," Eleanor ventured. "What does your grandfather plan to do when we get to the river?"

"I don't know," said Renee. "I'm worried, though, about his old bones, and he has a heart condition."

"I didn't know that," she said.

"A good day to die," Leonard said.

"Jeez, Leonard," Renee said. "That's not helpful."

Eleanor searched for another question despite her vow not to. Her mind was blank.

"So, Leonard," said Easton. "What do you do for a living?"

He leaned forward in the backseat. "I run an outdoor adventure store in a place you've never visited."

"Try me."

"Jarbidge in Northeastern Nevada."

Easton glanced in his rear-view mirror. Then he looked over at Eleanor. "Where you went searching for Rette."

"Yup, that's the place," she said.

"She told me about that." Easton stared straight ahead. A truck approached from the opposite direction. He lifted his fingers from the steering wheel in the customary wave.

Eleanor stared out the window at the undulating pastureland. A few cattle lay under the canopy of an oak. The grass was losing its green and an understory of brown threatened to take over. In another month the range would be dry. What remained would have scant nutritional value.

Renee cleared her throat. She spoke of a California tribe who'd saved a cultural site on the California border by doing exactly what they were doing today: bringing project developers to the site, hoping an elder's input would emanate its sacredness and change minds.

"The tribe organized two trips like the one we're taking to educate the BLM on the cultural importance of their sacred mountain. It was taboo for the tribe to talk about their ceremonies, but they broke their taboo and risked death to save the mountain from destruction.

"Their most powerful spirit was born there. Now, it's a protected national historic and cultural site and the people go there to practice their rituals without intrusions."

"What happened to the elders who told the story?" asked Easton.

"Haven't heard," said Renee.

The story hung in the cab's intimate space. Easton reached over and put his hand gently on Eleanor's thigh. Leonard, who sat behind Easton, had closed his eyes.

* * *

Easton helped Lawrence Standin mount up. He adjusted the stirrups and made sure the old man was comfortable without making a big deal about his fleece-lined saddle. Leonard would ride behind Lawrence. Three of the supervisors: Roscoe, Stephanie, and Jim rode in the middle. Eleanor put Renee on Jessie and she rode Fred, who'd be good if Jessie were in front. McKenzie on her buckskin Scotch brought up the rear.

Where was Ward? She called for him.

"I'm here." He emerged from the bush, buckling his belt.

"You can ride the bay mare," she said. "Need a hand up?"

"Nope, I'm good." He shoved his boot in the stirrup and pulled himself up and into the saddle with a grunt.

The first mile was a steep vehicle road. They turned off on a spur trail, where things were pretty at first with the pine needles layered over the dirt beneath. When they hit granite, the horses' metal shoes scraped as they climbed rock that had been blasted decades ago. Jessie stumbled, throwing Renee forward. She gripped the saddle horn and recovered. Ahead, Stephanie's horse balked.

"Kick her," McKenzie shouted.

Steph kicked her heels into the horse's side with no effect. Renee trotted Jessie to the horse's rump and the horse moved ahead.

Ward's mare spooked and skittered sideways. He moved with her and got her back on the vague rock trail with an agility that surprised Eleanor.

As they climbed granite, she gave Fred a loose rein, trusting his footing. The sounds of scraping hooves and creaking leather were somewhat unnerving. Easton took it slow and when they crested the hot, rocky incline and found themselves on sandy level ground, the group's relief was palpable. Stephanie's face was flushed with the heat and excitement. Lawrence seemed comfortable, as if the memory of former riding days were returning, seen in his heels and the way he rested with his palms stacked on the saddle horn, holding the reins, shoulders slouched, back straight. The panoramic view was something a person couldn't imagine without boots on the ground, or in this case, horses.

High country peaks were snow-capped. The air was cool and clean, but in the distant west, a brown layer hung over the agricultural lands.

Fred snatched for grass as Easton led a single file descent to the other side. When they arrived at the base of the mountain slope, the path softened into a glen of leafy green willows. A curtain of aspen by the river rattled as leaves pivoted on their stems. Renee turned in her saddle and smiled at Eleanor.

At the river, a horizontal line of bright yellow pollen stained the boulders, marking the high-water mark, roughly a foot above the present flow. Scraggly plant debris hung from overhanging branches. At a shallow gravel spot in the river, Easton led them across, single file. The luscious splash of hooves stepping on stones soothed her mind until Fred pawed the water, considering a roll. Eleanor pulled up his head and pressed him across the shallows onto the shore, trotting up the short dirt bank.

This side of the river was lush with tall grass and purple clover. Honeybees, bumblebees and small native bees filled their proboscises, oblivious of the passing intruders. Easton led the group into a grove of cedar.

"We'll tie up here," he said. "Take your time. McKenzie and I will give you a hand."

Eleanor dismounted and held Fred's halter rope. She asked Renee if she needed help.

"We'll see." Renee leaned forward and swung her leg over the cantle and down to the dirt.

Lawrence's hips were stiff, and he struggled to raise his right leg high enough to clear the horse's rump. Eleanor stood by and eased his leg over the horse. Leonard stood on the opposite side as Lawrence lowered himself toward the ground, one hand on the horn and other on the cantle. He couldn't bend his stirrup knee enough to reach the ground.

"Fall into me, Grandfather, I have you." Leonard had his hands at Lawrence's waist when Lawrence let go of the horn, fell back and piled on top of Leonard, both landing in the dirt. The supervisors turned quickly from their conversations and stared. Renee put out a hand to Lawrence and pulled him to his knees. Leonard rose quickly. He shoved his arms under the old man and hoisted him to his feet. Eleanor dusted the old man off, and they stood for a few moments, watching Lawrence walk to the horse. He grabbed his bundle from the saddle bag and went about setting up the meeting.

Eleanor and Renee led the horses to the shallows. Both horses drank. Eleanor let go of Fred's reins. He wasn't going anywhere with so much ripe grass and Jessie beside him. In the quiet, the buzzing seemed louder. A woodpecker tapped the deadwood of a snag. A series of knocks came from the top of a pine.

"What is that?" asked Eleanor.

"A grouse," said Renee. "That's their mating call. If we startle him, he has the potential to attack us. Just saying."

The two women stood quietly, staring at the river, comfortable with their own thoughts.

"How does this compare?" Renee asked, startling Eleanor from her reverie.

"To what?"

"Every other place you've been."

"This is pretty high up there."

"Compared to the beach?"

"Santa Cruz? I miss the cool nights, the sparkle on the bay in fall when the sun's low."

"How'd you make a living?"

"I wrote for the newspaper."

"You survived in one of the most expensive places per square footage in the country by writing for a local newspaper?"

"With an ocean view. My ex is a dot-com-er."

"Hard to leave?"

"Look around. This is beautiful."

"Why here?"

"Slower, and I always wanted a horse. The sad part? I wasted more than a decade of my life with him. I thought we'd raise a family, but, contrary to what he told me, he didn't want kids. I'd have left sooner if he'd been honest, which he wasn't." She turned and told Renee about his secret vasectomy.

"He convinced me I was infertile."

Renee's solemn expression affirmed the violation and rather than validating Eleanor, the truth of the harm done opened old wounds.

"He used to call me a brute."

"You're the furthest thing from a brute. What did he mean by that?"

"He didn't like the way I moved or the sound of my voice." She shrugged.

"Probably didn't like the sound of any woman's voice. Women with a hint of authority probably challenge his fragile sense of male authority."

Eleanor caressed her belly. "Turns out I'm plenty fertile. I'm pregnant."

"Easton?"

They smiled.

Renee pointed out the dark pebbles laying on the riverbed, the burble of crystal-clear water over rock.

"Breathe this air," she said. "Good for you and your baby."

Eleanor closed her eyes and tilted her face to the sun. She inhaled the river air and listened to the water cleanse her mind.

Her eyes opened. "Do you smell that?"

Renee tilted her neck and sniffed. "What?"

"Smoke."

"I don't smell smoke." She picked up the horses' lead ropes and handed Fred's to Eleanor and started back. "Let's see if Grandpa's ready for us."

Lawrence had thrown down his blanket on top of the damp meadow grass and stared at the ground. McKenzie and Stephanie stood on either side of him.

Renee laughed. "He's afraid once he sits down, he won't be able to get up."

Lawrence gazed at his granddaughter. "That's not it," he said. "I'm afraid of heights. It's a long way down."

Easton brought over a folding chair.

"You're a problem-solver," Lawrence said to Easton.

Leonard had gathered downed wood and was building a campfire. His face gleamed with sweat. Lawrence was dry as a weed even though he still wore his red flannel jacket with colorful stitching over his thermal.

"Leonard," said Renee. "We need a permit to build a fire."

"I took one out," said Eleanor.

McKenzie offered Lawrence water, which he drank. The rest of the group milled about. Lawrence held up a large abalone shell. He handed the shell and sage bundle to Leonard, who kept a small flame under the bundle until a curl of smoke rose. He went to Stephanie, fanning the smoke over her face with an eagle feather and around to her back, her shoulders, and down to her ankles. He stepped up to Elman and did the same. Elman closed his eyes and held up his arms. Leonard repeated the ritual for each member of the group, and they sat down in a circle with small groans except for McKenzie, who lowered herself in one graceful motion to the foot of Lawrence's lawn chair.

Leonard said a prayer in his mother tongue. Eleanor glanced at Renee and thought she looked radiant. Lawrence pulled out his pipe and smoked sweet tobacco as the river played its song of moving water through the meadow.

Lawrence thanked everyone for bringing him up here. He hadn't been here since he was a boy fishing, he said, and hunting deer with his own grandfather. He said they'd come here every season to gather acorns. Eleanor recalled the abundance of fallen acorns on that morning ride with Easton. The acorn he'd given her still sat on the windowsill in front of her office desk to remind her of their time together, not far downriver from where they were now. She remembered the fear that had overcome her and how her trust won as she sat astride him and let down her hair. When she looked across the fire, Easton was watching her.

You're smiling, he mouthed.

The fish.

Wood smoke spiraled from the small fire. A breeze carried it westerly.

"This was our acorn camp," Lawrence began. "*Chaw'se* you call grinding rocks where the women pounded acorns and made acorn soup. We fished from the river. Drank her water. We shared this field we're sittin' on with the horses. Not ours. Nobody's. We didn't have livestock because we lived on deer, elk, rabbit. I don't know what happened to those horses. They were pretty to look at. Way before my youth, the men went dancing somewhere far off from here and the women stayed, doin' their work, taking care of kids. Everything as it should be. There was a skirmish down mountain and a French gold miner was killed. Those men wanted revenge. They showed up with guns and started shooting every man, woman, and child they could. Hung the babies in their cradles from these trees to die. The survivors are my ancestors."

"Do you hear children?" Stephanie asked.

"I would, but I'm old and my hearing is poor," Lawrence said.

"They're laughing. And women are singing."

"Those are the children who played in this place," he said, "while their mothers worked."

Elman placed a hand on Stephanie's shoulder.

"My friend Elman," said Lawrence, "hopes that by touching you the sound will come through to him. Is that right Elman?"

Elman took out his handkerchief, blew his nose, and wiped his eyes.

A voice broke in. Elman put down his kerchief, and Lawrence turned stiffly to locate the disturbance. McKenzie stood quickly, protective of Lawrence, and Leonard put his hand to his hip, as if he were about to pull out a weapon.

Adelia Shepherd, dressed in uniform khakis and breathing hard, stood at the edge of their circle. "You have to evacuate. Now."

"What's going on?" demanded Renee.

"We have a wildfire over the ridge," she said. "You're not safe."

"How do we get out?" Ward asked.

"Not the same way you came in," said Adelia. "The fire's coming from the south and moving this way."

"Let's get the hell out of here," Ward said.

"Calm down," said Renee. "What's the protocol?"

"A rescue helicopter's coming in from the Columbia Airport, next county over," she said.

Lawrence stood from his lawn chair and straightened. "Looks like the white man is at it again."

41

EASTON UNBUCKLED CHESTER'S SADDLEBAG AND pulled out a coil of rope. A billowing white cloud rose behind the ridge in the direction they'd ridden from. Stephanie, her arms wrapped around her chest, exchanged words with Elman and Tindale. Ward headed for the bushes he'd visited earlier.

Easton was on his radio shouting their location when Adelia walked up to him.

"Chopper's on its way," said Adelia. "We'll lift each of you, one at a time. We can't take the horses."

"I'm taking the horses out," Easton said. "I'll drive them up the high trail and circle down to the pack station." He looked at Eleanor. "You're going with them. I'll be okay."

She wasn't sure about that, any of it. Not sure she'd go in the helicopter. Not sure he'd be okay. Not sure anyone would be okay. She looked up at the unmistakable sound of the whumping blades of a helicopter. The red nose appeared above the canopy of trees like a giant sky bug emerging from its chrysalis. It flew a wide circle and descended, but there was no space for it to safely land, so it hovered while a crewman was lowered from the helicopter on a cable attached to an exterior winch. He unfastened his harness and spoke a few words to Easton before selecting Lawrence as the first rescue. Lawrence shook his head, refusing, and offered Stephanie. The crewman helped her into the harness, and Eleanor watched as Stephanie was hoisted upward toward the chopper.

The sound of the blades was deafening, and Eleanor's hair whipped her eyes.

McKenzie stepped up to Easton and shouted, "I'm going with you."

"I need you to say with these people," he said.

She waved her arm toward where the horses were still tied in the grove. "I won't leave Scotch. I'm riding out with you."

"Alright."

"So am I," said Eleanor. "I'm going with you."

"No." Easton was firm. "You're taking the chopper, Lee." He pulled her close. "You have to go, please." He kissed her neck and smelled like sage.

"Lawrence goes next," said Leonard.

"No. My granddaughter first."

The ground man held the harness, and she stepped into it.

"I can't do this," Renee exclaimed. "I really am afraid of heights." Her skin blanched and her lips thinned.

"You got that from me, Granddaughter," said Lawrence. "The height will not kill you. The fire will." His hat blew off and tumbled toward the river. He let it go. "Close your eyes. Let these folks do their job."

The cable tightened and Renee shrieked. She shut her eyes and gripped the cable. Her feet left the ground and she ascended.

Adelia stood on the sidelines, appearing serious and regarding everything and everyone but Eleanor, whom she ignored.

Eleanor walked up to her. "How'd you know we'd be here?"

"We checked permits as soon as the fire was reported." She pulled open her vest and brought out a copy of the permit Eleanor had filled out. In that moment, Eleanor glanced at Adelia's open vest and saw the sidearm holstered under her arm.

"You have a gun," Eleanor said. "I'm not leaving if you have a gun." She scanned the group for Easton. He was talking to McKenzie now.

"Easton." Her voice didn't carry over the helicopter.

Adelia put a firm hand on Eleanor's shoulder. "Haven't you noticed? Every time I'm at a fire, a dead woman shows up."

* * *

As the distance between her and Easton lengthened, she felt increasingly desperate until someone was unfastening her harness and guiding her to a seat in the chopper. She was sobbing.

"What's wrong?" asked Renee. "You're worse than I am."

"She has a gun," Eleanor said. "I saw it. It's illegal for a Forest Service employee to carry a firearm during a fire."

Leonard was inside the chopper now and sat beside her. "I saw the gun."

The chopper lifted, angled sharply, and circled. Eleanor strained to see below.

"Your ole man's on Chester." Leonard's deep voice rose above the noise. "He's ponying the horses, and McKenzie has the rear with the rest lined up between them. That forest ranger with the gun is riding your horse."

"She's going to kill them."

He shook his head. "She's not."

The smoke had thickened. The co-pilot Jake was reporting three adults—a male and two females—traveling south on horseback out the upper Bear River trail, destination: the pack station.

Jake turned in his seat and shouted above the roar of the engine. "Easton knows this country better than anyone. They'll be okay."

Why did everyone say that? She wasn't okay. Easton was outriding a fire, McKenzie with him, "and I'm pregnant."

Grandfather handed his pack to Eleanor. "Hold this."

She clutched the bag and closed her eyes.

"Where's Jerry Ward?" shouted Stephanie.

Eleanor scanned the compartment and didn't see him.

"The dude with the attitude?" Leonard unbuckled his seat belt, leaned forward, and grabbed Jake's shoulder. Jake lifted his headphones and Leonard yelled, "We left someone back at the site."

Jake relayed the message to the pilot and the helicopter U-turned sharply. A surge of vertigo came over Eleanor. She dry-heaved and the helicopter circled and dropped into the thickening smoke.

Jake shouted Ward's name through a loudspeaker. The air was hot and visibility poor. Eleanor couldn't imagine how, if Jerry was below, they could discern him or how he could hear his name over the sound of the chopper.

The pilot circled once more, and with no sign of a human below, he took off toward the small plane airport on the north side of the next county.

* * *

The billowing cloud of smoke stretched across the mountains where, an hour ago, Lawrence told stories by the river and Stephanie heard spirits. The blaze would engulf the place, if it hadn't already. It would be days before the blaze was under control. The trees would be scorched to blackened spears, creatures burned alive. The spirits might survive. They'd survived this far, and Easton and McKenzie on the run—her thoughts hit the wall at Jake's pronouncement:

"We've lost their location." He held up his iPad and pointed to the topo map. "Here's where we evacuated your group. The pack station is here. Here's where we lost their location. No sign of them or the horses."

"They're likely passing through rock," Leonard told Eleanor before she could protest.

"I told you," Eleanor said. "She's a sick woman and she has a gun."

Her phone pinged. A text had come in from Mac. Mac rarely texted. *Reliable sources just confirmed Adelia Shepherd's the witness who saw Gunderson go over the falls. Sheriff named her a person of interest.*

"Oh, fuck."

"What is it?" asked Leonard.

"That forest service woman is a murder suspect, which means she started the fire because she wanted the body to be found."

"That doesn't make sense to anyone but you," Renee said.

"Doesn't matter," said Leonard. "I get it. When we land, we'll go find them."

Jake threw his keys to Leonard. "My Jeep's parked in front of the hangar. Black."

"Thanks, man."

The chopper was descending.

* * *

Leonard drove twenty miles over the speed limit, which wasn't fast enough for Eleanor, who navigated. Otherwise, they were quiet until they arrived at the pack station. A couple of horses were saddled and tied on the outside rail. Annie came out to the porch. They updated her and she offered a vehicle.

"Too loud," said Leonard. "And not accessible."

"Take the horses," Annie said.

"I can travel faster by myself," he said.

"I'm going with you," Eleanor said.

"Any two you want." Annie pointed to the rail.

Leonard took the big bay and she picked a muscled gray.

"Two things, Eleanor W.," he said. "Stop when you need to catch your breath. I won't be looking back. Two, when we're close, we get off the horses and walk. Got that?"

She reined the horse forward and kicked him. He reared once and took off galloping, running until she reached the end of the dirt road and hit the trail. She caught her breath and waited for Leonard to catch up.

They kept the horses at a slow lope and intermittent walks until they passed the first fork in the trail, where it dropped down to the Bear River. The flow was too high and fast to cross, so Leonard charged up the bank and bushwhacked, the horses' hooves digging in. Eleanor had been right about this horse. He was strong and had heart. The air had become gauzy with smoke. Ash fell like snow. They continued until coming to a blasted granite trail etched into the granite monolith. It was wide enough for one horse and the drop was straight down. The horses were used to the trail, but it was early in the season, and they likely hadn't crossed this year. She took a breath and single-file-followed Leonard's lead. They took it slow, and, after what seemed like an eternity, reached the other side and continued toward the large grove of cedar on the next higher ridge.

Leonard dismounted and led the horse to the shade of a sugar pine.

"We're bushwhacking," he said. "How are you holding up? I want an honest answer."

"I'm okay if we find them. No pain, no cramps. I'm not tired."

"It's adrenaline." Without a word, he helped her down from the horse. He removed bridles and saddles and blankets and stashed them in the brush.

He took a right angle off the trail, and they clawed their way up the mountainside, slippery with duff. He reached a granite outcropping and scrambled up its face. He put out his hand.

"Grab my wrist."

He pulled Eleanor up to him, and she followed his trail of holds to just below the top, where he reached down to hoist her aloft. The three-sixty view was blocked to the east, where the highest ridge uplifted, and a fringe of orange flames glowed hungrily through smoke.

He flattened himself on the rock and pulled a small pair of binoculars from his vest pocket. She lay down. The rock was warm but hard and made her aware of her thickening womb. She rolled to her side and breathed to calm her body. A wave of guilt passed through her. She pushed it aside for later when the adrenaline wore off and her body, she knew, would hurt to move.

"What do you know about this girl McKenzie?" he asked, turning his head to look back at her.

"She's perfect. Her boyfriend's a rookie firefighter, top of his class."

"Does he know she's here?"

"Possibly."

A perfect ash of black oak leaf landed on her arm as if the spirit world acknowledged her answer. She flicked it off. Leonard crept on his elbows to the edge and looked through the binoculars, turning his head to scan the forest. He held still.

"Do you see them?" Eleanor remained on her side, her arm cushioning her head, her other hand caressing her stomach.

"No. Not yet. I'm looking for color or movement. There."

He handed the binoculars to Eleanor. "Look for the red."

As she crawled to the edge, she remembered McKenzie had been wearing a red bandana They were a good twenty feet above ground. She took the binoculars. It took her a few to focus.

"I see it."

He took back the binoculars. "In the distance, three in a clearing. Could be Easton and McKenzie facing us. A third with their back to us." He passed the glasses to Eleanor. "Do you recognize the third?"

Easton came into focus, and she was seized with fear. McKenzie was next to him. "I can't tell who the third is."

"What's the third doing?"

"Standing."

"What else?"

"I don't know what you're asking."

"Describe exactly what you're seeing, and I'll make sense of it."

"One arm straight. One bent at the elbow. Elbow moving, like jerking. It's a gun."

"Roger that."

She handed the glasses back to Leonard.

He rolled onto his back. "Here's what we're going to do. When I say 'up' you're going to stand until your old man spots you, then get down flat. We're doing this fast."

"Okay."

"Stand, get his attention, drop. He'll look up startled. The third person will turn to see what he's looking at. I'll take it from there. Repeat."

Leonard stuck his hand inside his black leather vest and pulled out a pistol with a scope.

"I stand, get Easton's attention, drop."

"I take my shot."

"What if you miss?"

"I don't miss."

Leonard rolled onto his belly, leveled his gun, looked through the small scope, and took aim. "Ready?"

"Yes."

"When Easton sees you, drop."

"Got it."

"Ready?"

"Ready."

"Up."

She lifted herself from the rock and stood. She couldn't see the spot.

"I can't see him. How can he see me?"

"Here's what I want you to do. When I say, 'shout,' shout his name. I can see him. When I say drop, you drop flat. Repeat."

"When you say 'shout,' I shout Easton's name. When you say 'drop,' I hug the rock."

"You got this. Ready?"

"Ready."

"Shout."

"Easton!" she screamed and waited a beat.

"Drop."

She dropped and lay flat. The air exploded. Her hearing went numb. Leonard scrambled off the rock. She looked over the edge. He was down the cliff in seconds and hit the ground running.

She smoothed her hands over her stomach, promising she'd make it up to the life inside her as she inched her way down the gentler slope of the boulder.

42

WITH HIS BOOT, LEONARD SHOVED the person lying on the ground onto his back. Jerry Ward.

His shoulder bled and he groaned in agony.

"He shot Adelia." McKenzie straddled her legs for balance as Leonard cut the ropes binding her wrists.

"Why is he even here?" asked Eleanor.

"He had the runs and missed the airlift." Easton had a gash on his left cheek and a line of blood dripped from his jaw to the ground. "He showed up out of the blue and Adelia pulled her sidearm. Ward disarmed her and shot her with her own gun."

"Dumb fuck," said Leonard.

"Is she alive?" asked Eleanor.

"She was when we left her."

McKenzie let out a piercing whistle and hollered, "Scotch."

Easton pulled back his arms to give Leonard slack. "She's a few hundred yards back up the trail. Jerry, here, had to figure out what to do with the two of us, who'd witnessed him shoot a woman. Didn't look promising."

Leonard put away his knife and handed Eleanor the pistol he'd used to shoot Ward.

The gun was heavy, and she needed both hands to hold it.

McKenzie let out another ear-splitting whistle. The sound of pounding hooves grew louder, and seconds later the buckskin ran into the opening and came to a halt in front of McKenzie. She rubbed his face and kissed his cheek. Buried her face in his neck. Chester came up behind and Leonard glanced at Easton.

"Yeah," said Easton. "Take him."

Leonard threw a leg over the horse, turned, and took off, and Eleanor kept the gun pointed at Ward's groaning pile-of-shit body as Easton hogtied him. When finished, he gently removed the gun from Eleanor's hands and gave it over to McKenzie.

"Just in case." He guided Eleanor to a nearby pine, helped her slide down to sitting, and sat beside her. She lay her head on his chest to feel his voice as he told his side of things.

* * *

Annie's expression as she drove the ATV toward their group of bedraggled humans and sagging horses remained stoic, despite the sight of Adelia humped over the saddle horn and bleeding.

"What happened to the ranger?"

"Shot," said Easton. "By the guy in charge of the dam project. Got a bullet in him, too, but we left him up mountain."

"Alive?"

"Barely."

"I called 911 soon as I saw y'all coming," Annie said. "I'll call again and request a heli to pull him out."

They followed her to the lodge, where she told them to go inside the restaurant and have a meal. Eleanor wasn't hungry.

"The Fire Academy students are here," Annie said. "They're eating before they go out and clear brush around the pack station."

Chad came out onto the porch dressed in his yellow bunker gear. McKenzie saw him and passed her horse's reins to Eleanor. She ran across the dirt yard and clambered up the wooden stairs into his arms. He swung her in a circle and set her down, brushed back her hair. "Mitzi," he said. They kissed.

Eleanor led Scotch and Jessie to the long rail by the corral as Easton tied the rest of the horses. Leonard set up Adelia in a wicker lounge chair on the porch. Annie brought her blankets despite the heat. No way to tell if the bleeding was internal until she got to the hospital. Leonard remained in the matching chair beside her, waiting on the ambulance as Easton walked up to him and put out his hand.

"Thanks, man."

Eleanor held Lawrence's gaze wordlessly, conveying her gratitude with an energy she was sure he could feel.

McKenzie and Chad walked down the porch steps arm in arm. Eleanor stood in the doorframe and watched them head toward the river. Chad must have known McKenzie would be upriver on the field trip. He must've been worried sick when hearing about the fire. So why eat lunch with his crew instead of breaking out to find her?

Eleanor poked her head inside and found Annie handing plates of burgers and fries to the novices. "Annie," she said. "I'm heading to the river."

"Hold on," she said. "I'll give you a ride." She wiped her hands on her apron and threw the apron on the counter.

Eleanor climbed into the ATV. Easton swung into the back. "What are you up to?" he asked.

"I have a bad feeling."

"About what?"

She hesitated. "Those two." She pointed to Chad and McKenzie, who'd entered the trees near the river.

Annie climbed behind the wheel and sped parallel to the meadow, stopping at the end of the path. Chad and McKenzie, partially hidden by willows, stood on the riverbank overlooking the raging water.

"What are they doing there?" asked Annie. "The bank is undermined. It won't hold their weight."

Eleanor swung out of the vehicle and sprinted, yelling, "Get back from the edge."

McKenzie turned with a look of surprise. "What's wrong?" and walked toward her. Chad grabbed her arm and pulled her back. She wrested free and the bank collapsed. Chad disappeared. He resurfaced downriver, thrashing in the weight of his firefighter gear until the rapids rammed him into exposed tree roots that stretched into the whitewater like tentacles. He clung to a root as the rapids pelted his face.

Eleanor ran along the bank after McKenzie, who was already halfway across a fallen log that spanned the river. She lay down on her belly, and when Chad's strength gave out and he was swept through the roots into fast water, she lowered her arms and readied herself for him.

As he approached, about to pass beneath her, he held up an arm and managed to grab her wrist and hold on. His weight proved too much for McKenzie. She was pulled off the log into the river and rose struggling for air while Chad, panicked, grabbed onto her for buoyancy.

Downriver Easton stood on the last granite boulder before a slot where the rapids accelerated and crashed into a minefield of rock. He held a coil of rope he'd fashioned into a lariat and waited. The victims came down fast, and the paramedic tossed his bag into the river, shouting, as McKenzie fought off Chad and missed the save. Easton threw the rope, looping their shoulders, and backed off the rock, bracing himself against its edge. The paramedic joined in, and they pulled the two closer until the loop slipped. Easton yanked tight, securing McKenzie's wrist, and Chad climbed on top of her, scrambling to save himself.

When they lifted her from the river, she was unconscious. Chad lay in the dirt coughing and puking. The paramedic pinched McKenzie's nose, covered her lips with his own, and blew air into her mouth. Her chest rose and sunk. He blew again. And again. Leonard stood on the bank, watching.

* * *

Three ambulances were on the scene. Chad sat on the back of one, peeling off his firefighter pants. The paramedic draped a gray blanket over his bare shoulders, and Easton, arms crossed in a skeptic's pose, hovered over him.

Adelia had lost a lot of blood. Eleanor walked beside her as the paramedics carried her on a gurney down from the front porch of the lodge to the second ambulance.

"Adelia," she said. "Why did Jerry Ward shoot you?"

The oxygen mask placed over her mouth had steamed up, and Eleanor couldn't decipher what she was saying.

"Could you hold up a second?" she asked the paramedics.

They halted and she leaned in toward Adelia. "What are you trying to say?"

Adelia lifted her mask. "Is that bastard dead?"

"Which one?"

"The man who followed us. He took my gun."

"He was alive when they airlifted him out."

"Did he kill anyone?"

"He almost killed you."

"He was going to kill the girl. I tried to stop him."

Eleanor thought she may have misjudged, that it was possible Adelia was not the executioner but the avenger, desperate to stop the next murder. She grabbed Eleanor's arm and motioned for her to come closer. "Is she alive?"

The hair rose on Eleanor's neck as she recalled how it had taken the paramedic five long minutes of mouth-to-mouth before McKenzie heaved water. Her wet clothes had been removed, and she was wrapped in dry blankets. One of the paramedics, who knew her from high school, had coaxed bits of energy bar into her mouth. "She's in the ambulance now being treated for hypothermia and shock. She nearly drowned. But she's alive."

43

IT HAD BEEN A ROUGH day, and all they wanted was to go home. They asked Leonard to give them a ride in Jake's Jeep down mountain to her cottage.

They were tired, and words relieved the tension as they drove down the twisted two-lane mountain road.

"What were you saying to Chad at the ambulance?" Eleanor asked.

"It wasn't what I said," said Easton. "It's what I was trying to figure out—whether he intentionally tried to drown McKenzie or if his actions showed the true character of a pile of bear shit."

"What'd you decide?" asked Leonard.

"Bear shit. He used his girlfriend as a flotation device."

"He panicked," said Eleanor. "It happens."

"That river showed everyone what kind of man he really is under his good-looking surface," said Easton. "In a moment of crisis, he didn't care about anyone but himself, and if I know McKenzie's dad, he'll go after that dude and that'll be the end of McKenzie and Chad."

"What about Jerry Ward, holding you at gunpoint?" Leonard asked. "What kind of man is he under the surface?"

"He shot Adelia. Intentionally or not, he did it in front of two witnesses and freaked out when his life detoured to hell before his very eyes. A man like Ward who thinks he can stop a wild river from flowing but is too weak to own up to the weight of his mistakes has serious flaws."

Eleanor reached from the back over the passenger seat and took Easton's hand as they descended the mountain. She loved his hands. They were strong, capable hands and the skin of his palms were surprisingly soft considering his lifetime of physical work. Like his heart, soft on the inside. They passed the turn off to the far side of the Little Bear River where the coyote woman had witnessed the killer dispose of Marisol. Further down, they approached the Brown's Ferry Reservoir turnoff, and Eleanor strained to see beyond the conifers at the edge of the road to the charred remains of wildfire.

"In Chad's defense, he did work this fire," Eleanor said.

"Whoever started that fire probably knew something about putting it out," said Easton. "Overtime."

* * *

Leonard pulled into the mobile home park. He kept the truck in neutral and waited until Easton and Eleanor scuffed their way across the lawn and opened the cottage door. Eleanor turned to wave, but Leonard was already turning onto the road.

Granite. She'd left him with Sheriff Duncan's wife. She called and asked if the dog could stay with them overnight. Mrs. Duncan had already heard about the fire and set Eleanor's mind at ease with an "of course, no rush, Granite's in good hands, take care of yourself." She heard Granite's bark in the background, felt a pang of guilt, and let it go.

She and Easton peeled off their dirty clothes, threw them in a pile, and took a shower together, lathering each other, and toweled dry. They flopped down on the bed naked and climbed under the covers, falling into a sleep fit for the dead.

They woke when the sun crested the mountain, and the first shaft of light beamed through the treetops into Eleanor's bedroom skylight.

She stifled a groan when she rolled over to spoon Easton's back. Her entire body ached from the previous day's exertion. She stretched her arms to embrace him and winced from the pain in her shoulder where Leonard had pulled her more than once to the next fissure.

"Lee?"

He'd have something to say about the risk and what drove a woman to ride headlong into a fire and foul play when she was carrying her first child. He gathered her in his arms, and she smothered herself in his chest. The image of McKenzie drowning overlaid feelings of the flesh.

He didn't speak of recent events while they held each other. When they fumbled about her small kitchen making toast and brewing coffee, he talked about the horses. But the coffee quickened things.

"I'd say we did our share of rescuing yesterday," Easton said.

She rubbed the sleep from the corners of her eyes. "Yep, I think we're good for the rest of the year."

He slugged his coffee and wiped his mouth. She buttered her toast and put a spoonful of marmalade on top.

"What do you say we go down to the Rancheria and see how Lawrence Standin is doing today?"

"Good idea."

* * *

Lawrence leaned into a life-sized wooden carving of a coyote, chiseling a whisker on its long canine nose when they walked up his driveway into his converted garage. His hand brushed off the wood shavings before greeting them.

"How goes it, you two?" Lawrence said. "Glad to see you made it out unscathed."

"We're pretty good, all things considered," said Easton. "We wanted to check on you and tell you how sorry we are you took us up there to teach us about the place and chaos broke out."

"How are you feeling after yesterday?" asked Eleanor.

"Trail ride was fine. Stephanie made it worth the sore sit bones, and that lift to the heli? Good view of the fire."

"I'm so sorry, Lawrence," said Eleanor. "All your effort to save that place from human greed and a wildfire ruins it."

Lawrence leaned back. "Did it?"

He moved the carving so the coyote faced Eleanor.

"His eyes are so intense," she said. "He's looking right at me."

Granite growled.

"Easy boy," said Easton.

"Now sit over there." He pointed to a plastic deck chair, and she walked to the chair and sat down.

She gazed at the coyote, in awe.

"He's still looking at me."

Lawrence turned the carving back to face him and sanded the rough edge of the animal's listening ear.

"Just shows we expect things to be one way," he said, "but the next moment is unlike any before it and all things are possible."

"What are you saying, Lawrence?" Easton placed his hand gently on Lawrence's shoulder.

He blew on the coyote's ear and a little puff of dust flew from the wood and lost itself in the fresh air. "That forest fire went around the meadow."

44

LAWRENCE'S CLAIM WAS CONFIRMED BY the Forest Service fire investigator, who determined that the meadow at the proposed dam site where the supervisors had gathered the week before was too wet to burn. Jerry Ward sat in county jail awaiting trial for shooting Adelia. The Sheriff's office had no evidence of connecting him with the deaths of Marisol or Cleo. Ward's mother resigned from the Water Board and quickly moved to Modesto.

Eleanor was writing up mother-and-son Ward stories when a call came in from Sheriff Duncan.

"I need you to come down to the ER and identify someone."

"Who?"

"Don't want to predispose you."

"Okay. On my way."

* * *

The nurse led Eleanor to a curtained room. Behind the curtain Sheriff Duncan and Deputy Perelli stood at the bedside of an old woman. She was hooked up to an IV and appeared have scrapes and contusions on her face and arms.

"Do you know her?" asked Perelli.

"I gave her a ride to Walmart. She needed to buy formula for a litter of coyote pups," said Eleanor. "Someone had shot the mother coyote in what looked like a drive by. She's the woman who left the rod across from the crime scene. What happened?"

"Someone attacked her," said Duncan. "We found her at the county line passed out and near dead beside the river."

"Do you know her name, Wooley?" asked Perelli.

"I only met her twice and she never gave me her name."

"Did you ask?"

"Yes, I asked. She has trust issues."

Perelli shook his head. "Lucky we got there before the coyotes ate her."

"You saw the coyotes?"

"Five of them. Young ones. All howling."

"They weren't going to eat her. They were waiting for her to feed them." She noticed the zip tie around the woman's wrist attached to the bedrail. "Why's she cuffed to the bed?"

"Perelli," said Duncan. "Why is she cuffed?"

"Person of interest."

"We don't cuff people of interest."

"Sir, she's 5150 and the closest thing to a witness we've had."

"Remove the cuff, Deputy."

Perelli pulled a small cutter out of his back pocket and sliced the tie. Eleanor took the woman's arm from above her head and held it. Her hand was filthy and clenched tightly into an arthritic fist.

"Do you know what happened to her?" Eleanor asked.

"Not sure. She's hasn't woken up."

Eleanor stared at the poor woman, whom she'd last talked to at the laundromat. The nurse came in and checked the women's vitals and changed her IV.

"Is there anything I can do for her?" Eleanor asked.

"Sure." She checked the IV drip. "A cool washcloth on her forehead might break her fever."

Eleanor brought over the chair and set it close to the woman. She bent over and whispered, "Hey, Coyote Woman, it's me, Eleanor Wooley. You need to get well for your pups."

The Sheriff and Perelli left the room and stood in the hallway out of hearing range. The nurse brought in a washcloth and a kidney-shaped plastic bowl full of cool water. Eleanor dipped the cloth, wrung it out, and lay it on the woman's forehead. Her feverish skin quickly warmed the cloth. She repeated the process, drawing the heat until the fever broke. The woman's eyes opened, glazed and fearful.

"You." She moved her fisted hand to her chest. "Open it."

Eleanor was unsure what the woman meant. "Open what?"

She thumped her hand on her chest and Eleanor's best guess was she wanted Eleanor to open her fist. She pulled back a brittle finger. The finger was so rigid and fragile she feared it would snap.

The woman grimaced and her lips rolled back from her gums, revealing missing dentures. "Open."

Eleanor tried again. She pried back a finger and once that was down she laid out the next. Embedded in the palm was something gold. She pulled down another finger and saw a fine line of blood surrounded a cross where the edges had cut into her flesh. Eleanor looked around the room for tissue and seeing none applied the washcloth to the cut.

The woman exhaled a long breath and died.

45

ELEANOR WALKED SLOWLY TOWARD THE round pen where Easton lunged his horse, Chester. The gelding's rich brown coat shone in the sun as he loped in a circle. She climbed the fence and sat on the top rung, hooking her boots under the lower rung.

"Do you see his topline soften and round?" Easton asked.

"I think so."

"He's relaxed." Easton lowered his arm. Chester stopped and faced him, then walked up to Easton for praise. "Good boy." Easton walked toward Eleanor with similar submissiveness, his head down because she knew if he looked up, he'd grin like a fool.

He squeezed between her knees and kissed her belly. "How's my girl?"

"Happy," she said.

Chester plodded over to Easton and nudged his back, bumping him closer to Eleanor.

They laughed. "Go on, git." Easton swung his arm to stave off the horse when something caught his eye, and his smile vanished. Eleanor turned. The Sheriff's SUV passed through the gate and drove so slowly across the dirt yard she heard the tires crunch pebbles. Easton slipped through the fence rails and Eleanor leaned into his outstretched arms to get down. Hand in hand they neared the car until Sheriff Duncan got out. Granite walked up to Duncan wagging his entire back end. Duncan acknowledged the dog with a vague pat on the head.

He offered his hand. "Easton." He tipped his hat at Eleanor. "Hello, Eleanor. It's gonna be a hot one."

"What brings you out here, Sheriff?" Easton asked.

"Bad news, I'm afraid," he said.

"Why?" said Eleanor. "What's going on?"

The men looked at each other.

"I haven't told her," Easton said.

"Better you tell her."

"Tell me what?"

"They're bringing me up on charges for stealing government property and trespassing."

"The horses?"

"Afraid so. They have me on video."

"I was there, too," she said.

"Lee, stop."

"Sheriff, we didn't steal anybody's horses. We freed them from a gruesome death."

"I didn't hear that," said Duncan.

Easton crossed his arms and scuffed a boot in the dirt. "So Sheriff, I have a request."

"What's that, son?"

"If you could push forward the court date so I can bring my cows down mountain I'd appreciate it. It's too much without me present to round up the cows, and we can't leave them up there for the winter. Forest Service wants them out by September."

Duncan nodded. "I'll see if I can pull the strings and delay the hearing for good reason. Meanwhile, you might want to pack a small bag. If you have any medications or such, be sure to bring them when the time comes."

Duncan got in his SUV while Easton and Eleanor walked to the house. She took a backward glance and watched an indifferent sort of dust rise from the earth as he drove off.

* * *

Easton opened the hall closet and took out a small duffle, already packed.

"You knew this was happening?"

"Hoped it wasn't. But the time's come. You coming up mountain for the roundup? I could use your help."

"Of course." She was too shocked to cry. Instead, she went into the kitchen to make a new pot of coffee. She stood by the sink, staring out the small bay window holding an empty glass coffeepot, trying to remember what she was doing. From the window, she saw two mares in the field with their babies. She'd never seen horses out this window before. Easton slipped his arms around her waist, rested his chin on her shoulder.

"Pretty, aren't they?"

"I never noticed them in that patch of field."

"It's a small window. Easy to miss the horses."

"I'm so worried about you, Easton."

She gazed a while longer, desperate to keep his chest on her back, his breath in her hair, and the light stubble of his chin on her skin—before they took him from her.

46

EASTON GOT ON THE PHONE and started calling his buddies to ask for their help in an early high-country roundup. Usually the county's horse people were eager to help with a neighbor's roundup. It was an exciting way to connect with their western roots and leave their day jobs at bay. But this roundup was last minute, and folks had plans they couldn't change. McKenzie Wilson's dad, Jed, and her grandpa Farley, were available and wanted to help out, and McKenzie found one of her friends to take her shift at the coffee shack so she could join. That made five.

The forecast for the day was one hundred and five in the foothills and a cooler low nineties up mountain in Easton's forest allotment. The two of them rose before dawn and made coffee, packed lunch, loaded three horses—Chester, Jessie, and Fred—an extra in case someone needed a fresh mount.

The winding ride into the middle forest was uneventful. They drove past the Forest Service conifer farms and intermittent creeks where no one but an occasional recreationist and even rarer rancher might show up. They unloaded the horses onto a weedy patch of meadow adorned with weather-beaten remnants of an old cedar corral and broken down loading chutes from the days Easton's dad and granddad used to bring their cows up to this same territory. The meadow extended clear to the nape of the forest where black oak let down their acorns and Jeffrey pine and white fir clothed the mountain.

A dilapidated lean-to was missing timbers and roof shakes and served no purpose but as a reminder of the era when cowmen brought their livestock up mountain to graze the summer grass before plant biologists documented the damage cows did to fragile stream beds and meadows. Ranch families, like the Jodes and Wilsons, passed down their grudge against government control to the next generations, despite an environmental complacency they'd never admit to that spurred the protections.

As far as Eleanor could see, Easton had broken that cycle. He restored natural grasses and measured the height of the grasses before rotating the cows. McKenzie, who sat her horse beside Eleanor, was breaking the cycle, too. Despite what Eleanor was certain were regular scoffs of disbelief from her family, McKenzie, time and again, showed herself to be an informed environmentalist who straddled the line between Western tradition and progress with grace.

Something about the gather had created an intimacy between the two women. Perhaps sitting on horseback mindfully doing nothing before the push created a nervous buildup and sharing eased the tension. Suddenly, McKenzie was confiding in Eleanor that she'd broken up with Chad, and her breakup had been anything but graceful.

"I've never seen him so distraught." She stretched her arms back and placed her hands on the cantle. "He got on his knees and begged my forgiveness." She turned her face to the sun.

Eleanor waited, letting the girl share without asking the question, *did you?*

She straightened. "I told him I forgave him, but I was so turned off after the river." Her far-off gaze said she was reliving that day when the Bear River came close to claiming her life.

"You made a good decision."

"And my dad hates him. That was hard."

"I bet. McKenzie, look. What's your grandpa doing over there?"

Eleanor watched Farley Wilson, standing at the open passenger door of his truck, take out a small bottle of what looked like ibuprofen.

He put the bottle to his mouth and threw his head back. Followed that with a swig of something from a silver flask.

"Grandpa," she laughed. "It's his arthritis."

Farley led his horse to the fence and climbed onto the second rail to get high enough off the ground to mount. Once in the saddle, he straightened his hat and lowered his heels, moved his horse into a trot, and joined Easton and Jed. The men road three abreast clear to the scruff of the mountain.

Easton had a plan. They'd go straight up the mountain and drop down to the gorge on the other side, where the cows and their calves drank from the stream and ate grass. The men and McKenzie and Eleanor would gather and drive the cows through the gorge, around the backside of the mountain and down toward the meadow where the herd would gather and dwell. They'd keep the livestock calm before moving them into the chutes and loading them into double-decker trailers.

Eleanor spotted a cow to her left. Jessie was on it, turning into the brush to give chase until the cow dashed beneath the limbs of a tree into the weeds, hovering in the brush. Inches before Eleanor's ran smack into a low branch, she pressed the saddle horn and Jessie backed out. She chalked one up for the cows and returned to the trail up mountain where the rest had already ridden and were now picking their own drives.

When she reached the ridge, McKenzie was shouting. She saw her wave from below as she drove cows through the wash. She was yelling instructions, which Eleanor understood to mean she'd left several cows behind and needed her to bring them up. She scrambled down the mountain and at the bottom turned Jessie to the opposite end of the wash, where she circled around and cut off the rogue cows. One broke to the side and others followed. She and Jessie ran in front of the cows and turned them, running them down to the others, her head filled with the thunder of Jessie's hooves and ragged breathing, mixed with leather sounding against her horse's skin. The gully asymmetrically rose from the stream and its ledge crumbled every few yards into the bed. Bunches of sagebrush grew at odd angles from cuts in the soil, their roots exposed and thickly gnarled trunks about to topple. As Jessie bound down the ledge to the stream, Eleanor broke through fear and gave over her trust, relying on her horse to stay behind the cows just enough to push them toward the others.

McKenzie pointed, shouting. "Get over to the opposite side before they split off and we'll bring them down slow."

Eleanor trotted Jessie to the far side of the herd until she stood in full southern sun, facing them. One of the rogue cows stared at her. Her bovine shoulders hunched to her thick neck and her calf leaned into her side. The cow trained her eyes on Jessie. Without warning, she sidestepped and charged past Eleanor, who knew now what that cow had been thinking. "Greenhorn." She let it go and moved the cows, knowing the one who'd made the dash would return to her calf.

The meadow was thick with cows. Her goal now was to do her part to keep the herd calm as they waited for the livestock trucks, which sounded easier than it was. Jessie was high strung and restless. The cows lowed, their eyes darting, those on the perimeter contemplating a break. The trucks groaned and roared painstakingly up mountain from miles away. The cows heard them, and they knew this threatened separation from their calves.

Easton rode out of the meadow and talked to the driver, who put out the first ramp. He and Jed pushed the cows into the chutes, up the ramp, and into the trailer. When the top floor was full, they filled the lower floor. The truck geared up. Cow dung streaked the sides of the trailer. The truck and trailer drove off with the bleating of mama cows separated from their calves drowning out the engine's roar. A second trailer filled its place, repeating the work until the last cow was loaded. At last count, six were missing.

Time for lunch. Eleanor removed a ham and cheese sandwich from its Ziploc. She passed a sandwich baggie to Easton and peeled an orange. Gave him half. Jed and McKenzie ate leaning against the outside of their truck. Jed pointed at Farley riding off to flush out the missing cows.

"That's why we call him Far Off," Jed explained.

An hour later Eleanor was taking photos destined for the *Tribune*'s feature page of Farley driving in the half dozen missing cows. In the high of his success, everyone—including Eleanor—forgot what the fates had in store for Easton.

47

EASTON'S COURT DATE CAME ON the same day Goldenrod and Jessie displayed their mutual interest. Eleanor got wind of the romance when she carried a hay net to the paddock and found Jessie in the furthest corner pressed against the fence, head and tail raised, whinnying loudly. Far off, Goldenrod, out of sight but definitely within the horses' scent and sound range, answered her calls. Eleanor noticed the milky drips down Jessie's apple buttocks and realized there wasn't much she could do to ease her horse other than bring her inside the barn, where she'd fret and pace. So, she left Jessie in the paddock, free to prance and squeal and listen for the whinny of Goldenrod.

* * *

They entered the old courthouse located off Main Street and met Easton's lawyer, Patrick Shine III, Esq., in the hallway. He was a big man with a kind face who was known for bringing a jury to his client's side. But Easton wanted the trial decided by a judge. He didn't want the attention a jury would draw, and he didn't want that attention to spread to Eleanor, pregnant and unmarried. Shine believed a jury would come down in Easton's favor, especially if they knew Eleanor was bearing his child; Easton's family history went way back in a town that prides itself on history, and he didn't have enemies. A new generation of Jode would be a source of joy for Gold Strike's ranch community, Shine said.

But Easton declined and, on his lawyer's advice, pleaded not guilty to the charges of trespass and horse theft, tampering with federal property and returning wild horses to public lands.

At Easton's request, Farley and Jed Wilson accompanied Eleanor to the courtroom, one on each side. The judge hadn't entered the room when the two plaintiffs walked down the courtroom aisle looking like a couple of ne'er-do-wells. The skinny, rat-faced one with whom Easton had gotten in a fist fight looked meaner and more despicable than he had at the BLM corrals. His buddy, the portentous one, was as slovenly as Eleanor remembered a year ago when he'd invaded their camp asking if they'd seen any horses that didn't belong to them.

Farley twirled his white cowboy hat between his knees as the two men walked toward the front of the courtroom.

"If it ain't Buzzard Barney and Jacques Le Bouef." He said it loud and cranky so everyone in the courtroom who'd ever watched *Boys of Moo* with their kids, or as kids, heard.

The two plaintiffs sat beside their attorney. Even the Carhartt jacket couldn't hide the butt crack that showed above Le Bouef's jeans.

The judge, a tall, respectable looking man whose kids attended the local high school, walked in, and everyone stood. Jacques hitched up his pants and Barney looked like he had a lip full of chew he didn't know where to spit. He reached for his lawyer's empty paper coffee cup and put it to his mouth.

The attorney for the plaintiff called up Easton, who looked every bit a serious rancher in his blue plaid, long-sleeved Western snap and the dress Wranglers he wore for formal occasions. His stomach was flat above his Western belt, and he wore his good leather boots, placing his brown felt hat carefully crown-side down on the stand and running a hand through his hair.

"Now, Mr. Jode, could you tell us what happened that day out at the Moraga Plateau?" began the lawyer.

Easton described the ride on that warm summer day—from putting up their tent at the horse camp on the east side of the Sierra and then riding though the BLM wild horse range and into national forest lands until they came upon an old slaughterhouse on private land—as challenging.

"I saw those mustangs crammed together in that small pen, undernourished, wounded, and it broke my heart."

"What exactly does that mean, Mr. Jode?" asked the lawyer. "It broke your heart."

"It caused me emotional feelings for these horses, coupled with the knowledge they were doomed to slaughter."

"Did you think you could save them?"

"I did think I'd at least want to give it a try to rescue these mustangs from the likes of the defendant, a known kill buyer."

"Just what is a kill buyer, Mr. Jode, and how do you know my client is one?"

Eleanor was surprised the attorney would ask such a potentially damming question.

"I looked up the list of kill buyers, those men who buy horses from auction or kills pens or, in this case, through the BLM who pays them one thousand dollars per horse, and they turn around and sell them through the slaughter pipeline or haul them up to Canada themselves."

"You have proof of this?"

"It's online. His name." Easton pointed. "Anyone can find it."

"Is it an official government list, Mr. Jode, or fashioned by an animal activist group with no proof?"

"I see where you're going with this. It's created by folks who have the best interests of horses in mind."

"That's not good enough to ruin a man's reputation, Mr. Jode, and Mr. Cobb isn't the one on trial here. You admitted you ventured on to Mr. Cobb's private property to steal those horses that belonged to the federal government and soon to belong to Mr. Cobb?"

"Objection," said Shine. "My client didn't steal any horses."

"Objection sustained," said the judge.

"Why would you assume these horses were being warehoused for slaughter? Was there a sign stating as much?"

He shook his head. "Nope. I kept my eye on his purchases, though."

"You had your eye on him. You were stalking him and planning to steal his horses that he got fair and square at adoption."

"Objection," said Shine. "No evidence Mr. Jode stole horses."

"Sustained."

"But you were intentionally on Mr. Cobb's private property, and we have the video to prove it. Thank you, that'll be all."

Easton took his hat and carried it with him to his seat beside Mr. Shine, casting an embarrassed glance backward to Eleanor, who put her hand to her heart.

Patrick Kline called plaintiff Daggert Cobb to the stand. Cobb reached for the paper cup for one last spit before giving testimony. He walked up to the front of the room like a man with a sure bet and turned slightly to give Eleanor the evil eye.

"Mr. Cobb," he began. "You say Mr. Jode here stole your horses. Were they yours or did they belong to the US government?"

"Well they're mine, but technically the BLM's for another while."

"And did the BLM pay you to take those horses?"

"Yeah, they paid me five hundred for each of my four mustangs."

"Is it true what Mr. Jode says, you planned to sell them to slaughter?"

"Nope, not knowingly anyway. Sometimes they end up there when they're in bad shape."

"These horses sound like they were in bad shape by the time Mr. Jode came upon them."

"Question?" said Cobb's attorney.

"How would you describe the health of those horses on that day Mr. Jode rode up?"

"Healthy enough. They got a few scratches, and the flies drinking from their eyeballs is ugly, but that's horses for you."

"Mr. Jode said they didn't have access to water. Is that true?"

"That's a lie. I got a water trough I keep full."

"Mr. Jode said it was low and there wasn't enough for all those horses you have packed in there? How much water does a horse need a day, Mr. Cobb?"

"I don't have that figure handy."

"Let me answer that. Eight to twelve gallons a day, depending on the weather, and it was hot and dry out there. So you got twenty-five horses times ten gallons and that's two-hundred-and-twenty-five gallons minimum per day for those horses. You know how much that tank holds? A standard tank?"

"It's a standard tank, yeah. Don't know exactly."

"One-hundred-and-fifty gallons."

"Yeah, well, them mustangs don't move around much."

"I'd say that's an understatement, Mr. Cobb. Let me ask you this, you ever see wild horses out on the range?"

"Yeah, they're all over the place."

"How would you describe them when you try to catch them on your own?"

"Uncatchable. They run in bands, hide in the trees. You need helicopters and professionals to round them up for auction."

"You mean adoption, right? That's what you did. You adopted them."

"Yeah, adopted."

"I thought you could only adopt four per person. That pen was crammed with horses that couldn't even move from what Jode says, backed up by that video you have."

"Well, my partner Danny, he adopted four."

"Sounds like quite an enterprise."

"Objection," said their lawyer. "My clients aren't on trial."

"Let me rephrase. Is it true when a wild horse has a choice, they travel in search of fresh water and grass? That's what they do, instinctually?"

"Pretty much."

"When you went looking for them, you came upon Easton Jode and asked him if he saw those horses. Did you see any horses that looked like yours in the vicinity?"

"Nope."

"That's because Easton Jode didn't steal those horses. You're dismissed."

The attorneys rested their case and Eleanor felt lightheaded as the judge leaned forward to make a determination. Farley Wilson took her hand and gave it a squeeze.

"It's clear to me, there's no evidence Easton Jode stole anyone's horses, especially not from Daggert Cobb, because he didn't legally own those horses. There's no evidence he stole those horses from the BLM, either, but the BLM does have a black mark in my book on their incentivizing adopters such as the likes of these two with cash. Nor is Easton Jode guilty of letting the horses go. Wild horses by nature roam free and it's their God-given instinct to be free that sent them out of that crowded filthy pen in search of water and grass. Nor did he release them to public lands. He was on private property. That said, it is clear Easton Jode did trespass with intention on the private property of Mr. Cobb and into Cobb's corral, and Mr. Jode did break the lock of said corral so he could enter said corral as the video clearly shows. Trespass and breaking and entering another man's premises is against the law, and, especially in this state's rural parts, a prosecuted crime. For that, Mr. Jode, I sentence you to one year with the possibility of parole in the Rio Cosumnes Correction Center where they have a wild horse saddle training program so that you can put some of your considerable empathy and lifelong skills with horses to good work." He pounded his hammer once. "Court adjourned."

A year! Eleanor clutched her chest as the judge left the room and Easton rose. Farley Wilson hung his bare head, and she felt Jed take her elbow and help her stand. Easton turned and looked at her, shook his head, and mouthed "I'm sorry."

She said aloud, "I love you," and watched the bailiff cuff her man and lead him out the side door of the courtroom. She gripped the bench in front of her and wailed. Jed and Farley surrounded her. One man on each side, they put an arm around her waist and walked her, sobbing, from the building.

48

ELEANOR CALLED IN SICK. GRANITE slept on the bed pressed against her. She spent the day walking from one room to the next, trying to figure out how to fix the situation and forgetting why she'd come into the room in the first place until, exhausted, she went back to bed and cried.

The next day she didn't bother to call in to work. She didn't read her emails or texts or her voicemails from Mac. On the third day, she ignored a phone call from Charlotte, who hadn't seen her at meetings, and one from McKenzie, who wondered why she hadn't come by the drive-thru. Part of her wanted to be at her cottage where living alone was expected, but she didn't have the energy to leave, and the ranch house held more of Easton. She lay back on pillows and watched dust motes dance in a ray of sun that slipped through the finger leaves of the walnut. At the loud knock on the front door, she turned over in bed and pulled the sheet over her head, wishing the visitor to leave.

"Hello," a man's voice shouted.

The footsteps on the stairs advanced along the hallway and stopped in the doorway. If someone were here to do her harm, she didn't much care.

"Eleanor?"

She turned toward the voice. "Mac?" She pushed her mess of hair from her eyes.

"Are you contagious?"

"I hope not. I wouldn't wish this on anyone."

"We're worried about you and wonder if the wives can make you a couple of meals."

She wondered if he knew and thought he must since this was a small town and Billy had to have checked the Sheriff's blotter and read the crime report.

"We know about Easton, and I never thought I'd say this, but he's merely in jail. He's neither dead nor dying."

"Merely?" She fumbled with the sheets and swung her legs to sitting. "They gave him a year."

"Relatively speaking, that's not long and he'll get off early for good behavior, so you'll resume your full life together as soon as he's out. If I recall correctly, you're lucky you're not in the clinker yourself. How's the morning sickness?"

"Better. I'm a little moody is all."

"You think? Let's get up, find the kitchen, and make some coffee."

She sat at the table, and he asked where the coffee was and how to operate the electric percolator. He found the cups, poured them each a hot mug and sat down. She thanked him.

"You're welcome," he said. "When do you plan on coming back to work? The newsroom isn't fun and the coffee's even worse without you."

"I'm sorry, Mac."

"About the coffee?"

"About this."

"The Sheriff has a lead on the murders. They found a witness who saw the perp throw the first woman's body in the river."

"I gave him that lead."

"I was hoping you could follow up," he said. "And I'm thinking a feature on how the murders are affecting the town's sense of well-being to keep the story from going cold. Talk to some of the parents, the women's center, college instructors. See where it takes you."

"A story like that could stir things up. Let the sleeping dog lie."

"That's valid."

"I know the witness the Sheriff's talking about. She died. I was with her in the ER when she passed. Before she died, she made me open her fist. She was holding a gold cross so tightly it cut her palm. Pretty sure she pulled it off her attacker. And I think I know who the cross belongs to."

"You tell the Sheriff?"

"The Sheriff was there. I told him and Perelli about the cross but not my suspicion. I don't know what they did with it."

He folded his palms over his chest. "That's interesting."

"I don't know where to go with it."

"We'll think of something soon as you get back to the newsroom. That baby growing inside you wants to feel the clackety-clack of your laptop, so they know things are normal."

* * *

After Mac left, Eleanor wandered into the living room. Easton had bought a new wooden rocking chair that came with cushions and placed it near the fireplace. She sat in the rocker and watched the walnut tree slap the window in a dry afternoon breeze. She couldn't take care of a ranch, and she shouldn't stay out here in the boonies alone and pregnant. The nearest neighbor was a mile away, her doctor much farther.

She thought of the Hermit. The way he stood there at the gunfight and told her she was in danger. Returning to work felt like the safest, most sensible thing she could do.

* * *

Leonard Parker texted her and said he had a story for the paper. He met her at the cafe across the street from the newspaper. She ordered iced chai and he an iced caffe latte, large.

He removed the straw from his drink and placed it carefully on a napkin. "I closed our investigation of Bull Livestock Company and wanted you to know before word got out."

"Thank you, Leonard." She asked him to summarize.

"They're up to twenty-five animal injuries or deaths unreported this season. Electric prods, sharpened metal spurs and belts, a couple of roping calves they put down after overusing them. That euthanized gelding from the wild horse event was only one of a dozen fatalities."

"I can use my photographs of that poor horse when I write the story."

"I have a few photos we've taken over the years to illustrate some of the shit they do. My nonprofit is officially suing Bull Livestock on a documented pattern of unreported injuries and violations of the official rules of the PRCA, which don't do a hell of a lot to deter abuse, but we also have them for fraud dealing with a known kill buyer who sells the company BLM mustangs before he has title."

He took a few gulps of his latte and wiped his mouth on his sleeve. "After the rodeo's done with the horses, Bull sells them back to the same kill buyer."

"Know the name of the kill buyer?"

Leonard pulled out his phone and scrolled. "Hold on, gotta find my notes. He's a listed kill buyer who works on the Sierras' east side and regularly gets his friends and family members to buy mustangs. He also has connections, or had, in Gold Strike County."

She waited, suddenly impatient.

"Here it is. Daggert Cobb."

"You're kidding me."

"Not kidding. The dirtbag adopted four horses in his young step-daughter's name."

"Narcissa?"

"You know him?"

"Daggert Cobb is the creep who'd testified against Easton and got him a year in jail."

"That's some coincidence, Nell W."

"That man lives on the dark side. He adopts mustangs and forces the horses to live in squalor. That's why Easton set them loose."

"He sells to Bull Livestock, and the horses that survive the rodeo circuit go back to Cobb for slaughter in Canada, making a few extra bucks hitting a couple of rodeos on the way. And Bull gets a percentage of slaughter sales. This Daggert Cobb is bad news."

"He's ruined my life."

"Maybe not. He'll be especially visible on the kill buyer list after our lawsuit. Write the story and get the prison's attention for Easton's early release. Meanwhile, get the BLM to admit they're adopting out to known kill buyers. I'll send you the report by day's end and then my time in Gold Strike has come to an end."

She felt a pang of regret. "Where are you headed?"

"Going the long way home by way of a Mexican *charreada* in West Dallas where they practice horse tripping and *coleadero*."

She didn't know the terms.

"An unsanctioned rodeo where the contestants practice tail stripping—cowboy grabs a steer by the tail and wraps it around their boot and stirrup and forces the steer to the ground. The flesh on the tail's torn off the underlying bone resulting in an excruciating injury call 'degloving.'"

"That's terrible."

"Yeah, it is. Then I'm home. I got an adventure business to tend to and eleven horses to feed."

She propped her elbows on the small table and leaned toward Leonard. "I have a question."

"One question."

"Where'd you learn to shoot? You're an amazing marksman."

"I grew up playing cops and robbers."

"No, really."

"I have my secrets, Nell W."

They walked out of the cafe and stood on the sidewalk where they hugged goodbye. She looked up at him and he kissed her cheek.

"Come on out to Nevada and bring your old man," said Leonard. "He can't be holding a grudge against a guy who saved his life."

She crossed the street to the newspaper building and glanced back for a last look. Leonard stood where she'd left him with his hands in his jeans, staring blankly up the street.

* * *

BULL LIVESTOCK COMPANY SUED
FOR FRAUD AND ABUSE

The story ran above the fold and continued to an inside page with photos of abused rodeo animals. As soon as the paper went out, Mac submitted the story to the California Journalism Awards for investigative journalism and breaking news. They'd have to wait a year for the results.

"'Til then, Eleanor, you're a contender." He slammed his bottom desk drawer, anticipating the first of many irate phone calls from animal lovers who would protest images of dead or suffering animals in the newspaper. It happened every hunting season. Now the outrage would surface in rodeo season.

49

THE PLACE SMELLED LIKE HORSE. And the flat, dun-colored earth that spread in all directions spoke for the Great Central Valley. A few random trees grew from the dry ground. The premises were peppered with large and small pipe fence corrals holding a few robust mustangs.

Two huge, open-ended, off-white dome-roofed arenas lay ahead. This was horse business, for sure, but the tall cyclone fencing topped with concertina wire and the guard tower with a gun turret left no doubt where she was.

Eleanor entered the largest of the two structures. The corrugated siding along the arena's dirt was at least nine feet high. Two banners hung from the siding, identifying the Sacramento Sheriff's Wild Horse Program and urging folks to adopt a BLM wild horse the inmates had gentled and saddle-trained. The dome roof was state-of-the-art, supported with heavy metal framing and offering as much shade as possible for the equines and their incarcerated trainers in the hot valley heat.

She headed to the bleachers, where roughly two dozen people sat. Horse lovers, no doubt, judging from their jeans and shirts, hats, and scuffed boots. The front row was taken, so she walked up the aluminum steps and took an end seat in the second row. She scanned the premises looking for Easton. She saw prison officials and a few men in helmets and vests walking their horses around the arena. She didn't see Easton. Law enforcement officers stood at each exit and three men in civvies sat at a table in front of microphones.

The man in the middle announced the start of the event, welcoming the guests and lauding the Wild Horse Program, called R3C and sponsored by the BLM. He introduced the first horse, a buckskin gelding with a dorsal stripe whose freeze brand on the left side of his neck was so fresh she could make out the symbols. The rider wore the number one on his vest. Someone raised a card and offered a thousand dollars. Another raised her by the minimum two hundred. People loved buckskins, and this one reminded her of Scotch and brought her back to that Mother's Day when McKenzie tore around the Gold Strike fairgrounds arena on that hot, spring afternoon a lifetime ago.

"Sold."

The horse and rider left the arena.

"Easton Jode riding the mare Obsidian," issued over the loudspeaker, and Eleanor's stomach lurched.

He walked a shiny black mare with a white blaze into the arena. He scanned the bleachers. Eleanor stood and turned sideways. She ran her hand over her belly. He grinned, tipped his hat, and wasted no time showing off the mare's training. They went through the horse's gaits, and then stopped. The mare stood still, pausing until Easton nudged her into a sidestep—useful in opening gates, a skill Eleanor failed miserably at. He moved the horse left and right, as if cutting cattle, making deep dips to one side and the next, raising cheers from the crowd.

The auctioneer asked for bids and she raised her chit.

"Five hundred."

Someone bid one thousand.

She raised her hand. "Fifteen hundred."

Easton wanted this horse. He'd called her weeks ago and asked her to bid on the mare. The BLM had gathered her from the Moraga Plateau the same time Goldenrod was captured. He believed they were family.

"One thousand seven hundred and fifty."

"Twenty-five hundred," Eleanor yelled. "And that's my friggin' old man."

Whistles came up from the crowd and the auctioneer exclaimed, "Sold. To the little lady with the voice of an angel."

Easton touched his hand to his helmet, blew her a kiss, and placed his palm to his heart. Then, to more clapping, he led the mare out of the arena. A gentleman who sat in the bottom row stood and turned around to help Eleanor down the bleachers. After the paperwork, they let her bring home the mare that day. A couple of wranglers loaded the horse into the trailer. Eleanor and Easton had picked out their own name for the horse. Belle. She balked once, then stepped up fine.

"You have a safe ride, ma'am," one of the wranglers said. "Your old man's a good guy. Best of luck to both of you." He glanced at her stomach. "All three of you."

Eleanor drove out slowly, the big domed arenas and guard tower in her rear view mirror. She was bringing home something of Easton's, which in a very small way anesthetized her sadness.

50

SMOKE AS WHITE AS BED sheets billowed behind the ridge on a backdrop of bright blue sky, which meant wildfire. Eleanor thought of McKenzie, who'd sunk into a depression after her abduction at gunpoint and near drowning in the same day. Instead of entering the university, she was taking a gap year. Meanwhile, the man who'd held her at gunpoint, Jerry Ward, was in prison for felony assault with a deadly weapon on Adelia Shepherd. However, the Sheriff's Office found no evidence Ward had anything to do with the deaths of Marisol Rodriguez or Cleo Gunderson. The court determined Ward had wrested the gun from Shepherd in self-defense, panicked, and shot her. Panicked even more when he realized two people had witnessed the shooting.

The killer was still at large. And who knew when they'd be caught. The Trailside Killer had evaded authorities for thirty years. On the other hand, Edmund Kemper confessed his killings within a week of murdering his own mother, and Aileen Wuornos was caught two months after she killed her last victim—number seven over a span of one year. The best Eleanor could hope for was catching the murderer before they killed again.

She ordered an iced mocha at the intercom and drove up to the window. McKenzie stretched out an arm and handed her the drink.

"You're hauling a trailer," McKenzie said.

"I just got back from visiting Easton. The jail put on a horse auction, and I bought the mare he trained. Easton thinks she's from Goldenrod's band."

"I want to see. Can I come out to the ranch and visit?"

"Please do." She noticed a bruise on McKenzie's eyelid. "What happened to your eye?"

She took a deep breath. "Chad's mother."

"Chad's mother? I thought you broke up with him."

"I did, but he bribed me with finally taking me to meet his mother."

Eleanor checked her rear-view mirror. There were no cars behind her rig. But a Ford 150 was parked at right angles to the fence on the lot's western boundary. An older man in a cowboy hat sat in the passenger seat.

McKenzie frowned. "I can see why he didn't want me to. Her house smelled like cat urine and the walls dripped with secondhand smoke."

"She hit you?"

"Quote-unquote 'accidentally.' She fell out of her wheelchair. I was helping Chad get her back in and she elbowed me. That was after she yelled at me for touching the Bible on her coffee table."

"I'm sorry you had to go through that."

"She's mean as a rattler, I swear. Her parting comment to her son was, 'You get rid of her, boy, before she bears your child.'"

"How's Chad with all this?"

"I don't care. He didn't defend me, not once. I stopped seeing him for good and he doesn't like that one bit."

Eleanor put her hand out the window. "Good for you." McKenzie slapped her palm. "You call me anytime, night or day, McKenzie."

"I don't want to stress you out with my romantic problems."

"You'd be keeping me company while I get through my own romantic problems."

They laughed shortly and she drove out.

McKenzie shouted, "I love your mare."

Eleanor waved and checked out the man in the 150. That's when she recognized Farley. She spotted the shotgun in his window rack. He put up his hand in a short wave.

She rolled down the passenger window and shouted, "Hey, Farley."

He opened his truck door, stepped out, and walked up slowly, his stiff, achy bones working themselves back into place. He stood a foot from her open window in his short-sleeved plaid western shirt, red suspenders holding up Wranglers.

"Where you going with that horse?" he asked.

"I'm bringing her back from the jail auction up north. Easton trained her."

"You're smiling, little lady."

"Thinking of Easton when he saw me and this belly." She ran her hand over her stomach, which pressed against the steering wheel. "What are you doing here?"

"I'm scarecrow for the night making sure the turkey vultures don't get any bad ideas."

She put the truck in park. "Is that shotgun in your window rack loaded?"

He glanced backwards to his truck. "That?" His faded blue eyes held hers. "Carrying a loaded shotgun in a vehicle would be illegal, now, wouldn't it?"

"Sure would."

She studied his *they give me shit and they're dead* face. It was all over him, like on roundup and in court.

"McKenzie's lucky to have you for a grandpa."

He pursed his lips and nodded. "You need some help unloading that horse?"

"Thanks, I can manage."

"You sure, now?"

"You're better off here, Farley."

"Well, okay then." He turned and walked back to his truck.

She worried. Farley was protecting his granddaughter because of Chad. Men like Chad didn't react well when a woman stood up for herself. Or broke up with them. She knew the type. Apparently, so did Farley. Men who act out when they're denied access to their *objet d'amour*. They cloy. They beg. Apologize, profess, and promise to change. But they don't change. Their badness magnifies and obsession transforms love into loud and violent eruptions and torpedoes of destruction.

51

NOVEMBER. AN AUTUMN BREEZE SWEPT the ranch. The red earth was thirsty and the grass dead. Leaves the size of plates had fallen to the ground, forming a perimeter of yellow beneath the maple tree. She pulled her knife and cut the blue bailing string with ease, thanks to Clifton's sharpening. She stuffed three flakes into four different nets and threw them in the horses' stalls. She grabbed alfalfa pellets for Jessie and Fred and brought them to the corral where they walked toward her. She listened to them crunch the pellets, deciding she'd ride Jessie out to the pasture to catch a glimpse of Goldenrod and his mares. Granite could follow along.

Her phone rang. Unknown number. She answered.

"Hi," said a small voice. "Is Eleanor there?"

"This is Eleanor. Who's this?

"This is Narcissa."

"Narcissa! It's so good to hear your voice."

"I'm using my friend's phone."

"I see."

"I'm wondering how Goldenrod is."

"I was just heading out to the pasture to check on him."

"When you find out, would you call me back? I might not be here, but you can leave a message at this number with my friend."

Eleanor hesitated. As much as she cared for Narcissa, the little girl was the stepdaughter of the dirtbag responsible for Easton's imprisonment. Initiating a conversation would be unwise.

"I can't do that, Narcissa. I'm so sorry."

"Someday when I'm old enough I'm going to visit you."

"I certainly hope so, Narcissa. Goldenrod and I look forward to that day."

"Bye."

"Bye, sweetie."

She put on her stretch jeans, thinking about the little girl who lived on a sheep ranch with her awful stepfather. She lay on the bed and raised one leg at a time to pull on her boots. Her breasts overflowed in her bra and stretched the cotton T-shirt in a way that made her wish Easton could see her now.

She and Jessie rode through the dry prairie down to the creek that ran through the aspen grove.

Jessie's ears perked and she lifted her neck when she saw the mustangs. But she was past her season, so that was the extent of her interest. Goldenrod drank from the creek, and a few of the mares stood in the shade of the aspen grove. That's when Eleanor saw the black mare, Belle, lying in the grass under the aspen, her belly a mound. Two bays stood side by side, one facing the mare, the other facing the opposite direction, like sentries standing guard. The mare, Eleanor realized, was about to foal. A two-for-one. Easton's mare was already pregnant when she'd made the winning bid at auction.

She got down from Jessie and draped the rope on a manzanita bush.

"Stay," she told Granite, who lay on his belly and watched her walk off. She crossed the shallows, cautiously sidestepping slippery rocks. At the far end of the field, the rest of the herd stood with the stallion, grazing a patch of still-green grass at a bend in the creek.

They turned their necks and stared at the sound of her splashing.

She paused where the water ran over pebbles and leaned over her ample tummy to wash her hands. She stepped onto the creek bank, nearing the mare while the pair of bays kept watch and didn't move.

She approached slowly, hands still, breathing to calm herself because horses sense anxiety. The mare knew her from the weeks Eleanor had confined her to a barn stall, per program guidelines, to help her adjust to her new surroundings and build trust.

She walked near enough to make out two small black hooves at the rim of the mare's vagina. The mare's back hips sucked in contraction. She squealed once, raised her head with effort, and laid back down. The little hooves hadn't moved.

Eleanor knelt beside the mare and ran her hand softly down her mane along her freeze brand and down her neck. "Good mama," she murmured. Eleanor moved down the back and looked under the mare's tail—the hooves still hadn't moved. She positioned herself as Easton had that day in the barn and inserted her hands into the mare's opening. Her fingers felt for the hooves and lifted their edges from inside the vagina's rim and the legs slipped through. On the next contraction the head emerged, enveloped in a vellum birth sack.

Unlike what Easton had done that day in the barn, breaking the sac so the foal got its first breath of air, Eleanor left it untouched by human hands. The mare would know what to do. Eleanor sat back on her haunches, forgetting her own discomfort, and waited. The foal's shoulders passed through, and with the next contraction the newborn slithered onto the ground.

The mare stayed down, resting. Eleanor knew that was good. Belle turned her neck and looked at her newborn, sniffed, and lay back. With a burst of energy, the mare stood. Eleanor stepped back. The bloody placenta hung from the mare as she turned to her baby and licked the opaque membrane down to the coat. She'd foaled a palomino colt with a wide white blaze down his nose.

Eleanor walked back through the grass and across the shallow river, imagining telling Easton the good news, and decided to rest and watch before heading to the barn. She unbuckled Jessie's saddle and chanced to look over the cantle. Goldenrod watched her from a distance. She lowered her gaze and lifted the saddle, walked it on her hip to an oak, and propped it against the trunk. She kicked aside the acorns and pulled off the blanket, laying it over the ground in front of the saddle. She unbuckled Jessie's bridle and let the bit slip from her mouth. The rope halter was frayed. She draped the lead rope over the horse's back, making a mental note to repair the halter. She lay the bridle on chaparral and sat down.

The foal tried and failed to stand on his newborn legs until he stood. He nosed his mother's belly and found a teat. The mare and foal had triumphed in this primal passage, and Eleanor had a literal hand in their success. She wondered who'd be present when her time came.

Her phone chimed. She hoped it was Easton. Her screen showed McKenzie was calling.

"Hey. How are you, McKenzie?"

Eleanor's stomach flipped and the baby moved a limb under her rib. She stretched out on the blanket and rubbed the pointy bulge until the baby shifted. "What's up?"

"Well, I'm wondering if I can come out and talk to you. You said anytime I want to talk about romance troubles I could, and you can talk about yours."

Granite put his head on her thigh and panted. She scratched his ears. "Wonderful. I'm happy to talk to you and really look forward to your company, McKenzie."

"I'll wait until I get there to tell you."

"Sounds good. I'll make us some tea."

"Are you at the Jode ranch?"

"I'm just walking back from the mustangs. I helped Easton's mare give birth. A palomino colt."

"That's awesome. I can't wait to hear about it. I should be there within the hour."

"Gate's open."

Eleanor rolled onto her hands and knees, feeling the weight of the baby and the pull of gravity. She straightened her back, and one leg at a time came to standing. She threw the blanket over the saddle and left it there, under the oak. Rain wasn't predicted in the near future and today's sky was bone blue. Walking helped position the baby for delivery, her doctor had said.

She held Jessie's lead rope and Granite walked at her side.

"C'mon, let's head home."

52

ELEANOR PUT JESSIE AWAY AND brought the halter to the house with her, thinking about McKenzie and her comment "I never did like that nickname." For the hell of it, she Googled Mitzi. AI came up on the screen with the words "a German pet form of Mary." She walked out of the barn into the blazing sunlight, stunned. A GMC truck had parked out front of the house. She didn't recognize it, but the Wilsons owned several ranch trucks. Mud covered the tires and splashboard.

She walked inside the house and hooked the halter on the coat rack beside the front door before walking into the living room and calling out, "Hello."

Chad stepped out from behind the door and slammed it, shutting out Granite.

Eleanor spun around and froze. "What are you doing here?"

"Making things right."

The dog barked and she went for the door, but Chad barred her.

"Not so fast." He pushed his chest in her face.

She stepped back. "You need to leave."

He stared at her belly. "Actually, I need to clear up a few things."

"Get the fuck out."

He grabbed her shirt and dragged her by the arm and pushed her into the rocking chair by the fireplace. She lifted the pillow from beneath her and clutched it to her stomach. Her mind raced. The pepper spray was in her backpack, hanging on the coat rack next to the rope halter. Her knife was in her back pocket.

"I know why you're here." She had to keep talking.

"I'd like to hear what you think you know."

"You think I turned McKenzie against you."

"Thanks to you, she's not even talking to me."

"Thanks to *you*, she's not talking, which is smart."

"What do you mean, smart?"

She heard Granite scratch at the door. "For starters, you're an insane, violent predator, and she's on to you. You killed three innocent women and you're building your courage to kill McKenzie."

"That's a harebrained theory based on no evidence."

Eleanor shifted in the chair and felt the knife in her back pocket, determined to keep the conversation flowing because as long as they argued he wasn't hurting her or the baby. "I have plenty of evidence."

"Like what?"

"Same evidence the cops have. Circumstantial."

"You're not a cop."

"But I know a cop. I told Sheriff Duncan about the three Marys."

He flinched, as if she'd thrown dirt in his face. "What about them?"

"You're using the three Marys of the Crucifixion as a template for murder."

"And I bet you weren't convincing," said Chad. "That's—

"—crazy. Duncan thought so, too, but I didn't know who the third Mary was until now. You're on his radar and we know you're missing a gold cross that showed up in a dead woman's bleeding palm."

He took a deep breath.

"She died for your sins, Chad, and McKenzie has an identical cross she won't wear because you're so fucking toxic."

"You're lying."

"It's your mother, Chad. You're a pitiful, religiously and emotionally abused boy because of your mother. Is that why you hate women?"

He spit on the floor. "Only women like you who don't know how a society is supposed to work." He hunched his shoulders, clenched his gloved fists and crossed himself. "And women who think they're superior, who're eroding the power of full grown men and their place in the kingdom of patriarchy."

"But your own mother runs the show in your kingdom."

"Leave my mother out of it."

"She raised you to believe you're a messiah." She saw in his face the truth of her claim.

"—shut up."

"Chad." She said his name firmly. "I understand why you'd hate women after her and why you'd distort religious teachings, but killing women because you wrongly believe you're called to do so for a higher purpose won't change anything except their lives and yours."

"Actually, that's not accurate. Fulfilling the Trinity alters reality."

"The Trinity is a symbol."

"Not a symbol. A spiritual conduit. And whatever blocks the way—" He took a step closer.

"—Stop." She put up a hand, and he slapped it away.

"You are such a bitch. Women are designed to be submissive to the men who protect you."

"If that's true, where were you when Jerry Ward tied up McKenzie and—"

"—I said shut the fuck—"

"—and held her at gunpoint?"

"I didn't want her to go on that trip and she knew it."

"You panicked and nearly drowned her. Not exactly firefighter behavior. In fact, cowardly. You're a coward, Chad."

He tilted his head and spread his arms. "Fuck you."

"You murdered Marisol and Cleo, and you know why?"

"I sanctified their souls."

"Because your mother doesn't want you to be happy. And you plan to murder McKenzie, or Mitzi, as you call her, the third Mary."

"Magdalene."

"Where is she now?"

"I don't know. The whore won't see me."

"Have you hurt her?"

"Not yet, but once I'm done with you, it's her turn, and you've made it easier." A tic rippled across Chad's left cheek. He lunged at Eleanor and lifted her to standing. Rawhide gloves clenched her throat. She screamed and tried to pry his fingers from her neck, but her efforts made him tighten his grip.

In a last-ditch effort, she dropped her hand from his fist and reached behind her back into her pocket and slipped out her knife. With one flick, the blade opened ... *hard as you possibly can*. With all the force she could gather, she jammed the blade into his back, pushing through the resisting flesh. Tendon and muscle crackled. He screamed and released his grip and slumped to his knees.

She raised her arm and aimed for that spot at the base of the neck. The front door flew open.

"Eleanor."

She whirled around. McKenzie strode through the doorway, wearing an overcoat and jeans, pointing a shotgun. She stepped up and pressed the gun into Chad's back. "Don't move or I *will* shoot you, you fucking piece of shit."

"Where's Granite?"

"In my truck. Eleanor, get something to tie his hands."

She remembered the halter.

"Tie his hands behind his back." McKenzie pressed the gun harder, and he winced.

Eleanor had a better idea. She pulled the halter over Chad's head and stuffed the noseband between his teeth and up into the corners of his mouth. She cinched the tie down tight at his throat and pulled the lead rope until his head lifted from the carpet. Then she tied his hands.

Eleanor heard the sirens, faintly, and soon the squad cars screamed into the yard, one after the other. The Deputies entered the house, guns drawn.

"Anyone else here?" Deputy Perelli asked.

"No, McKenzie and me," she said. "And him."

"Put the gun down, Ms. Wilson." Perelli hoisted Chad to his feet and stared, perplexed at the halter cinched over his face.

"Didn't think you had it in you, Wooley." He unwound the ropes from Chad's hands and undid the halter. Two other deputies kept their guns pointed until Chad was cuffed.

"You're under arrest." Perelli recited Chad's Miranda rights before escorting him to the patrol car. Chad spouted Biblical verses and dammed women to hell as Perelli pushed him firmly to the back seat, a hand on Chad's head.

"Could I have a word with him?" Eleanor asked Perelli before the door shut.

"Make it fast," said Perelli.

She leaned toward the open passenger door. Chad's shoulders slumped forward, his wrists cuffed behind him.

"I'd say this disproves your theory."

He wouldn't look up, but Eleanor was certain he heard.

EPILOGUE

THE FOLLOWING WEEK, ELEANOR'S DOCTOR announced she was dilated, and on December 2 Eleanor gave birth to an eight-pound baby girl. McKenzie was present for the delivery and came out to the ranch to feed the horses, help with the housework and deliver her mother's homemade meals. She confided in Eleanor that she felt tainted by Chad and couldn't forgive herself for not knowing who he really was.

Eleanor placed a hand on her shoulder. "McKenzie, sometimes we don't see what's in front of us."

Eleanor waited to name their child until Easton was home. He was released days later for good behavior. Every afternoon he wrapped the baby in a front-pack for her nap and rode Chester around the arena until she fell asleep. He kept on riding long after she woke up.

*　*　*

The time had come to name their child before the year ended. They were used to naming things. In fact, this had become a ritual between the two of them—one they enjoyed. Naming the dog, naming the horses. Now, naming their baby girl.

Easton pushed for an outdoor ceremony in that place of alpenglow she'd never seen. But it was December, and she didn't enjoy the cold. He convinced her, though, that the walk would do her good, so she layered herself in thermals and down, and found her wool mittens and hat. She bundled the baby in fleece and bunting. They left the house before dawn and ambled along the two-track through the pastures where frost-coated grass lit the dark. Granite walked beside Eleanor and Easton carried the infant in a sling.

They walked past Goldenrod's band of mares and heard them whinny. Easton left each gate open after they passed through. They walked side by side, holding hands most of the way. When they passed through the fourth gate, Easton told her, "We're almost there." He'd said that twice before, so his reassurance had no effect on her. But she discerned the silhouettes of cliffs and oak canopies in the coming light.

Easton stopped. "We're here."

He gestured to a flat rock. They sat down facing the dark and distant cliffs with what would soon be sunrise at their backs. The baby cried. Easton scooped her from the sling and passed her to Eleanor, who was warm now. She unzipped her layers and offered a breast. The baby suckled as the sun rose, and the first ray transformed the serpentine cliffs to a brilliant pinkish orange. *Beautiful.* She felt vibrations as the horses thundered across the land, nearing them.

Easton reached behind her. He pulled out the thermos from her backpack and poured a cup of hot coffee, which they shared.

"How about Coral Leigh Wooley-Jode?" she asked.

"Hmm, let's think about this. What about Flicka?"

She laughed, "No."

"Why not? We started out on horseback."

"We met at a bar."

The Bear Clover Inn.

"Clover," he said.

"I love it."

And he lifted the baby to the dawn's rosy light.

ABOUT THE AUTHOR

ROBIN SOMERS spent her middle years in Tuolumne County in the Sierra Nevada, where she wrote for the daily newspaper, taught high school English, and kept an American Paint Quarterhorse. She is retired faculty at the University of California, Santa Cruz, with an MFA in Creative Writing from San Jose State University. She shovels horse poop and hangs with horses at Canham Farm horse rescue in Scotts Valley, California. She is a Volunteer Ambassador for American Wild Horse Conservation. *Three Marys* is the second book in her Wild Horses Mystery series. The first book, *Eleven Stolen Horses: A Wild Horses Mystery* (Sibylline Press 2024) won Finalist in the category of Best Westerns from *Pacific Coast Book Review*. She is also the author of *Beet Fields*, a murder mystery re-released in March 2025 by Sibylline Press, inspired by her son's organic farm, Dirty Girl Produce.

She lives in Santa Cruz with her husband and frequents the Sierra Nevada where her Wild Horse Mystery series is set. Find her at robinsomers.com

ACKNOWLEDGMENTS

I'M SO GRATEFUL TO SIBYLLINE Press: To Suzy Vitello, my very kind editor, for her valuable feedback on this story. It's a better story for sure because of her intelligent mind and keen knowledge of fiction. And to publisher Vicki DeArmon for guiding this ship to harbor. To Alicia Feltman for her beautiful cover and Sang Kim, publishing manager, for organizing me. To Anna Termine, the rights and special sales director for Sibylline Press.

For the constancy and brilliance provided by my aptly named writing group GLOW, consisting of Paula Mahoney, Sarah Savasky, Enid Brock, Simi Monheit, and Becky Wecks, thank you for our enduring weekly in-person meetings. My love for you goes beyond words.

Gratitude also to the late Tuolumne County Sheriff Dick Rogers, who was an uncommonly kind police detective when I knew him. The story of the Me-Wuk in this book was inspired by G. Ezra Dane, who in his old-time storytelling voice wrote and published *Ghost Stories* (1941), a collection of Gold Rush era narratives, including how Uyeayu, the White Man, massacred the first people and "devastated the land of the Me-wuks to dig up the Gold."

Thanks to Captain Tim Sturm of the Calaveras County Sheriff's Office for information on wilderness crime scenes and law enforcement jurisdiction and protocol; to retired Smoke Jumper Josh Starbuck and Laura Quick for taking care of my dog so I could work a few precious hours a week at Canham Farm Horse Rescue and Rehabilitation. And to Julia Hyde, owner of Canham Farm, for her vast knowledge of caring for horses and providing me with the opportunity to hang with them. Lori Halliday, owner of Horse and Heart, whose ever-expanding heart has touched mine. Thanks to ranchers Price and Barbara Mailloux for a long ago round up of cows from the high country. I've never forgotten.

Blessings to Patty Kelly Tolhurst, who helped me pick out my first horse. Patty was last seen in Twain Harte, California. She's been missing since 4/18/2024.

Beloved pediatrician Dr. Casey Schirmer provided information on mature age pregnancy. Schuyler Raine-Mustain offered generous intellectual consultations and divergent thinking on matters of the psyche when I sat in his chair and put my head of hair in his hands. Thank you to Pat Kaunert, retired USFS employee for the Stanislaus Forest, for details on Forest Service protocol, and Rachel Benevidez for putting a name to the brilliant rosy glow on the face of rocks and mountains at sunrise or sunset—alpenglow.

John McNicholas, Jr., a.k.a. "J.Mack" planted the seed for writing a book about a sacred, wild and endangered scenic river. He was an early champion of saving the Clavey River, one of California's last free-flowing rivers. And thanks to an undisclosed friend for permission to apply their name to a terrible character (who is nothing like my friend). Thank you Charlie Schirmer for inspiring a vital character. Loads of gratitude to my friend Susan Watrous, an amazing last chance editor, who knows how to slow down my rush to the end.

American Wild Horse Conservation has been a resource about all things to do with wild horses. I'm honored to be a volunteer ambassador. The AWHC's tenacious efforts on behalf of keeping wild horses free roaming on their federally protected lands and safe from kill pens, kill buyers and slaughterhouses are fruitful. As I was writing this book, Amelia Perrin of AWHC and Sky Dog Sanctuary won their lawsuit against the Bureau of Land Management's adoption Incentive Program. As of now, this abusive program is on hold. AWHC is working to pass the SAFE act, making slaughter of horses for human consumption illegal; it currently sits in the House Committee on Agriculture.

To Dennis, my love and soul mate, father of our two children, thank you for driving me into the hinterlands to chase my dreams.

QUESTIONS FOR DISCUSSION

1. A darkness has crept over Gold Strike as its young women become endangered. *Three Marys* delves into the harm to an entire community when a serial killer is on the prowl. What are the subtle and obvious changes in the town folk from the festive beginning of the book over the course of the narrative? And how does Eleanor Wooley work to restore the light?

2. What are the parallels between human abuse of environment, animals, and women and what are examples of people who stand up for the vulnerable elements of a society? Is this a literary device limited to fiction or do these parallels and examples of heroism exist in reality? Explain.

3. We learn in Eleanor's backstory that she's survived a uniquely abusive marriage. Analyze her decision to protect her hard-won self by remaining single. What are your hopes for her personal evolution in this area of her life as the story develops?

4. One of the heart-wrenching and unresolved relationships in the book is Eleanor's acquaintance with Narcissa, the young stepdaughter of Daggert Cobb. Is there a chance their paths may cross in the future and what do you imagine that looks like?

5. Easton has done something illegal in his recent past, though some might consider his action heroic. Nonetheless, he pays the consequences. Does the punishment fit the crime? How does his punishment further the obvious and more subtle trajectory of the narrative?

6. Several characters from *Eleven Stolen Horses* reappear in *Three Marys*. Who's your favorite? What ways have they evolved and what do they contribute to the story?

7. Which characters in *Three Marys* do you want to see again in the next *Wild Horses Mystery*. And why is that?

8. At first glance, a road trip to Nevada may seem entirely disconnected to the events occurring back home in Gold Strike. How does this trip—and the Goldenrod subplot—cohere to the main plot of *Three Marys*?

9. Youngsters—both two-and-four-legged—play a part in *Three Marys*. Make a list of the young in the book and consider how each contributes thematically, emotionally and ethically.

10. Last, imagine the future of Eleanor and Easton in the next, say, five years. Let me know your ideas if you care to by contacting me via my website: https://www.robinsomers.com. I look forward to your input.

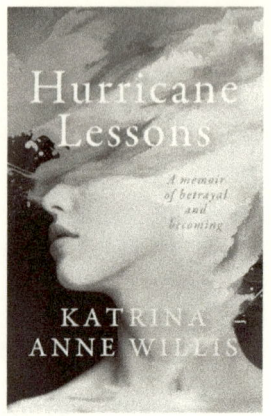

Hurricane Lessons: A Memoir

By Katrina Willis

MEMOIR
256 Pages • Trade Paper • $19
ISBN: 9798897400140
Also available as an ebook and audiobook

When 46-year-old Katrina falls for her female Pilates instructor, she's forced to confront the truth about her sexuality and the cracks in her decades-long marriage. As lies, manipulation, and abuse spiral out of control, she must decide whether surviving the storm means saving her marriage—or herself.

Girl in a Box: A Novel

By Jean Gordon Kocienda

HISTORICAL FICTION
360 Pages • Trade Paper • $21
ISBN: 9798897400126
Also available as an ebook and audiobook

In early twentieth-century Japan, rebellious poet Yosano Akiko defies tradition, fleeing home to pursue love, art, and freedom from Tokyo to Paris. Through hardship and passion, she becomes a pioneering feminist voice—only to face the personal cost of her relentless devotion to poetry and independence.

Griftopia: A Novel

By Suzy Vitello

FICTION

394 Pages • Trade Paper • $21
ISBN: 9798897400164
Also available as an ebook and audiobook

Orphaned sisters Pearl and Scarlett Freischin, each reeling from scandal and loss, must find a way to survive as their fractured family teeters on the edge of ruin. Desperate and nearly destitute, they turn to a string of dubious online schemes, exposing the darkly comic underbelly of modern hustle culture.

Last Summer at Feather River: A Novel

By Karen Nelson

FICTION

304 Pages • Trade Paper • $20
ISBN: 9798897400188
Also available as an ebook and audiobook

Ten years after a tragic accident closed her family's beloved Camp Feather River, Brooke returns to care for her grandfather and confront the past she's long avoided. As buried secrets surface, she begins to suspect that the so-called accident was something far more sinister.

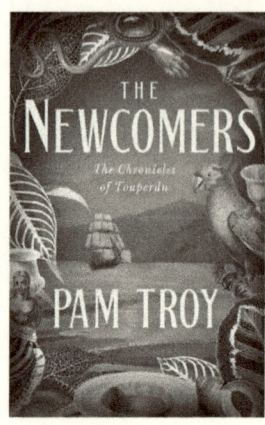

The Newcomers: The Chronicles of Touperdu, Book I

BY PAM TROY

FANTASY
472 Pages • Trade Paper • $22
ISBN: 9798897400089
Also available as an ebook and audiobook

In 1880, two immigrant families—a Creole chef seeking peace and a matriarch of witches craving freedom—journey to the mysterious Isle of Touperdu, hoping for a fresh start. But as they soon discover, the island's promise of refuge may be an illusion, forcing them to confront what they're willing to sacrifice to belong.

Sibylline Press is proud to publish the brilliant work of women authors over 50. We are a woman-owned publishing company and, like our authors, represent women of a certain age.